AF490893

HANNAH

one woman's quest for vengeance and enlightenment

DAVE O. DODGE

Preface

Every day of my childhood I watched from my bedroom window as twin rivers flowed together in unison that created the mighty Merrimack River. For centuries, its waters have sustained generations in New Hampshire, shaping the land, the people, and the quiet rhythms of life. It is a constant presence threading through the valley bearing witness to survival and sometimes death.

Hannah Duston, her story, her legacy and her moral ambiguity have always been in question. Her actions have forever been embedded into the fabric of life along the Merrimack, sometimes glorified and sometimes vilified, but without a doubt always in question.

Sugar Ball Island is not far downstream from my view, far enough away to forget about what happened there so long ago. But close enough to pass by it often. The view from the highway is her statue looms in a silent testament, to both survival and death. I have always taken a silent reflection on those days, often with my own questions. Does violence create violence, or does retaliation normalize it? The moral weight doesn't go away, and could it take another shape; where guilt and grief can bring enlightenment.

This is a biographical novel, not a verdict or an opinion. I have searched the darkness of her life and used my imagination to illuminate it. I have tried to bring an emotional truth to her story, balancing the facts, and listening to stories of folklore. My intention was not to cast judgments or make any assumptions.

Violence doesn't just shape her world; it reshaped it, so she could become a woman at peace with herself and her God. This is one woman's quest for vengeance that created her enlightenment.

I dedicate this novel to Brian and Gwen, whose true friendship is matched only by their generosity, support and hospitality. Sometimes a writer does not have to look very far to fund the reason for telling a story.

"She thought she was not forbidden by any law to take away the life of the murderers, who had embrued their hands in innocent blood."

Reverend Cotton Mather
Magnalia Christi Americana
Book VII -1702

It had been, without a doubt, the longest night for the *John of London*, with barely twenty crossings on its register, mostly sailings across the north Atlantic to Boston. It was the worst night in the memory of its seasoned captain, George Lamberton. The wooden four-mast galleon was built by Trenckmore Shipbuilders near Shoreham-by-Sea in England in 1620. A sleek design with a keel made of oak and masts of pine, it was built for anything God might present to it. For Lamberton, he knew that morning, God might have played a hand with the challenges he faced to keep the course steady. It also helped to remind his passengers of God's fury and to entice them all to pray harder.

The relentless winds from the north battered the wooden galleon, tossing it side to side, showing no mercy for its cargo or its passengers. The sound the ship made as it creaked and groaned was a strange language that only experienced sailors could understand. With every fall over the waves, the vessel spoke a strange tongue that the crew could understand.

The ship had set off weeks ago from Hull Harbour, England and was still nowhere near its destination. The journey had taken longer than anticipated due to the tumultuous weather and the last-minute passengers. It was called the Great Migration, and many were seeking a new life of freedom in a land across the Atlantic. Lamberton seized every opportunity to make a coin; keeping stowaways off the ship's register was an easy task and provided added profit in his pocket. Some entries were best forgotten; his blind eye to those made no difference once the ship docked.

The Captain had kept records in his journal, measuring the fathoms and watching the night sky when the stars showed themselves. That morning when the sun broke, he reviewed his notes once again before heading topside. Lamberton was convinced that the *John of London* was close to land, perhaps in a day or two. He had hoped that the outer cape where the Massachusetts Bay Colony was established would come into view soon.

Dawn had broken, the light from the rising sun illuminated the helm, and he wanted to be at the snout, high above the bow with his spy-glass. As any experienced sailor was taught, the winds that caused the high seas would abruptly change as the ship sailed closer to land, and the prevailing breezes would shift. Lamberton was exhausted and was ready for rest, but his duty had been an overwhelming force to see the voyage through. He was also motivated to receive his salary once he successfully reached Boston Harbor.

He relinquished the ship's wheel to his Chief Mate, another experienced sailor who by his own right should have his own vessel. The wheel at the helm was located on the quarter-deck in the rear of the ship. Lamberton felt a sense of dread as he headed to the bow. He was trying his best to avoid the Reverend Ezekiel Rogers, the leader of a flock of Puritans on board from Lincolnshire. They were migrating to a new world of freedom for their beliefs.

With spyglass in hand and the second mate in close pursuit, he maneuvered across the deck in the direction of the snout that sat precariously in the front of the ship; it was the best vantage point for him to see what lay ahead. The wind had started to subside as the sun rose, and he could feel the heat from the sun on his back. The sky was clear, and the blue was the color of his wife's eyes; how he longed to see her again. Her image pleased him, as did the fact that they had made it through another night. His one thought was that he hoped the passengers below fared as well, despite the crowded conditions below deck.

"Captain Lamberton, Sir," a shout from a man's voice came across the deck, not unlike being fired from a cannon. He knew it was the Reverend.

The Captain increased his pace; he had not yet made it to his destination. The Reverend Rogers was more agitated than usual. The rough night caused him and his flock a sleepless one, he had conjectured.

"Sir, please stop," Rogers said.

"Good morning, Reverend," Lamberton bit his own tongue. "How am I able to assist?"

Crossing the Atlantic Ocean was a perilous and life-altering journey for anyone taking the leap of faith to do so. Thousands of English Puritans, driven by religious persecution and the hope of building a new life, set sail for New England. The crossing often lasted weeks; that morning, they marked 31 days; the *John of London* was now into its fifth week. The Reverend took offense to the length of the sail and the dwindling supplies provided to his brethren.

Rogers also took offense to cramped quarters, the unsanitary conditions, and the lack of fresh water. These conditions were not isolated to Lamberton's ship, as all wooden sailing ships that were part of the great migration had very similar complaints.

Families often traveled together, and they braved seasickness, violent storms, multiple diseases, and the constant uncertainty of survival. There had been limited food on this voyage, and the good Reverend negotiated 19 more passengers than he first contracted. Lamberton had aired his grievance, but his words had fallen on deaf ears with the shipping company; some fares were mostly paid in advance, and these were not. Passengers dying at sea would alleviate some of the crowded situations, which was an outcome that the shipping company and the greedy captain took into consideration.

"The water is stale, where is all the fresh water, sir?" Rogers was looking directly at the Captain.

"Not to be contrary to your needs," Lamberton replied. "What is the number of your flock?"

The Reverend took a deep breath and knew exactly where the Captain was going with his dialogue. That might have been the first journey for most on board, including the Reverend, but it was not Lamberton's.

"We are fifty-six God-fearing souls." He answered with a hint of regret.

The number had gone down by one after last night's horrific ordeal. Along with stale drinking water, there had been no real medical care, so even a minor illness could prove fatal. Despite these hardships, most Puritans relied on their faith and the possibility of God's enlightenment to see them through any storm. Those risks kept many passengers determined for providence.

It was a spiritual mission for the Puritans; the voyage across the sea was not just a physical journey but a transcendent one. They believed they were chosen to build a Godly society in the New World, free from the corruption of the Church of England. The Atlantic crossing became a test of their devotion, endurance, and belief in divine providence. Prayers were said daily, sermons delivered at sea during calmer days, and many had seen the successful conclusion of the voyage as an indication of God's favor.

"Might I remind you, sir, of our conversation the night before our embarkation?" Lamberton stood his ground.

The good Reverend knew exactly what he was implying. Over sold, under stocked, and stuffed like potatoes in a sack, his followers forged forward. New England and Governor Winthrop's vision of a *City on a Hill* were the driving force for most below deck.

"Yes, I am reminded," he replied. "We have done our best to conserve. How many more might perish before the sight of land was upon us?"

The Captain looked at him with the gravest of looks; there was no projecting God's will. The possibility of land or death was equal in his mind. Hopefully, the latter would not come into fruition on this voyage.

"Reverend Rogers, I will instruct the Quarter Master to bring you two barrels of water and a sack of hardtack." He reluctantly told him.

He knew four souls had perished since leaving the east coast of England, and what he did not want was any more to follow. In his heart, he knew land was close; with no more storms or rough seas, his assessment was likely two more days with a strong wind. The sails all needed to be unfurled and raised to achieve his plan.

"Thank you, Captain, may God guide us all to a conclusion of this exodus from England," Rogers told him.

"Your deliverance is my utmost desire," he replied. "Go with God, now I must tend to my duties.

The Reverend had distracted him to the point of needing a tankard of rum, but he would wait for breakfast. He mused to himself, did he not think that he wanted to see Boston as much as the good Reverend wanted to? "Only a few on board knew that deep in the cargo of the ship was a printing press, this invention, that was now indispensable in England, would be introduced to the Massachusetts Bay Colony, residing at Harvard University. It would be the first in the colonies, as rumor had it, one had been shipped from Spain to Mexico City a few years before.

The captain reached the bow and assessed the view ahead of them. Calm waters, clear skies, and full sails. It was only a matter of time. Rum and some johnnie cake were the next order of the day for him.

When land finally came into view on the following day, the weary travelers felt a mixture of relief, awe, and solemn commitment to the religious covenant that had carried them across the ocean. God had favored them; they had been delivered from the corrupt church of England, as the Reverend John Winthrop said: *The City on the Hill.*

It was Winthrop's desire to create a model society that reflected his religious and social ideas. A community governed by its principles along with God's graces and Puritan values. He envisioned the colony as a beacon of righteousness and a place where they could live according to God's will.

It had been a few years since Winthrop first preached his sermon in South Hampton, England. He outlined his master plan, quoting from the Old Testament and Jesus's *Sermon on the Mount*. His metaphor was taken from the book of Matthew: "*as a city on a hill, the eyes of all the peoples are upon us.*" Boston was a perfect choice, having three distinct hills in full view of the harbor to the east and the woodlands to the north.

The elation that their journey was coming to an end was infectious. It was felt throughout the ship, from Roger's flock to the boy in the crow's nest who first spotted land. Everyone was thankful that no more souls had perished and was grateful to the Captain for increasing their rations a few days before.

The Reverend was on deck; his sermon that morning was one of possibilities and forgiveness. He spoke of where they had come and where they were going. He instructed them all to be vigilant, never compromising the work of the Lord and the providence that would be bestowed upon them.

The Reverend Rogers, a graduate of Christ's College in Cambridge, had left his ministry in Rowley, a small village in East Yorkshire, before enticing his followers on the ultimate pilgrimage to New England. Like Winthrop, he had his own church, St. Luke's Church in Rowley but had left it after seventeen years when he refused to alter his beliefs on Puritanism. His flock of twenty families was small but no less devoted. He had a plan to create his heaven on earth in a new location; Rowley, the newest charter in the Massachusetts Bay Colony, it would be called.

Along with the twenty families, there were a few adventurous and loyal members of St Luke's, some single. One in particular was Michael Emerson, a young man with a desire to be a good servant of the Lord, as well as one to seize any opportunity that might be presented to him. Emerson was one of the last-minute passengers to join the sailing; he was thankful to be leaving England and his past behind.

Emerson had not yet seen his twenties, yet he had signed on to this venture without hesitation; the new world meant a new outlook on his young life. He planned to remain part of Roger's brethren as long as possible, or until a better opportunity presented itself; he wanted it all.

Each night, the young Emerson would lie in his corner in the bowels of the ship, wrapped in a tattered blanket on a bed of straw, and he would allow his mind to wander. He projected a new life away from the confines of his grandparents, who had raised him, away from the memory of his parents, both dying of the sweating disease. He was only ten, but the tragic outcome was that he watched both his parents, racked with pain and sweating profusely, as it took their lives in less than two days. There was nothing he could have done for them. Watching their life slowly dim in their eyes only hardened his resolve.

He was disillusioned by that event, even inquiring about God's will, for making him feel like an orphan. It did not detour him from his goal. He knew God would provide, as he always believed during his few years on earth. He wanted to believe that. The Puritan movement had swept him up like a crashing wave in the North Sea; meeting the Reverend after burying his parents sealed the deal of his faith. He was pleased with himself; after all, he had for the first time laid his eyes on the ocean. It was the day before sailing out of Hull Harbour; now he fancied himself a veteran who had crossed the North Atlantic.

New England and the Colony would provide for him. It was said that land would be available to all who were deserving. Women were plentiful, and a wife soon could be for the taking. He had tasted the forbidden fruit as taught in the Bible only once, and he enjoyed it immensely.

The young girl, whom he did not know well, was the daughter of the tavern keeper who would entice him only to cast him off. That had made Emerson angry and given him other ideas. One night, he waited for her to leave the tavern, he grabbed her and forced her into the dark alley; her screams were muffled by his hand. The relief he felt was an awakening of his soul, and the reality of the charge of ravishment only gave cause for his hasty departure. The incident happened not two days before convincing the Reverend to let him join his flock.

He knew the pleasure he felt in his groin only transcended to his soul; the new world would provide for him. Puritanism considered the practice of sex as one of the most revered acts within the confines of marriage.

A wife would be considered heavenly adoration, and as soon as possible, he would choose a bride.

Michael Emerson had ideas that some would call unconventional and unbecoming of a follower of Rogers, but he did not care. Some might call them evil, those feelings that he possessed were deep inside his being, buried upon levels of grief, guilt, and gluttony: his own tragic Holy Trinity.

ONE

The water's edge was teaming with life, and plants emerged from the fresh and fertile soil after a long winter of rest. Renewal came with the warming sun, and along with that, the ice flows melted, releasing the frigid water. The current flowed slowly and meandered downriver, taking its time before it arrived at the land which the locals called the crotch. There, the river would be joined by another, creating the *Merrimac*.

The Abenaki had chosen that very spot along the river called *Wiwininebesaki* by those who came before; it was the place upon which the Great Spirit had smiled, creating the perfect location for them to live. The river encircled the village, creating almost an island, providing a natural barrier of security while slowing the current for easy fishing. Weirs, a device made of birch twigs fashioned in a basket-like shape, were strung across the waters so that the salmon or trout could more easily swim into them, providing substance for the tribe.

The rivers belonged to the Great Spirit, and the native peoples that lived along them respected it. Their customs that had been handed down for generations were revered and embraced. The knowledge of nature and of its bounty was not limited to just the men of the village, but also to the women. Grandmothers taught their daughters, who in turn taught their daughters. Like the men of the tribe who taught their sons how to properly use the bow or stalk a deer, the women knew where to gather food along the water's edge from the bountiful native plants. This was a necessity when the crops of planted squash or corn were not ready for harvest.

Waban, a tall, slender Indian woman with long black hair, was dressed in a deer skin wrap-around skirt. She emerged from the long house not far from the village center. She was the eldest child, barely fifteen summers old, but looked older than her years. Confident and smart, she commanded a presence amongst the younger children. Waban had her daily duties, one of which was helping the others to empty the weirs in the river. The fish they caught would be divided among the others, the oldest getting to choose first. Carrying a basket, she made her way to the narrowest bend in the river where the others gathered for their chores.

The sun was up, and its rays were forcing their way through the forest canopy to warm the morning air. It was spring, and the sense of rebirth after a hideous winter was all around. Waban knew that the fish were returning up the river and that the weirs would prove to be bountiful. Getting her chores done was first on her mind.

Walking along the river's edge, nature was restoring it to its glory before the snows came. It was becoming lush with an abundance of grass and plants to create a verdant shoreline. The smell of the open fire lingered in the still air. Waban knew the elder women in the village were cooking some meat, no doubt a recently killed deer after its hide was removed and stretched on a rack for drying. Deer skin was soft and durable; everyone in the village would benefit from it, along with the meat. The Abenaki knew never to take more than they could use from the forest, for fear that the Great Spirit might show retribution if the bounty was wasted.

She gathered the others at the river's edge, and together they worked in harmony, pulling in the weirs, emptying the fish into baskets that were also made of birch twigs. The fish that morning had been a combination of perch and trout; it was a productive expedition for her. She was first to choose because she was the eldest. Once the traps were put back in place, she picked up her basket and returned to the long house.

Her home, the only one she knew, was a long house, sometimes they called it a wigwam. The structure was constructed large enough to provide shelter for her entire family, as well as some others that resided with them. It was made with an assortment of animal hide, birch bark, and young saplings that were bent to create a curved roof, which during the rainy season proved to be very beneficial. In all, there had been twenty-one souls living in the long house, from her grandmother of sixty summers she was told, to her newly born brother, barely one summer old.

Waban's life had been hard at times; the unforgiving winter weather, the threat of disease from the white man, were a pale comparison to the tales she heard that came from the south. The English had broken a treaty, and war had emerged along the ocean's coast. Tales of slaughter, starvation, and the demise of Chief Metacom made their way north all the way to the crotch of the rivers. The Frenchmen were to the north, and the English were to the south, which caused her to reflect on how these changing times would affect her family and her life.

Her grandmother was sitting on a stump near the entrance of the longhouse; she was pounding some deer meat on a flat stone, making a mash. Next to her was a deerskin pouch filled with crushed spicebush leaves. Waban knew that she was making *Pemmican*, another way to preserve the meat, combining the ingredients with rendered fat, which could last for months without spoilage.

"Nokemes, tell me how you are today?" Waban asked the old woman.

Her grandmother did not look up, but acknowledged her with a light-hearted grunt. Nokemes was focused on her work and did not need a distraction. She was mixing in the rendered fat from a bear into the mixture; the correct amount would preserve it, too little would cause it to spoil.

Waban didn't wait for further talk; she brought the basket of fish to the other side of the longhouse, where someone would clean them and dry them in the sun. Fish was also preserved for later times.

Waban dropped the basket and walked to the center of the village, where the fire was now out, and the strips of meat were laid across the smoking embers. The smoke would cure the meat and give it flavor. She was looking forward to a meal with fresh smoked meat and cornmeal cakes; the meal would come before sundown, but not for a while.

There were other men of the tribe gathered near the smoking fire; they were in a deep discussion about something that gravely concerned them. Though Waban was smarter than most her age, she also knew her place. For a squaw to enter a tribal talk of just men was forbidden, or at best, frowned upon by the men. She casually squatted next to the meat, pretending to monitor its preservation caused by the rising smoke, while listening to the louder discussion that was happening.

Bampico, a warrior barely twenty-five summers, appeared to be angry. He was the center of the discussion, trying to make his point heard to the other men. The group consisted of some of the elders of the village and some younger warriors whom she did not know. These men were older and wiser, and often the young warriors would seek their advice before adopting their ideas.

From where Waban squatted, she could clearly see the disapproving looks on the older men's faces. Bampico had a commanding presence among the others. His bare chest and deer skin leggings created a masculine figure, one that she had admired for some time. Her curiosity got the best of her, and she moved closer to the group without notice from them. She could hear their voice more clearly and was surprised by what the dialogue was.

Bampico was known throughout the village as a strong, defiant, and resourceful warrior. He was smart with a keen sense of the forest and was one with the land. He also had heard the same stories from the south, the conflicts between the English and the tribes there, and it was devastating to him. His message to the elders was that something needed to be done. The English had discovered the rivers and their resources. Their settlements along the rivers were now being established by the religious group known as Puritans. These white settlers were not in harmony with the land, which angered most Abenaki.

"They may come here, the crotch, and our way of life is threatened." He told the group.

"What are we to do?" One elder asked Bampico.

"We are strong and wise; the rivers have taught us all to respect life and to seek harmony," another replied.

They all agreed that the white man from across the sea would venture into their domain, their lands. They were worried that the loss of more life to strange diseases, and the lack of game in the winter, would leave them, once again, hungry and cold. A winter like the last should not be repeated.

"I will go north to the other white man, the French," Bampico announced.

Stories that travel north from the English were as prevalent as the ones that trickled south from a place called *Kanata*, where the Frenchman met the Iroquoian. This tribe was not part of the Algonquin, with whom the Abenaki aligned. The Iroquois had their own language and culture and were also living along another mighty river that also connected to the sea. Bampico had heard that the French were friendlier and more resourceful to those people.

"They have men dressed in black; they are called priests," Bampico told the group of men.

He went on to repeat the story he had heard about these priests who were part of something bigger, the Jesuits. They came across the waters with the French, and they were helpful to the tribes. Teaching them about their God, their ways. Governor General Frontenac was the voice of authority in what is now called New France, a vast territory of natural resources and an endless supply of wilderness.

Frontenac was supportive of the native peoples there and got them to align with the French. He also approved of the Jesuits in their efforts to convert these heathens to be good Catholics. The French hated the English and their advancements north, and the Indians proved to be a necessary ally, to be the distraction, preventing them from expanding.

"I will go and learn from these men dressed in black. I am strong and can learn their ways." He continued. "I will return with knowledge."

Bampico knew that the journey would be an easy one; in fact, he knew the dangers of the forest and what it would take to reach the French. His determination would guide him along with the Great Spirit from above.

Waban was saddened to hear what the men were talking about: were they in danger of the English? Would their lives be interrupted? Would their sacred river, called *Merrimac,* be the vessel of the intruders? These questions went unanswered in her mind, and now she would worry about Bampico and his quest north to *Kanata.*

Waban got up and ran into her longhouse. She was frightened by what she heard and more concerned about Bampico's quest. If he leaves the village, she may never see him again. He will journey far to seek his knowledge and alliance with the French. Without explaining to Nokemes, she grabbed a pouch made of deer skin and filled it with corn meal that was being stored in the long-house, along with some of the mashed meat, *Pemmican* for his journey. She would meet him the next morning before he started his way north.

It had been a chilly start to the morning; dawn was breaking, and so was Waban's heart. She was the first to wake in the wigwam. The smoldering fire from the night before was still emitting a trail of smoke that rose through the hole in the center of the structure. She dressed quietly and slowly pulled the animal hide flap open that served as a door. The sun was in direct alignment with it, a shaft of sunlight to briefly illuminate the interior. She quickly pulled it down and crept quietly to the river.

It was a serene morning; the light, the birds, and the sound of the river created a magical setting for the meeting. Bampico, as he promised the night before during the meal of the night, would wait to bid farewell to Waban before crossing the river.

Waban stepped on a fallen branch, and the sound it created caused Bampico to smile. He knew she was close by. He turned in the direction of the village and saw her approaching with a small bundle.

"I will miss you, Bampico," she told him.

"I will as well, for you have been a friend and one that I hope to know better one day," he replied.

She handed him the pouch with such generosity that he knew it came from her heart. There were assurances that they would never see each other again, but he would leave knowing that their hearts had touched each other's.

"Strength lies not in the battle, but in the knowledge of the understanding," he told her.

He picked up his quiver of arrows and tied the pouch of food around his waist. He was not going to show Waban any emotion or physical contact, for to do so would mislead her, and it would be unjust for both of them. His desire to learn the ways of the French to assure the longevity of his people was greater than his need for emotional satisfaction.

Waban stood motionless, and Bampico turned and walked to the river's edge. There, at its closest point, was a birch bark canoe tied to a fallen tree. He would traverse downstream to the crotch of the rivers and then paddle upstream along the *Pasomkasik* River, the second to create the *Merrimac*. The *Pasomkasik* was known for its swift waters and fast current. Bampico would go as far north as possible before he would be forced to continue on foot.

Waban stood silently as Bampico paddled downstream out of sight. He never looked back and never saw the tears in her eyes. An emotion that she rarely felt, and one she didn't quite understand.

TWO

Daybreak in June comes the earliest in the colony, the days are the longest, and hopefully the most productive. The rising sun is a gentle reminder of God's wonderment as it rose gently across the hills in the distance, creating an unmentionable feeling of rebirth. The early morning light can be the most spiritual of the day. The warming of the air caused the mist that lingered over the cold waterway to dissolve, creating a crystal-clear view of the river. The light that refracted off the water created a glow of forgiveness for all those able to seek it.

It was late spring and a time for renewal; the ground was beginning to show signs of life, and soon the river too would be alive again, nurturing those who sought its benefits. It is said that all life came from the water, and all life needed it. The river was truly a blessing for the homesteads along it.

She could hear the seagulls off in the distance; they sounded happy. The distinctive noise the birds made, like *cow-cow-cow*, was wafting through the apple orchard that was downstream. That had been a sure sign of spring for her. There was no more ice dam or any other hindrance that would not allow the fish's instinctual need to return upriver to spawn in the days that would come. The circle of life, as told in the good book, was there in front of her; she was pleased.

Despite the challenges, the Merrimac River in June was also a symbol of endurance and stability. It flowed through lands claimed and contested, through cold and thaw, and through lives shaped by hardship and hope. Beneath its current, the water moved slowly toward spring, just as the people who lived beside it moved cautiously into an uncertain future. The river was a witness to history, silent and immense, reflecting the stark beauty and struggle of colonial New England. That day, it was spring's final grasp; summer and all its warmth would be upon them soon.

She knew her time on the water's edge was nearing; the sun rose, the mist faded, and the ferns nearby with their fiddleheads emerging from a deep sleep were slowly facing the rays. She, too, turned her face to feel the warmth of the sun; the dreaded winter had passed, and she and her family hoped they would never look on such hard times again.

Settlers along the river in 1693 lived a rugged existence. God had called them to that place, and every day she and her family tried their best to remember that. It had not been a perfect existence, but she felt she had done her best for her family at the end of each day. There with her homemade rough-hewn timber and little comfort beyond the hearth, she created a life.

The connection they all had to the Merrimack River was practical; it provided water, fish, and, when not frozen, a route for canoes and small boats. The river was extremely long, she was told; in fact, no one she knew had any idea where it came from. It was rumored that many other waterways converged to create one large one.

It was said often, especially on the Sabbath, that past the river's edge was the "devils' country," a dark and evil forest that one should never venture off into. As a Puritan, she and the rest of her family, along with her neighbors, listened intently to the sermons on the Sabbath. Each week she and her husband and her eight children would trek to the meeting house to listen to the word of God for hours; it was required of them.

The town of Haverhill had been established along the river in 1640. It was part of the Massachusetts Bay Colony, which was founded sixty-five years before, in 1628. It had been the Reverend Nathaniel Ward who had brokered the deal with the local Indians. Sachem Passaconaway had sealed the deal for the settlers, granting them the deed. The collective group changed the area's original native name of Pentucket to the birthplace of the Ward in England.

The sound of the gulls grew closer; they were making their way upriver from the ocean that was only sixteen miles away. She thought to herself that the birds must be hungry; their insatiable appetite reminded her of her son Thomas Jr., who was barely ten. He had a love of food that was unmatched among her other seven children. Smiling to herself, her thoughts were of a mother's need to comfort her children, which is second only to the need to protect them.

The Duston farm was on the very edge of town, beyond Thomas Sr.'s apple orchard lay a land of unknowns to her. The region was still sparsely populated. It was, after all, the frontier of her world. Behind every rock, every tree, lurked The Devil. She didn't want to believe it, but she knew the Reverend was no doubt right.

The native people of the land were an unruly lot, she thought; it was clear to all the settlers that they needed to be on guard at all times. The chasm between the English and the French grew wider and deeper, and it was fueled by events that occurred back across the seas, a place she had only heard and read about. The situation grew worse with the pact the French made with the Indians from the north; it was said some were converted to the ways of the Catholics, a truly blasphemous way of life.

Settlements like Haverhill, Amesbury, and Andover stood as precarious outposts on the edge of English colonization, with wooden garrisons as a form of protection facing the dense and dark woods to the north. Relations with native tribes, particularly the Abenaki and other Algonquian-speaking peoples, were strained as the colony grew further into their hunting lands, which only angered the Indians, not to mention the French. King William's War continued to rage up and down the colony, from Boston to Maine. The rift between the English and the French grew precarious with each passing month. With the alignment of the local natives, the French had an advantage; no one was safe against those savages.

Protection was a commodity that, at times, was very rare for her. With each passing season, the threat of disease, hunger, Indian attack, and God's salvation, weighed upon her like an unseen force of nature. Her reflection, just of the previous year, was enough to cause her fretfulness. The problem of witchery had taken hold in the colony; no longer was it a problem from across the seas. The accusations had made it to the colony; no one was safe. She began to lament about her own family, a cousin, an aunt, a neighbor, all forced to give testimony on The Devil's work.

"How could this be happening still?" She questioned in her mind.

Witchcraft and those who were accused numbered in the 100's; nearby Salem Village was the epicenter of it all. Rumors and gossip plagued the lives of the Puritans, which was only fuel for the fire that burned in everyone. Witchery in every form was on trial last year, starting with a slave named Tituba who caused a stir that even the Lord himself could not abolish.

She walked over to the edge of the river, the sun still warming the morning chill from her body, and sat down on a fallen tree. The roots of the young maple had released from the ground, no doubt during one of the storms in December. The snow that had fallen was causing much havoc in the village. The bark felt warm and reassuring as she sat there in silent meditations of her life, not feeling any guilt that the Bible was not part of her reflection.

The apron she was wearing was freshly laundered, as was her waistcoat; she was not going to soil them as she had plans for that day, plans that she dreaded. She picked up a piece of bark from the fallen maple tree and tossed it into the water. Her actions were done in vain, as was the bark that represented a layer of protection from the elements that didn't seem to work for the fallen sapling. Like her own troubles, she hoped the bark would sink out of sight, causing no more introspection, but, alas, it did not sink but slowly meandered downstream, floating out of sight.

Well, she felt slightly vindicated that her troubles might go away, but not after a journey downstream, it appeared. Suddenly, from behind, she heard a noise from the forest, a snap of a twig. She was startled and looked in that direction, but there was nothing in sight. Her first thought was of the almighty. Why, on such a perfect morning, would he send a wild animal to descend upon her? Or maybe it was The Devil himself disguised as a painted warrior ready to snatch her away into the depths of Hell.

Standing up, along with the hair on her neck, she looked around for anything she could find for a weapon. There still was nothing in sight from the direction of the noise; she dared not look away, as confronting the demon face to face would be her resolve. Her fists were clenched and ready for what came her way.

"Ye show me my fate, for Ye are ready," Hannah whispered.

A small deer with a white tail emerged from the woods, slowly walking towards the river's edge without taking its eyes off her. They both stood in silent defiance, each equally afraid of the other. The deer moved closer, and she watched it with a sense of relief and was pleased that it had not been a more menacing force. She had hoped that all her distresses would be that easy. She sat back down on the tree ever so slowly; she wanted to savor the moment, nature's display of the simplest form of harmony.

Suddenly, without turning away, the young doe saw something that frightened it immensely, and like all wild creatures in fear, darted off in a split second back into the dense forest. That action had startled her once again, and the hairs on her neck assumed the previous position. Before having the chance to turn around, she felt the unthinkable on her shoulder, a hand.

"Hannah, how be ye?" The voice questioned.

She jumped off the log, letting out a gasp so loud the poor deer running through the forest could have heard her. She was no longer frightened, but relief was the emotion that was overwhelming her at that very second.

"Hannah, I came looking for you," he told her. "It's nearly half past six."

"Thomas Duston Sr.," Her voice stern and annoyed. "How dare you scare The Devil out of me?"

They both smiled and felt a false sense of tension. She tried not to show resolve between them as he reached out to embrace her. She took his advance and let his arms engulf her with a sense of security and protection, something she had been seeking that morning.

"How does one feel on such a lovely spring morning?" Her husband asked.

Hannah kissed him on the lips. They were deep in the woods, away from the prying eyes of anyone. She knew it was not a sin, but still, in the climate of their lives, every precaution was made to present themselves as God-fearing, loyal members of the community. They smiled and sat down holding each other's hands.

They had been married for over fifteen years, having fallen in love almost at first sight. It had been a neighbor who introduced them in the village, and it blossomed into uncontrollable lust. They met in public, with proper guidance from her mother and father. It was the secret meetings that had gotten out of hand. Christmas, a holiday that the Puritans did not celebrate, was observed by them more conventionally during 1677 with the conceiving of their firstborn that arrived the following August. This was not an unusual occurrence in the colony, but it was easily rectified with a marriage between the Emerson clan and the Duston family. Baby Hannah was born healthy and legitimate.

"Hannah, it's time," Thomas said. "We have a full day of journey ahead, and everything is prepared in the wagon."

"Yes, it is almost past the time, let's make haste." She replied.

They got up and walked back along the narrow path to the homestead. The path was no doubt an old Indian route through the thicket, not suitable to walk side by side. Thomas, who was carrying his flintlock musket, had been commissioned as part of his time with the local militia. Before the hard times of late, the native peoples were friendly and helpful to all the settlers. But that was years before, and neither of them could remember a time when they were not on alert. He was worried when Hannah had walked from his view earlier, but the sense of relief he felt when he saw her watching the deer was safe and serene.

"It will be a hard day tomorrow for you," he told her. "Saying goodbye is never an easy task."

"Yes, master, I will do my best to show divinity and forgiveness, "she replied.

Why did she say forgiveness? Was she harboring thoughts of malice? He thought to himself. There had been so much trouble, emotion, and resolve during the trial that he assumed they agreed on the matter of her sister Elizabeth Emerson.

"Whatever the outcome, I will be with you." He placed his hand on her shoulder; it was his familiar touch that relaxed her.

The homestead came into view, and the smell of the hearth's smoke lingered over the house like a blanket. Hannah could see the wagon and the horse near the front door. Thomas had been right. They were ready for their trip south. The children were all there to greet them and to bid them a safe journey. She grabbed Thomas's hand again, and they walked towards them.

Boston was a long trip away, normally done with a night's rest, but that morning their goal was to reach Charlestown before nightfall. They would stay at The Three Cranes, a tavern they had stayed at before, and be ready the next morning to take a skiff across to Boston to visit the Gaol, the city's notorious jail.

The "old stone prison," as it was referred to, was the name of the Boston Gaol, the same name used in Ireland, England, and even Australia. Gaol was synonymous with regret, and oftentimes death. The prison was constructed in 1635, with walls that were made of stone three feet thick, windows unglazed and covered in iron. It was a dark, dank place not fit for habitation. Walking the corridors above or below ground was reminiscent of a Bible passage, "though I walk through the valley of death."

Images of *The Pilgrim's Progress* by the English writer Bunyan came into Hannah's mind whenever she thought of that place. She had read the novel about Christian's journey from the City of Destruction to the Celestial City on top of Mount Zion. Perhaps Elizabeth would find that Boston, atop a different mount, would be her salvation. She thought not.

It was a bittersweet moment for Hannah as she waved goodbye to the children, knowing they were in good hands with an old family friend, Mary Neff, who had been a part of her family for so many years. Whether the times were good or miserable, old Mary was there to smooth over the brittle parts.

Thomas maneuvered his prized horse along the edge of the garden. Hannah knew it would be time to turn the soil and plant soon. A new season to reap the rewards from the good earth; it would be a time with the promise of closure and hope. What lay ahead had little chance of a positive outcome, but they would endure and manage whatever the outcome. Spring could not be held back, and soon the apple orchard would be in full bloom.

THREE

That morning, God was with them. The sky was clear, and the sun was warm on their faces as the cart rattled along the narrow dirt road south. The springtime rains were late that year, which was a blessing for them. The rain showers that come each April are truly a gift from God, a heavenly consent to all farmers to tend their fields. But a nightmare for anyone traveling on any thoroughfare. Mud season was The Devil's own; he himself claimed this fifth season. With the ground still half frozen, the rain that was bestowed took its time to recede into the soil, creating impassable pools of thick mire ready to swallow your cart's wheel. Only the wheelwrights looked at the mud as God's providence.

Their journey to Charlestown would be a long one, almost thirty-five miles. It was indeed more than a day's journey, Thomas thought. His determination to make the journey as fast as possible would have them traveling past sundown if needed. He had always had a plan, something he prided himself on.

That morning, the oxen were back at the farm in Haverhill in the barn, and his prized horse was leading the charge. The ride would be faster and more comfortable, he had been sure of it. The stallion had only been a part of the Duston family for a short time, a newly acquired asset to the Duston farm. The stallion was strong, healthy, and very loyal; all the traits the men of Puritan faith looked for in horses and in wives.

Thomas was far more devoted than Hannah, but his wife knew that devotion and obedience were virtues all good women of Massachusetts Bay Colony possessed. It had been nearly fifty years since Winthrop's vision of the *city on the hill* was established. What had started as an experiment of faith and devotion had grown into a colony of thousands of followers of the master plan. With hundreds of homesteads along the route, if any trouble had occurred, help was not far away.

There had been long tracks of wilderness, dense forest where the trees on the side of the road attempted to overtake it, reclaiming the dirt path back into the woods. With more and more pilgrims arriving, there would be little chance of that happening with the increased daily activity on the highway.

King William's War was in full swing across the great ocean, and the residual effect created more uncertain times back in the colony. Protection was always a part of the equation for anyone living north of Boston; the guard you kept could not be let down at any time, and your safety and that of your family were of the utmost importance.

Thomas was a veteran of King Philip's War, which ended over twenty years prior. He was part of the militia back then, having seen the devastation the Indians could inflict upon unsuspecting farmers and their families. He had been happy with the demise of Metacom, the Wampanoag Chief known to the English as King Philip, at Mount Hope. He was also pleased that the dismembered head was placed on a spike at the colony in Plymouth for all to see; a reminder of treachery against God and the crown would not go unpunished.

King William I, the sovereign of the colony, aligned himself at Augsburg with other nations, which only further fueled the disdain between France and England. This had devastating effects throughout the colonies. The relationship between New France and New England grew immensely, creating another Indian war, something not one Puritan wanted. How could something as frivolous as beaver pelts determine the fate of so many doing the work of God?

Thomas had his flintlock musket close by at all times, loaded, ready to be used in a split second. He rested it, leaning against the cart between him and his wife, Hannah, where they sat in silence that morning. An Indian raid was the farthest from his mind; what clouded it was his thoughts of his wife and the emotions she would be experiencing the next day.

"Master Thomas, why so quiet?" She asked her husband, placing her left hand on his knee.

"Keeping a keen eye out is all," he lied. "Tis a fine morning, we are making very good progress."

Hannah smiled and did not want to meddle. Thomas was strong and often very stoic in stature. She could tell his emotions; they would be displayed in his gait, his stance, and how his face looked. He was a handsome man; she had felt lucky that he was such a fine man. Over six feet tall, broad as the barn, and a devoted servant to

God and his family. Her adoration for him was unyielding, as was his appetite for her during intimate times.

Thomas had a voracious thirst for all things when performing God's plan to procreate. Hannah did not mind; in fact, it was one of the few things that had given her great pleasure. Most topics, especially ones of such nature, were taboo to speak aloud, so she whispered them to herself, so that she and God were aligned in their times of familiarity.

"Your stallion is doing a fine job," she told him. "We should arrive at the Three Cranes during the mealtime with God on our side."

This had only been Hannah's second trip to Charlestown. She had prided herself in remembering the details of any journey, whether on a byway or a foot path that was once used by the savages before the arrival of the Godly.

"I will be pleased with a tankard and the daily supper. Thomas turned to her. "Shall we pray?"

Thomas thought if ever there was a time to seek the guidance of the heavenly father, it would have been that morning. He was feeling a sense of guilt that came from deep inside his being; his decision had gone against all he was taught. With matters of family, devotion, and the law, the lines were blurred, and often the incorrect conclusion was unresolvable.

Times had been tough for both the Emerson and the Duston families. The events were numerous, and for years, the struggles they dealt with at times were insurmountable. That morning, they were off to visit Hannah's younger sister in the Boston Gaol. She had been held in the old stone prison for over two years, a tragedy that might have been prevented if he had shown more empathy for his wife's little sister. Thomas pulled back on the reins of the horse, stopping it in the center of the gravel path. He gently took Hannah's hands.

"Lord Father in Heaven, please show your mercy and offer your guidance to us as we embark on another delicate family situation. We seek salvation for our dear sister Elizabeth and forgiveness for her for any transgressions that might have occurred. We seek your absolution for her soul as she enters the eternal world of your kingdom," He paused. "Amen."

"Amen," Hannah spoke softly. A tear slowly trickled down one cheek.

Hannah herself was a strong and capable woman. She was the backbone to the Duston household, holding it together, reserving any emotion she might have for a silent meditation as she had earlier that morning at the river's edge. Not as tall as her husband, but equally as strong, defiant, and resourceful as any good wife of the time had to be. To Thomas, there was not another Goody in the village who fared to his; Hannah had proven to be the right choice as he had told her so many times previously.

With a snap of the reins, the horse began to move again. Thomas was aware that the road ahead had become smoother and wider as the traffic had increased over the years. He snapped them again. Making haste, Charlestown was still far off, but he knew it was achievable.

The prayer had helped Thomas recollect the events that came years before. For Hannah his decision about Elizabeth had sealed her fate and stirred a burning desire for her to scream, something that she would not do.

Her composure was very important to her; emotions for women needed to be overmanaged. The society in which they lived was one of observations, from the clergy, the family, and most importantly, the neighbors. The eyes were always present to report; the brethren were acutely aware during those troubling times. There were countless times on the Sabbath that the sermon would remind them that Winthrop's vision was for *all to see*, a model society of Puritan Faith.

Those sermons on Sundays at the meeting house would be lengthy, sometimes three hours, and most times there would be two orations. The Reverend of Haverhill was often long-winded and incapable of using fewer words to make his message clear. It was Hannah's desire always to show her devoutness to the church and to set an example for her children. The duty of a good-wife was that of education and proper child rearing of her family. They would squirm and agitate each other until Thomas's stern look caught their eyes, and they settled back into a silent trance, listening and trying to understand the word of the Lord.

Hannah's mind wandered as Thomas was in full control of the horse and heading south. She thought about Elizabeth and how so very long ago the trouble was made aware to her and Thomas.

Michael Emerson, the father of Hannah and Elizabeth, was an unruly and disrespectful man to his wife, his children, and his church. These were strong feelings that she never spoke aloud; only once did she confront him on his disheartening behavior. He was as ambivalent then as he always had been. His taste for cider and rum, which when taken in moderation, was allowed among them. God often made allowances. Her father had taken drink to a new height, and when it occurred, The Devil himself occupied his thoughts and actions. The Emerson household knew not all the prayers in the book could deter the evil that would be unleashed.

The benefit of the doubt of his improvement during better times had long passed in Hannah's mind. She tried to understand his behavior, and perhaps it was from whence he came, watching his parents pass from the sweating disease and enduring the long and dangerous trip from England all by himself. These factors had to play a role in the way he viewed the world. His taste for rum and cider had only intensified his malice towards his family and his church.

Years ago, on a stormy night, the bang on the Duston homestead door was deafening. Bang, Bang, Bang. Thomas leaped out of bed, and Hannah followed. The distance was short back then, the one-room house was where they slept, and it was near the door. His musket was close by, and he was prepared to use it.

"Hannah, Hannah, let me in!" She thought the voice was Elizabeth's.

"Betty, be that you?" Cracking the door slightly, Thomas stood behind her with the musket aimed.

The door was flung open, and Elizabeth fell into the room, still in her night clothes and barefoot. She was soaking wet, her dressing gown covered in a combination of mud and blood. Betty was the name Hannah would call her little sister, something her parents frowned on. Her face was also covered in blood, one eye swollen shut. Hannah was confused. What had happened? Did she fall in the muddy road? Was the blood from that? Why did she have no shoes? In times of distress, it is amazing how fast one's mind can process thoughts.

Thomas lowered the gun and retrieved a blanket from the bed, and wrapped it around her. Elizabeth was not even ten years of age; no child should arrive at your dooryard in that condition. The chill from the rainy night created a wave of damp, cold air into the house. In one motion, Thomas slammed the door, preventing any more heat from escaping, and then placed a chunk of wood on the burning embers in the hearth. He had a feeling it would be a long night. He had been correct.

"Was it Father?" Hannah asked, tightening the blanket around her little sister.

Betty nodded; not a word of explanation was needed. The Devil had visited the Emerson home once again that night, and that had been the evidence. Betty was distressed and ashamed; her sister was her only ally. Hannah moved her sister down to the floor in front of the fire and retrieved a piece of linen and the water bucket. Thomas found another quilt to place under his sister-in-law's head.

Michael Emerson would never win any prize for his fathering of his children; in fact, perhaps facing arrest would be a better option. That is exactly what happened: Hannah's father was charged by the magistrate for "cruel and excessive violence" for beating and kicking his nearly 11-year-old daughter. The charges came with a fine of 5 schillings and the subject of much conjecture and gossip from the "eyes" in Haverhill and the nearby townships.

That had been fourteen years ago when Hannah had pleaded with her husband to take her sister into their home. She knew Elizabeth needed to distance herself from the evil in her father. A blind eye from Hannah, her mother and namesake, did not help the appalling situation. The oldest often was given the same name as their parent.

Thomas refused to accept her little sister for reasons that were most apparent to them both. Besides being another mouth to feed, Elizabeth had a troubled spirit, which was something he was not ready for. Their own family was growing, and there was no stopping them from procreating; it was the will of God.

Had her husband had a change of heart, perhaps they would not be on route to Charlestown to the old Gaol to see her sister. Forgiveness is something that Hannah herself had always tried to employ in her reflections and meditations. It was not a trait that came easily to her. Many passages in the Old Testament referenced "an eye for an eye." One of the few that pleased her. Michael Emerson, The Devil that he was, would get his due on judgment day, a day that could not come soon enough, Hannah thought.

"What ye thinking about?" Thomas asked her.

"Oh, I am just trying to recall a time when the trouble did not exist," she told him. "Was there ever a time when our door at the house opened, and it was a welcome one?

Thomas placed his right arm around her ever so slightly and allowed her head to rest upon his shoulder. The movement of the cart was soothing to her; it had caused her to release a deep sigh of anguish and remorse. She felt better.

The road ahead was well-worn and becoming more passable. Thomas thought one day this would be well-traveled, and the Surveyor of the Highways would care for it properly. They passed their brothers and sisters of the brethren along the way. A nod from him was a simple hello, and he sent God's blessing to them without a word spoken.

Hannah drifted off to a state of slumber, with her head on her husband's shoulder, not quite asleep and not fully awake. The sounds from the cart, creaking and groaning as it passed over the gravel, created a sense of reassurance.

Elizabeth, her little sister, once again drifted into her consciousness, clouding her once again with dread. It had been two years previously when another knock at her door came, this time from her loyal friend and household helper, Mary Neff.

"Hannah, oh my dear Hannah," Mary said, distraught and shaking.

"What is it, Goody Neff? Hannah asked.

"I'm so sorry, I had no idea when they asked me to accompany them to your father's house."

"What say you? Speak not in riddles," Hannah knew if her father was involved, it had to be something very wrong.

"She had the babies, twins they were." Mary, with tears in her eyes and anguish across her face, stared into her friends' eyes.

Hannah helped Mary in the house, which was now larger, and the great main room was fully furnished with the talents of her husband, and the never-ending supply of pine trees on their property. The furniture served its purpose, as there were no sleeping quarters in the main room. The children all slept in the loft and the second room was where Thomas and she lay. The Duston house was prosperous and growing as was their family, with already six children; Hannah was pregnant again.

Mary Neff was sobbing, something that women seldom did; she sat down on the bench at the eating table. Hannah fetched the dipper from the hook on the hearth and ladled a full cup of water from the wooden bucket.

"Drink slowly," she instructed.

Mary was in a state that Hannah had never seen. It reminded her of the time when someone in the village center mentioned her name and witchcraft in the same sentence. Witchcraft, or association with the word, was as damaging as the actual accusation; it had been the start of the troubling times in the colony, especially for Salem.

"Mary, take ye, settle your mind," She told her. "Your unquietness will trouble your heart."

Mary drank from the dipper; it had helped. Her breathing slowed, and she was able to speak. The story that unfolded was a horrifying tale that Hannah thought to be untrue. Once again, Hannah felt the pain of a lonesome heart for not being nearer to her Betty; though only a few miles away, the Emerson household was not a welcome destination in her mind.

It had been the Sunday before that Mary was summoned by Nathaniel Saltonstall, the local authority, along with a few others, to her childhood home. Her parents, Michael and Hannah, were at the village meeting house for the weekly Sabbath, but Elizabeth was feeling poorly and remained home.

Mary started to tear up again, but she tried her best to tell her strange tale to Hannah. The eyes of the town had been upon the Emerson house for some time, it had seemed. The right moment to confront her sister had been when the house was empty, with her alone. Elizabeth had grown noticeably large, as if with child. She had denied it and tried her best to conceal her condition. She was, in fact, pregnant.

"Did ye know?" Mary asked her friend.

Hannah was dumbfounded and riddled with guilt. How had the weeks turned into months that the sisters never met? Her sister, six years younger, was in the family way by a married member of her congregation. A shameful act and one that would not go unpunished.

The story, as told, went from a dire situation to the unimaginable; it emerged that the infant had become twins and was born in secret. Elizabeth lay in her trundle bed, not two feet from her sleeping parents, and performed the miracle of life without anyone being aware. Her sleeping parents claimed never to be awoken to any sounds of newborn infants, pain of childbirth, or any other disturbances.

"Where is my sister now? Hannah asked. "The children, does my mother have them?"

Mary began to cry again; the story was not over. Using the sleeve from her apron, she did her best to dry her tears. That Sunday, which had just passed, when Mary, Reverend Saltonstall, and the others abruptly descended upon Elizabeth, they found no infants, no sign of them.

"How did you become aware?" Hannah asked.

"It be ye was after she was touch her stomach, tis be tender. I was ordered to inspect her," she said.

Saltonstall was an ardent member of the clergy and, at the time, an influential force for witch hunting in the colony. It was said that he would become a judge if the accusations came to fruition. Refusing Nathanial Saltonstall, when he instructed you to do something, was not a choice Mary Neff would be able to refuse.

Elizabeth's skirts were lifted as she lay on the bed in her parents' room, and Mary was able to inspect her woman's area. Mary could not help but notice her ankles, swollen and tender to the touch. She was fatigued and could not attend the services on Sunday, and the discomfort in her belly was overwhelming to her when she pressed her fingers to it.

Mary, an experienced midwife and healer herself, knew she had given birth and would have to make the investigating party aware of Elizabeth's non-condition. She explained to Hannah that as she was confirming her findings to Saltonstall, another man came into the house carrying a sack, which looked soiled as if it had been buried.

"Oh, Mary," Hannah sat down, feeling weak herself. "Please tell ye that they were not in the sack."

Mary nodded. It seemed the eyes were upon Elizabeth for some time, when her belly grew rather fast, an unmarried woman of twenty-six living in a house with history; the eyes kept a vigilante watch. Their vigil for righteousness was unyielding, especially for the Emerson clan.

When the belly suddenly was no longer, Saltonstall was brought into the fold, and an investigation proved to be worthy. It was made aware that on that Sabbath, she was seen in the back yard with a spade, a most unusual sight for a young woman where there had been no patch of garden.

Elizabeth, a woman already with a past, claimed that they were stillborn and that her parents were not aware of their existence. Having been unwed, the infants were not legitimate and could not be buried on consecrated ground. She hid the bodies in a trunk, and on the morning when her parents left for the meeting house, she sewed them into a sack and buried them near an apple tree behind the Emerson homestead.

"A story I take no pleasure to tell ye, Hannah," Mary said, exhausted. "No sister shall have the burden of another like this."

"Mary, the tale is scarce to be believed," Hannah continued. "It maketh me as sorrowful as it does wroth."

Memories, especially the bad ones, have a way of staying foremost in your mind, and with Hannah, those memories play out every time she closes her eyes. They cause heartache and rage within her. Something she did not like, but something she could not prevent.

Hannah's eyes were still shut; the day was passing fast. The memories of her sister, and the tale that Mary Neff told to her nearly two years before, caused her heart to singe, one that would never heal. Slowly, she opened her eyes, and Thomas was focused on the task at hand, trying to keep the cart moving forward. How long had she slumbered, she thought? She sat up straight and stretched her neck in the opposite direction from Thomas's shoulder.

"There ye be, how was your quiet time?" Her husband asked.

She smiled at her husband, but he could sense the tension in her face. The situation was dire; they both knew it and wanted nothing more than to be back in Haverhill on their homestead, far away from this madness.

The smell of smoke from nearby homes was becoming more plentiful. It was a cooler than a normal evening for June; fires were lit, suppers were cooking, and soon the light of the day would fall behind the hills of Boston, casting Charlestown into darkness. They would find a paddock for the horse and cart. A small skiff across the Mystic River would be the last part of their trip. It would be a dark crossing, but the boatman would know the route, having done it many times a day. From there, a short walk to the Three Cranes Tavern would be easy; a hot meal and a good sleep were next.

Hannah smiled and spoke not a word. It was her way of coping with the impossible. Steadfast in her resolve, she would see that day through, for tomorrow would be upon her soon, and that would bring another tale of treachery to her soul.

FOUR

It was at night, when darkness fell upon the city of Boston, and the view from her window was no longer visible to her. That had caused her the most regret, and sadness would overcome her with a sense of hopelessness. The lack of lighting turned the city into a dark labyrinth of cobblestone streets and alleys cast in shadows. It happened most nights, except when the full moon rose; it was on those evenings that Elizabeth could watch from her prison cell the city she dreamed about rejoining one day. A fantasy that she held tight to her heart.

It had been nearly two years since Elizabeth Emerson had been taken to the Boston Gaol to await her trial. She had never seen the daylight from outside since the day she was convicted of infanticide of her twins, and the long wait for her sentence finally came a few months prior. On that night and with the absence of any moonlight, she knew her demise was imminent. Her execution by hanging was to be the following day on Boston Common; it would be directly after a sermon.

She was so troubled, deep in thought and nearly despondent, with no will to live, that Elizabeth did not hear the metal dish of food slide across the cold stone floor.

She turned to see the keeper of the prisoners standing there once he spoke. He had an imposing frame that was cast in shadow from the torch he carried, a giant of a man compared to Elizabeth, who was five feet tall. The guard, strong and intimidating, was not without empathy, though he tried never to show it, except for occasions like that morning, when he knew what would be happening.

"Goody Emerson, eat. You will need your strength to endure what is to come," he told her.

She never replied. He turned and walked down the narrow passageway of the prison. The light from his torch was slowly fading as he descended the steps to where he stood watch through the night. She could hear murmurs from the other prisoners as he passed with the torch, each sounding more desperate than the next.

Once more, she was cast in almost complete darkness. Elizabeth crawled over to the wooden door where the food was slid under. Reaching for the metal plate, she took it carefully back to her makeshift bed of straw to eat its contents. She thought that her appetite would not lend itself to take the meal, but the salted fish and fresh bread were a welcome change from the gruel of oats and water that normally came at night.

It had been two years and a month since she was taken from her home on Mill Street in Haverhill, where she lived with her parents and her daughter, Dorothy, who was born out of wedlock ten years before. That had been another tragic time for her and her entire family. The brethren frowned upon illegitimate children, but the father of her child was never disclosed, and she lived in virtual exile since her year eighteen.

Oh, how she missed the embrace of her Dorothy, the cuddles, and especially her smell. Her child had been her joy, despite how she was conceived. Her child was hers, and no one could change that; her only hope was that with the next day's event, her little Dorothy would no longer be the product of Puritan judgment and begin to thrive in the community. She had hoped her death would be penance enough to discharge her from the shame of her mother.

Elizabeth finished her meal, using the last bit of crust to clean the tin plate. She lay down on the musty straw; she had hoped that sleep would overtake her soon. She also wondered, that if there was a God, why would he not spare her the next day and take her while she slept. She knew there was no God, no matter how many times the Pastor would preach about the almighty; her opinion on the matter was not very favorable.

There in the darkness, she lay unable to sleep and unable to cry. There had been no tears left in her; she was fast becoming a former image of the young mother she once was. Not only was she branded an unclean woman, but she had become a murderess, the worst kind.

Infanticide had been a burden in the newly found colony in the city on the hill. The church looked down on unwed mothers, unclean women, and illegitimate children, who had no place amongst a God-fearing community of Puritans. Women who found themselves in such a predicament, either by lust or violence, had few choices to eliminate the problem.

There were those elders in the community who knew the ways of the old world; once they came, they could take care of the issue, and then there were those who tried to take care of it themselves, causing more bodily harm. The few who cried violence against them were then ridiculed for stating rape, an equally distasteful accusation. To prove malice on the man's part, there had to be a witness, one who would testify, which always proved to be an unlikely combination.

Elizabeth had been in a quandary for years, from the beating she received from her father at the age of eleven, to an unwanted pregnancy at twenty, and now this situation, six years later. Her entire life seemed to be marred by unexpected events and violence. Neither of which she felt was entirely her fault.

As a Puritan woman, her role was to demonstrate religious piety and obedience. The church preached male authority, and women of the community needed to be submissive and display humility. This was Elizabeth's lot in life, a no-win situation; she had felt the wrath of her father's rage from such a young age.

When she found herself pregnant with Dorothy, she had no one to turn to except her mother, who, for some strange reason, showed her little sympathy. Her mother had her hands full with her other children, so she informed her husband, Elizabeth's father. Something she dreaded as much as her daughter did. Sometimes the truth is closer than one would think.

Michael Emerson's reaction was not as violent as either of them had expected; he was enraged and strangely somewhat embarrassed. The shame once again would be put upon his household, this time from his daughter, and by his own doing.

"How could this happen, shame, shame!" He raised his voice and his hand; the crack that it made as it connected with his young daughter's face could be heard throughout their modest dwelling.

"No husband, do not let history repeat itself!" Hannah, the senior, cried out, stepping in front of Elizabeth.

"Step away, The Devil in her needs to be punished. I will free her of this affliction," he demanded.

Elizabeth did not move; tears rolled down her red face, but her stoic expression was unyielding. She was no longer going to be the submissive daughter who accepted many acts of violence from her father or any man.

Her father knew that no amount of beating would be the punishment she needed to solve the problem, but he always knew that the situation could have been prevented with perhaps a more watchful eye.

"Name the father," he cried. "Tell me now, I will drag him to the town stock for this travesty."

Elizabeth would not say a word, but looked intently into her father's eyes. Her glare was enough for him not to pursue it further that evening. The next morning, he thought he would have devised a plan to render the situation.

"Go to bed, think on ye for ye lay with The Devil and ye will reap the penance," he told her.

Elizabeth gladly retreated to her bed; there she wept alone, for she had nowhere to turn but to The Devil himself. What plan will her father devise in the day's light? How will this turn out for her and the child growing in her belly?

Michael had seen her with a young man on a few occasions; they had been seen walking to the meeting house on the Sabbath day, and they were acquainted from the days in their school years before. He convinced himself that the perpetrator was Timothy Swan.

Right after breakfast, he grabbed his cloak and hat, and he abruptly left the Emerson home. Elizabeth heard the door slam and jumped out of bed to the window. She had no idea where he was walking to, but by the gate of his walk, anger ruled his demeanor.

Not but a few streets away was the Swan Home. Michael walked up to the wooden door and banged loudly. Samuel Swan came to the door, the look of confusion on his face detailing the dislike he had for Emerson.

Michael rattled off his accusation about his son, Timothy. The father of the alleged perpetrator was mortified by the very idea that his son could be responsible for this deed. Samuel's demeanor became apparent to Emerson. It was an offense. Asking Goodman Emerson to leave his property was the first thing that came to mind, but not until he said his peace.

"You be but a wicked soul, Emerson, no doubt a servant of Satan himself; you have brought shame many times onto your house," Swan said. "Your past transgressions are known; off with you, before I send for the constable."

"How dare you speak of such nonsense; I am no servant of The Devil." Michael shot back. "How can you be so sure of your son's ill manners?"

"I charged my son Timothy not to go into that wicked house of yours," he told Emerson. "My son would not abide by such jade."

With that, the door was slammed, and Michael turned to walk back across the village green to his home and to his troubles. With no solution in hand, Elizabeth would bear the child, and they all would bear the burden of the fine from the village court.

Still awake in the bed of musty straw, Elizabeth could not sleep. The event that led up to that night was so overpowering in her memory that she was forced to re-live it in her mind. She was glad that her parents were far away in Haverhill, perhaps not even knowing that the next day would be her last. She had hoped to hear word from her sister Hannah, who was the backbone of her resolve over the past years. Perhaps she will come, one more glimpse of her, and to plead once to watch over her Dorothy, for she fears that one day she too might fall to The Devil himself.

There had been a glimmer of hope when the esteemed Reverend Cotton Mather showed interest in her case. He, along with his father, was well admired and revered in the city of Boston, as well as the entire Massachusetts Bay Colony. They were co-pastors at the North Church, sometimes called the Second church, as it was newly built after a fire had destroyed the first.

Mather, the junior, had inquired during the hearing to her solicitor if he could interview Elizabeth in her cell. Since there was no admission to the killing of her babies on her part, she would not be received in the kingdom of Heaven. Damnation for her soul was something Mather, as any good Reverend of the Puritan faith, thought he could avoid.

Cotton Mather was a force to be reckoned with, a graduate of Harvard and the son of the most learned pastor in Boston, the Honorable Increase Mather. The Mathers together represented the Puritan faith at its purest, as every member of the church knew. His interest and his influence could get Elizabeth a pardon from the Governor himself.

The witch trials of Salem had not quite ended that June, though rumor had it the Governor had decided enough was enough and wished the accused be released within a fortnight. Reverend Mather played an important role with his writings and sermons, condemning the accused and forcing confessions from them. For a witch to confess her sins and repent was a feather in his cap, as well as preventing the execution of those who did not. It was a different outcome for those who would not confess; confessing to an untrue charge would surely be damnation in hell; not confessing brought another sort of damnation, public execution.

There had already been too many deaths centered around this time on the north shore of the colony, especially in Salem. Elizabeth was not aware of the severity of the accusations until one day, almost a year prior, when her cousin, Roger Toothaker, was brought into the prison, accused of consorting with The Devil himself. She had only been made aware of his presence when his daughter was also accused of the same crime, and she passed by her cell and was locked in another with the other accused women. It was no surprise that more disfavor had fallen upon her family.

Roger was a fiery man with a tall story for every occasion. He boasted of being a folk healer and that he could detect a witch in their midst. He lived in Beverly, a few miles from Haverhill and closer to Salem. He once told a neighbor of his exploits that a long time before the witch hunter appeared, he and his daughter discovered a witch living among them. He detected her and proceeded to eliminate her from the village and the earth. They killed her together.

The story was as sensational as the rest of the accused; the courts saw through it swiftly and dismissed the charges against Martha Emerson, his daughter. She received a heavy fine. She tried to raise the funds for her release. Roger's fate did not prove so beneficial. During his short time in the Gaol, he had fallen gravely ill. Without any medical care, he died shortly after his incarceration, before the court could hear his case.

During her meetings with the Reverend Mather, Elizabeth sought to shame him and his God about her cousin and all the others who were executed. But she feared his condemnation of her own alleged crimes might prevent any chance of a pardon. Still, she would not, and could not, confess to the murder of her own offspring. Many times Mather would visit the dirty cell where she was imprisoned. He would arrive with a bundle of papers, a quill, and a wooden stool that the prison had lent to him.

"I know not why ye return each time," Elizabeth would tell him. "I never laid a hand on those babies, dead they were."

Elizabeth was slowly being worn down by Mather on each of his visits. His presence was as unsettling as were his persistent questions. The visits distressed Elizabeth with aggravation each time he visited. Having to relive the incident for the good Reverend was more than she could handle.

"Yes, I hid them from my father," she finally broke down. "Stillborn is what midwives called it; those babies were already on the way to Heaven without ever taking a breath."

"Goody Emerson, tell me why you hid the infants for days before burying them," Reverend Mather asked her. "What were ye hiding?"

By that time Mather realized that there would not be a confession unless his tactics changed. In order to get the young mother to tell him the truth, he was going to have to manipulate her. He described in detail the process of the execution, how it was done, and that her soul would be in hell for all eternity. Her daughter, Dorothy, and the entire Emerson clan would be the center of gossip and ridicule. The eyes would always be watching; peace for them would not be possible.

"Enough, enough!" She screamed. "I did it, I did it, I did not want the shame of bearing children of The Devil. You write that, I will not."

Mather scratched some notes on the parchment and bid her good day. Elizabeth broke down in hysterics, sobbing and throwing the straw about the cell. A fit of anger mixed with remorse overwhelmed her. The Reverend cautiously stood up and backed away in the direction of the cell door. The guard had heard all the commotion and had already unlocked the door for Mather.

She fell face down onto the straw, her face wet from the salty tears; she sobbed. "What have I done?" Words escaped her in a whisper that ought to have been a prayer.

Mather wrote it, and she made her mark on it during his last brief visit. It did not help, and the sentence remained. Mather was not a man of God in her mind, but a messenger for The Devil; for without Satan, the good Reverend would have nothing to preach about.

Elizabeth was cursed to think of all the misgivings that were bestowed upon her and her family before she was to be executed. It was a nightmare for the young woman to endure alone on a bed of straw in the dark of night. She closed he eyes and prayed to whatever God that might be listening for sleep to take her.

FIVE

The Tree Cranes Tavern had proven to be a worthy stop for Hannah and Thomas. Their late arrival was not an issue, and the evening meal served warm was adequate before retiring to the loft room on the third floor. The feather bed was a Godsend for them, and sleep was exactly what they needed. They did not know what the next day would bring, but they were determined to see it through.

At daybreak, Charlestown woke up, as did the Dustons. The sound of horses, carts, and peddlers had started to fill the dirty streets; footsteps along the wooden walks echoed in the morning air. Everyone had a place to go; it was the start of another day. It was Sunday, and unlike the hamlet of Haverhill, where life was that of devotion and day-long sermons, the city proved to be more than that.

There were many houses of the Lord, some not even finished, and the bare timbers could be seen across the Charles River. It would appear that Boston was growing at a steady rate, with the continued flow of freedom and fortune seekers in 1693 having only grown.

They made their way downstairs to the tavern's great room. A morning fire was smoldering in the hearth, and a cast-iron pot filled with porridge was bubbling away. The tavern keeper's wife was slowly stirring the pot of oats and currants, ready to serve those guests in need of breakfast. They sat and thanked her for breakfast. They ate it in haste, as they still had to cross the Charles River to get to the meeting house on time.

The flat-bottom skiff glided the short distance across the Charles; the boat was nearly full with others off to do business in the city. Thomas was amazed at how easy it was to maneuver from one side of the river to the other. They disembarked on the north side of Boston and asked for directions to the Gaol. Prison Lane, as it was called, was not far; he was sure they had plenty of time to get there.

The cobblestone streets were a challenge for the two, as the country road and old Indian paths that they used seemed easier somehow. The cut square blocks of stones wet with the rain from the night before, and the waste from the chamber pots, only added to the discomfort of the situation.

"Hannah, take my hand," Thomas said. "We will steady each other."

Hannah was dressed in her best clothes for that day, a linen undergarment over which her wool skirt covered her petticoat, and her favorite cloak, the one she always wore on the Sabbath to the meeting house. Her head was covered as it was expected with a linen cap that Mary Neff had embroidered with a row of small violets around the edge.

"Goody Duston, we are almost to the prison," he told her. "How ye be? Betty will be happy to see you on such a sad day."

"Thomas, I know not how to be; my little sister will meet her demise today," she told him. "My heart is broken, and my mind is in a state I have not felt before."

Thomas slowed down enough to embrace her for comfort with his form of security. She was grateful and wished the day to be over. The Boston Gaol was now in sight; the gray stone building was like a menacing demon looking down upon those who dared enter. With its ominous walls thicker than anyone could imagine, unglazed windows, and iron bars across all of them, it truly was something neither of them had seen before or had a desire to enter.

They were well aware of the people who resided in that structure. Pirates, thieves, witches, and baby killers, all of which both Thomas and Hannah had heard stories of. The large wooden door covered in iron spikes was ajar as if someone had seen them coming.

"Good day," Thomas yelled into the dark corridor. "We have come to pay respect to Goody Elizabeth Emerson."

The heavy door slowly swung open, making a creaking sound. If it were heard in Haverhill, the entire village would fear it was the gate to hell. The smell of the interior was so overwhelming to them that it caused them to pause and to have second thoughts about entering. Hannah reached into the pocket of her cloak and pulled out fresh swatches of linen that she had made over the past winter. She placed one over her nose and mouth, and gave the other to Thomas, who did the same.

They stepped out of the sunshine and into the darkness of justice.

"Master Duston, the prisoner Emerson is straight down to the end, then one flight up," he told them. "Make haste, she needs to be delivered to North Square by ten. The master Reverend Mather will be there to receive her."

Thomas nodded, but Hannah would not make eye contact as they passed him. They hurried down the long, dark, and dank corridor, holding the linen across their noses. The smell was so overpowering; the unclean bodies, moldy straw, and human waste were contributing to the foul, stale air.

They passed other prisoners, some in makeshift cells made of wood and others with iron bars and locks so large that Thomas had never seen anything like them. Some of the prisoners never looked up, and a few others reached out into the corridor as they passed, trying to touch them. Some pleading, some reciting the Lord's prayer. It was a scene that was expected but not actually experienced.

They turned the corner and climbed the narrow stairs up to the next floor. They were happy that a rope was attached to the wall as a makeshift railing. Hannah reached the top and froze in her steps. Tears filled her eyes, causing her vision to blur; it was as if her body was producing the tears as a defense mechanism to spare her the view.

"Betty, my sweet Betty," Hannah whispered. "What have they done to you?"

Elizabeth turned to face her sister; her feeling of shame overwhelmed her, and so she bowed her head. Making eye contact would be a fatal blow to her heart.

The situation was grave, her condition was almost unrecognizable to her sister, and fate was at the door. Nothing could be done; the deal was sealed, and making the best of the time they had was all they could do.

"Thank you for coming, sister. I do hope the journey proved easy?" She asked her older sister.

"Betty, my little sister," Hannah was tearful. "I had to come, tis a tragic time for all, and I'm at God's mercy to see this through."

"God, please do not speak of him," Elizabeth said. "He has forsaken me and left me to rot. I will be at the gates of hell soon enough. God has turned his back on me."

Hannah stepped closer to the iron door and reached in to touch her sister. She wanted her to know that comfort was readily available, at least for a short time. Elizabeth turned and stared out the window; the sun on her face was all the comfort she needed, and the view of the street would be embedded into her memory; that would be all she would take from that hideous place.

"Elizabeth, we came because we love you and want to show support anyway we can," Thomas told his sister-in-law.

"Betty, I brought you your favorite cloak to wear today. I thought it might give you some solace," Hannah was almost pleading. "In the pocket is a lock of Dorothy's hair, please take it."

Hannah pushed the cloak through the iron bars, and it fell onto the floor of her cell. Elizabeth was torn between her love for her sister and the disappointment she felt for Thomas. They both knew what a situation she had been in for years, yet the support they showed had not been sufficient to help. The Devil still found her; there was no escaping it in the Emerson house.

"Please, Betty, I need to know that inside that broken vessel of your being, that your heart and your soul are intact. I love ye dear sister, I will never forget you." Hannah continued to plead.

"And I love ye, as well," Betty told her. "I will take my love for you all the way to the bitter end." Elizabeth picked up the cloak and tied it around her shoulders. It did make her feel better, and it hid her soiled clothes that were barely rags. In the pocket was a locket of her firstborn's hair. It was tied with a ribbon and smelled of lye and lilacs; all children have a distinctive smell that only a mother knows.

Thomas was sad that Elizabeth did not address him, nor did not make eye contact. His actions so long ago on that rainy night proved to be the wedge between them, and now it will be there for eternity. His only thought was that thankfully his wife did not make the same judgment on him.

The sounds of footsteps were coming up the stone stairs along with the rattling of keys. The guard presented himself to the small group, and without a word, they all knew it was time to go. The beginning of the end was upon them. The guard produced an iron key that was over a foot long; he had several tied to his waistcoat. He waited for the Dustons to leave before he unlocked the cell door.

Hannah did not embrace her sister but simply met her eyes and smiled. Forgiveness from either of them went unmentioned; there was no need for it. She knew that her sister would soon be at the *Wicket Gate* and would be guided to the *Celestial City*; it was the way in the *Pilgrim's Progress*, something she read over and over and wholeheartedly believed.

North Square was but a short walk from prison alley; they crossed on foot, back to the north side of the city. There would be a mass held this morning at the newly built North Church with the honorable Cotton Mather delivering the sermon. Mather was, in his own way, yearning for approval and hungry for fame; it appeared in his sermons and his writings on the printed page, which came after, and which no doubt was for sale.

Execution day in Boston was very popular, especially for those accused of witchcraft or infanticide. That day would be no different; the morbid curiosity of the Puritan went deep into their mannerisms. With little other chances to peak their senses, death was the ultimate awareness of enlightenment. For whatever reason, executions brought the best and the worst out in the open.

Thomas and Hannah arrived at the church and decided to sit as close to the door as possible, in case an easy departure might be needed. It had been their first Mather sermon and their first execution. They dreaded both activities that June morning.

The church was nearly full, with most people squeezed into the pews in the front first. They all wanted to see Elizabeth Emerson, baby killer from Haverhill. Hannah could hear the whispers from those near. The mention of her cousin, the witch that died in the Gaol, and another cousin still imprisoned: those were comments made in hushed tones, along with the unanswered question of who the father of the babies was, and why he had never come forward.

"Thomas, did ye hear that?" Hannah whispered.

"Yes, indeed, many questions are not answered," he replied. "We may never know, but we must be strong against the workings of The Devil; our resolve cannot be undermined."

Hannah was confused by his answer; perhaps the visit to Betty had been overly taxing for him. It had been his decision and lack of generosity that kept her sister away from them so long ago. She had abided by his will and understood his reasoning; times were never the easiest then or now.

Something was happening; the entire congregation was becoming unsettled. From where they sat, they did not have a good view of the front of the church. The whispers continued, and she heard the side door open. Elizabeth had entered along with the prison guard from the Gaol. Hannah strained her neck far enough to cast her eyes on the backside of a golden cloak in the front pew. It had to be Elizabeth. That color she knew, as her mother dyed it last fall with the flowers of the Goldenrod. Betty loved that cloak.

The congregation grew quiet, and the Reverend Cotton Mather had approached the pulpit and placed his notes there. Hannah could see him and was surprised by his young age. Mather, dressed in a traditional robe with a white wig, was not more than thirty years of age. How could a man of his status have accomplished all that he had in those few years? He truly must be learned, a man of God. Everyone was waiting for him to speak. What would his message be, and would he absolve Elizabeth before her execution?

"There should be a fountain open for sin and for un-cleanness. Your sin has been uncleanness, repeated uncleanness. Impudent uncleanness, murderous uncleanness: you must, like the leper, cry out unclean! Unclean!" Mather's words were filled with drama and direct.

Cotton Mather was, without a doubt, a bit of a showman; his fiery sermons could stop any churchgoer in their tracks. That morning had been no different, and poor Elisabeth Emerson sat there for the entire world to see the remorse she felt displayed across her face.

Mather's sermon was entitled, "Warnings from the dead," and included Elisabeth's own words she had given during the confession which he aggressively extracted from her.

"I am a miserable sinner, and I have justly provoked the Holy God to leave me onto that folly of my own heart for which I am condemned to die," Mather was shouting at that point. "Those are not my words but those of the unclean." He pointed down to Elizabeth.

Thomas was shocked that such words would have come out of his sister-in-law's mouth; it did not sound like her. The young girl whom he had not seen in a very long time did not speak in that manner. She was surely misinterpreted.

"Husband, I would like to make haste from this place," Hannah whispered into Thomas's ear.

"Are you not feeling well?" He asked.

Hannah was tired of it all: the journey, the prison, and her sister's fate. It had all become overburdening to her mind. She was a strong woman, if at times stronger than Thomas and most men she knew. The limit of emotions had been reached; it was equally as painful to stay as it was for her to leave.

"I wish not to stay, and I wish not to see my younger sister's death displayed for these people to be amused by." Hannah was firm and did not wait for an answer.

She stood up slowly and took Thomas's hand. He knew to stand and leave as discreetly as possible. They were not recognized as a relation of the accused, and it was best for it to remain that way.

With their heads clear and their thoughts focused, they walked out into the sunshine. It was after the noon hour, and the sermon would continue for some time. It was too late for the journey back to Haverhill, so they would fill the day in Boston.

They walked west across Hanover Street in the opposite direction from the small ferry. They just needed to separate themselves from the morning's turmoil. As they got closer to the Boston Common, they could see a crowd gathering, vendors were selling rum in tankards; hard tack and corn cakes were also being sold.

"What say you about all this today?" Thomas asked the corn cake seller.

"Aye, but not one, but two hangings today. Twill be a full afternoon for the work of justice," he replied.

Hannah looked at her husband with disbelief. How were they not aware of the location of the execution? Gallows' Hill, as it was called, was on the Boston Neck, a narrow strip of land that connected the city to the mainland in the south.

"You said two executions. What be their crimes? Thomas asked.

The vendor was clear about the prisoners, both women, both sentenced for killing their own babies. One darkie slave from Africa and a young girl who murdered her twins from someplace on the North shore.

"See over there," he pointed. "That old Elm is the hanging tree when they do it on the commons."

Across the grassy knoll stood a large elm tree, larger than most in the area. It had seen many changes over the years and witnessed many executions. Next to the base of the tree was an open wagon with a negro woman sitting in the back. She was motionless as if she were tied to something. A large wooden ladder was leaning against the tree. It had appeared they were readying the tree to serve as the gallows.

That was all Hannah needed to convince her that their departure was overdue. The thought of being subjected to watching the life drain out of her sister was too much for her to bear. Hannah turned from the grassy common and started back in the direction of the skiff to remove her from that place. Thomas trailed behind; he knew not to question her decision.

It had been a trying day, and distance was needed between the Dustons and the city of Boston, which would help ease the pain. Hannah's anger smoldered in her like a sleeping volcano from the stories she had read. Her sister would soon be no more, and her niece motherless, two things that she had no control over. The feeling of being powerless was something she despised, something she felt would never be her fate.

SIX

It had been a long night for Hannah, and she was still not feeling her best. It had been five days since she bore her eleventh child; resting in bed was about all she could manage. Hannah had prided herself on her ability to bear children and return to her chores the next day. She was the consummate frontier woman, strong, fit, and with childbearing capabilities.

This time it was different. The birth of baby Martha had taken a toll on her body of thirty-nine years; it had been nearly twenty years since the first was born, Hannah, her namesake. It was a Puritan tradition that their off springs were named for other family members. Ten babies had been welcomed into the Duston home, with only eight surviving the harsh ways of the land before Martha was born five days earlier.

Complications had arisen, and husband Thomas was fearful of the worst. He had prayed that his wife and baby would pull through; another loss would have devastated Hannah and caused her more reflection on her faith and the will of the Lord.

Midwifery was a skill that only a few in the village had made the calling. Mary Neff came as soon as the message from young Thomas reached her door. On her hurried arrival, she had assured Thomas that Hannah's body was just growing weary, and more time was needed to see the birth through. The afternoon of the baby's birth was long and taxing on the entire household. Little Martha entered the world with lungs full, loudly crying as if saying, "I've arrived." Neff assured them all that rest was what Mother Duston needed.

The Dustons were grateful for their neighbor, Mary Neff; having her close by was a sign from God that they would always have help with their growing household. Neff was a widow and lived not a mile away with her son. She was an experienced midwife and healer of ailments. Mary had learned the ways from her mother, who was one of the first to settle in Haverhill so long ago. Life in the new world was an unforgiving challenge of both physical stamina and spiritual devotion.

Mary Neff had been a constant staple in the Duston homestead for many years, having been a source of solace during the troubling years for Hannah's sister. It had been nearly four years since that awful day on Boston Common. Like Hannah, Mary was also glad that she did not witness her final moments swinging from that elm tree, an image she rushed not to embrace in her mind.

March was the time of transition on the homestead; the ground was almost thawed, and soon Thomas and the children would be readying the fields for planting. Hannah was grateful that her daughters, Hannah and Elizabeth, were old enough to keep the fires burning and cook the food for the meals as needed. The younger children also had their duties to do: the chickens needed to be tended, and the livestock fed. Large families were crucial in the Puritan world; the Duston household was no different.

Mary Neff decided that morning to return to her home and gather more of her dried herbs to treat Hannah. Goldenrod, which had many uses, from dying linen to making a poultice. The wild plant could also be steeped into a tea for sipping. It was known that the swelling of the belly could be reduced, helping to take the pain away. It could also be used with the dried leaves of the raspberry bush to help restore energy, and strength would soon follow. Neff was assured that Hannah would benefit from the tea.

The day passed, Hannah slept most of it, and by the evening meal, she sat up in bed. She had started to feel much better, and some color in her cheeks had returned. She was hungry, and it was also time to nurse her baby. Hannah's husband thought his wife was blessed; he adored her full bosom, something she herself felt was a burden at times. With each child, she felt they grew larger and heavier; her milk, though, was plentiful. Mary was always close by to help her nurse the infant.

With the meal behind them and the sun down, it was time to stoke the fire for the cool night that was sure to return. March in Massachusetts was still considered winter by the calendar and by the temperature in the meeting house on Sabbath days. The children had all come into the bedroom to wish their mother a good night and kiss the new sibling baby on the forehead. Mary would stay by Hannah's side, sharing her bed while Thomas slept next to the hearth in the great room. He did not want to disturb her; morning would come early, and the day's work would begin.

Mary had brought in an empty chamber bucket and placed it next to Hannah's side of the bed. It would be too much for her to go to the privy on a cold night; it was the duty of a midwife turned nurse to anticipate any needs their charge needed. She took the baby, Martha, and swaddled her in another layer of blankets. A quilt made of scraps of wool would be a line of defense from the chill if the fire were to go out. Hannah had already drifted off, so she crawled into the bed and placed sleeping Martha between them.

Morning came with no warning. Thomas stirred and woke to a fire that needed tending. It would soon be daylight; the sun would rise, and the day would start. That morning, he had decided to get an earlier start than usual, and he dressed in his work clothes, wool britches, a waistcoat coat, and his hat with a flat brim. He did his best not to wake the household, but he also wanted the children to ready themselves for the day's work.

Young Hannah and Elizabeth had stirred and were climbing down the ladder from the loft. They were already dressed and ready to tend the fire, boil water for porridge, and heat yesterday's corn cakes for breakfast.

"Tis a fine morning," Thomas whispered to the girls. "Ye mother is feeling much improved; I fear she will be up and around soon."

They both smiled and nodded, noting that the chores needed to be done on time and correctly. Hannah Sr. ran a tight household; her incapacitation over the past few days was a slight relief for the children, but the respite would soon come to an end.

Thomas quietly opened the main door to their home, trying not to cause it to squeak or to let out any of the heat that filled the room from the fire. As he left the house, he retrieved his Flintlock Musket that was always positioned next to the door. He walked to the barn and saddled his prize horse. The stallion had been one of his best purchases and proved to be a loyal and useful addition to his growing homestead.

The Duston farm was the farthest from the village center. He had amassed twenty-one acres, built a home, and created a pasture where only forest existed before. Thomas was a hard worker and a solid provider for his family. He was a skilled marksman who had served in the militia during King Philip's war years before. He was also a brick-maker with his own kiln next to the barn in a lean-to that he had built. He was feeling accomplished as he mounted his horse.

He looked to the horizon; the daylight was about to reach the ground. He didn't need much light to see where he was going; he knew his land better than anyone. Being that far from town, the wilderness was next, the unseen forest, where the Reverend would preach about it being the Devil's Den, filled with savages and untold mysteries.

He slowly rode down to the pasture; he wanted to see it without snow so that he could determine when to get the oxen and plow out. Planting and harvesting the fruits of your labor were tasks as Godly as prayer to him in his mind. Twenty-one acres is no small amount of earth; it took time to cultivate and prepare it for what he wanted to plant.

Being close to the river, he had always kept a keen eye on it during spring, the height of the Merrimac, the mighty river could swell with the melting snow, causing land to wash away. He believed that his apple orchard, which he had planted a few years before, was far enough away from the water's edge that it could sustain the rising water.

The sun was not quite up, but he knew his property well; the sense he felt as he worked the land was very satisfying to him. Watching the current as it flowed past his fields was comforting. He noticed the faintness of the sun's rays that filtered through the trees; there was a faint mist that gave his view a sense of foreboding for some strange reason. He paid it no mind.

He surveyed his land as he strolled on his horse, taking his time to reach the orchard. The river was indeed at a normal height, along with its flow, in his opinion. He dismounted his horse and allowed it to drink from the water's edge. Daybreak was happening, and the fields were now becoming illuminated, but darkness was still in the dense forest.

He heard the sound of seagulls off in the distance; their distinct sound was a rarity, as the ocean was over fifteen miles away. He paid it no mind; perhaps the gulls were hungrier than normal, and the fish were running up the river. It was a springtime event; nature had a way of repeating itself.

Back on his horse, he meandered to the lower pasture that was next to the forest's edge. He was now further from the river, and the sound of the gulls was louder and coming from the dense wooded area. That gave him a concern, and he thought he would listen more intently.

Sitting on his horse, he tried to steady the animal, who had become agitated. Animals' senses were at times keener than man's. He listened to the sounds of the birds more closely, which caused the hair on his neck to stand tall; he suddenly comprehended that those were not natural bird calls; someone was making them. He then realized that there must be Indians in his midst.

Grabbing the reins, he made haste and galloped back up the hill to the orchard. He paused to look back, not knowing for sure, but he had to confirm his suspicion. Clearly, he saw the fiery light of torches moving through the thicket, and one had emerged at the forest edge. He counted five more torches in the dense forest and could make out eight warriors as dark as the night that began to lift into daybreak.

His first thought was to return to the house and gather them all up to the Garrison. The Marsh Garrison is but a mile from the Duston House at the rise of Pecker Hill which was built of the strongest of timber, massive logs, and reinforced mud bricks. It was their only line of defense against these savages. Onesiphorus Marsh and his son of the same name were the local militia, and the Garrison was well-armed for exactly that morning's purpose.

He could smell smoke that now lingered in the air as he rode across the fields. Looking over his shoulder, he saw black smoke billowing over the tree tops. It had to be a house on fire, he thought. There were more savages than he first saw, no doubt a planned attack on their hamlet.

Making it to the house, he saw two of the children near the barn; they had already started their day. His oldest daughter was carrying a bucket, no doubt off to milk the cow, and his son Thomas had a fork to muck the stall in the barn.

"Indians, there are Indians," the desperate father bellowed to his children.

The children dropped their tools and started to run to the house, which would be the wrong direction. The Duston house could not sustain an Indian attack. It was a sturdy house, made by his own hands, but he knew it would be reduced to embers as soon as fire was placed upon it.

"Marsh House," he screamed. "Fetch the others, go. Make haste!" Desperation caused his voice to crack.

They turned and began to run in the direction of the Garrison. His oldest daughter came out of the house after hearing all the disorder. She was in disbelief and knew she had to act fast. She grabbed her sister and the youngest Duston and began the run to the base of Pecker Hill.

Thomas reached the front door, which was open, and the remainder of the children, still in their night clothes, ran out and in their bare feet. The war-like cries from the savages were deafening to his ears and scaring the children. It was a scene not unlike something from the Bible; Armageddon was upon them. Those savages were out for blood, his family's blood.

He dismounted from the horse and loaded his musket, having seen his fair share of conflict during his time in the Militia; his confidence got the better of him. He would see this skirmish through and be ready to talk about; he was not going to fall victim that morning.

"Hannah, get up, get out." Thomas found his sickly wife still in their bed, Mary Neff trying to dress herself. The Baby Martha was crying as infants do when they are fearful. Hannah rallied herself out of bed, perplexed about what to do; she knew that the Garrison was too far away for her, Mary, and the baby to reach.

"Thomas, the children, the children!" Hannah screamed.

The thought of losing just one more child would be the end of her spirit; she had already lost two to sickness: young John, to consumption, and Timothy's twin, Mehitable, near birth.

Puritan life was hard any way one would observe it. Freedom of religion had its price for those who sought it out. The Emerson family and the Dustons all knew that their time on earth could be numbered at any moment, with no notice. The hardship of conflicts from the accusations of witchery, to the struggle of carnal desires, each of these sins has a mortal outcome.

"There," Thomas pointed to the door in the back of the house.

"Go," she pleaded.

She knew that if she were to survive, she would have to take the situation into her own hands. God at that point had turned a blind eye to them that morning. He did not forsake her, and she not him.

It was only a matter of minutes before the raiders reached the front door. The first savage had a stained faced almost black, with only his eyes showing in the morning light. Thomas raised the musket and fired; the hideous intruder fell backwards from the force of the shot. Thomas stepped over the bloody body and jumped on his horse. He did not look back and only hoped that Hannah and Mary were able to escape. The children were in sight running up the hill, making their way over the terrain of rocks, stumps, and grass. It was not an easy jaunt and one that was done with barely any daylight.

He galloped up the hill and jumped off his horse. He stood behind the animal and used it as a barrier between them and sure death. He produced his powered horn and rod. Reloading a musket for the inexperienced was a troubling task. But for an experienced militia man, it took seconds. The Indians were now at the house, swarming it from all sides, some with torches in hand, and one with a rifle. His thoughts were to Hannah, Mary, and the baby. There was nothing to do for them; he had to get the children up to the Garrison. Choices are made in life, some in seconds and some often with the gravest of results.

He stood his ground and fired the musket at the closest savage within range. He was dressed in a hide breechcloth, stained with berries, and wielding a tomahawk. The shrieking that he made was penetrating the morning air and could be heard all the way to the village. The ball hit him squarely in the neck, the blood spurted out like a fountain of life; he fell to the ground, and Thomas reloaded.

He had to move forward and not watch what was happening at his homestead. Quickly, he reloaded the Flintlock and jumped on his horse; he galloped up to the slowest of his children. Johnathon and Abigail were both struggling; the roots and the stumps from the clearing of the area were troublesome for the youngsters to climb over. Both were in shock and complete exhaustion; their father's arrival was just in time.

He slowed down the stallion only long enough to bend down and grab each one of them by their clothing, he lifted them onto the saddle. Abigail in front and Johnathon behind, both of them holding on for dear life. With his musket in one hand and the reins in another, he did manage to get one more shot off. The savage was charging uphill with a long knife in hand, ready to scalp his children with no remorse. The shot was not fatal, but slowed him down, with another behind him gaining on them. He had to make it to the Garrison; reloading the firearm was out of the question at that point.

A few yards from the Garrison, Onesiphorus Sr. and Jr. were there, rifles in hand. At that point, he knew he, as well as all his children, had reached safety. It was a blessed moment in his mind; for Thomas, it was also a calling from the Almighty Himself for his salvation. Without any distraction, he jumped off the horse, grabbed the children, and put them on the ground. They both were crying, for fear of the savages and no doubt the fate of their mother back down in the house. Thomas and Elizabeth ran from the Garrison and gathered up their siblings to the safety of the interior.

More men arrived at the top of Pecker Hill, some from behind the Garrison and some from the other side, each carrying a weapon. The few savages that were on the offensive up the hill started to retreat in the direction from where they came.

Thomas was out of breath; the entire series of events that morning seemed to have taken forever, but in reality, it was just a few minutes. He knew he had to return to the house, but feared the worst. His wife and newborn's fate was not determined and only speculated.

"Goodman Duston, let my son go with you," Onesiphorus told him. "They are on the run; we stood our ground."

"Let me reload; it will not take but a second," replied Thomas.

Catching his breath and gathering his thoughts, he reloaded the musket. Onesiphorus, the son, appeared on horseback, also with a loaded rifle. The task at hand would not wait, and they both regretted it.

The sounds of the screaming Indians were dissipating like the morning mist as the air warmed the cold ground. The smell of smoke was now overpowering, with house fires burning all around them. Thomas scanned the horizon and knew that many of his neighbors received the same fate that morning.

"Goodman Duston, look!" The young Onesiphorus shouted.

Thomas was now more disheartened; the house that he had built with his own hands was clearly engulfed in flames. The fire was a deliberate act of cruelty, as was the raid; these savages were under the direction of the French and had done what they had set out to do. It was the most troublesome of times, one that Thomas had thought had passed.

He mounted his horse and galloped in the direction of his burning home, with the worst expectation for what he would find.

SEVEN

Hannah stood beside her bed. She had just screamed for her husband Thomas to go. Regretfully, he left the house and pulled the door shut. It was not a second later that the startling sound of his musket went off, causing her to shriek; she could not tell who had fired the shot. She had no awareness of what was unfolding on the other side of the wooden door.

Mary was hectic with the baby, Martha, trying to keep her from crying, while she herself looked for her clothes. She knew that they needed to get out the back door and hide in the forest. The baby, Martha, was crying; surely those savages would hear her, Mary thought.

Hannah's mind raced. What was happening? Why in God's name would she have to endure more hard times? She thought that all the troubles had passed; the baby was a sign of new beginnings for the family and her faith. God had blessed her once again with a healthy child; was she mistaken?

"Mary, I cannot find my shoes," Hannah whispered to her nurse, with desperation.

The house was in near darkness, and the light from the fire was not sufficient. Panic overtook her mood, and the pain in her belly, which had lessened, prevented her from looking under the bed.

It had been six days since she lay there in their bed, the very one Thomas had presented to her as a wedding gift. Made of the pine from the cleared pasture, and with a feather bed that she had made herself. The baby, Martha, proved to be a challenge; she was grateful to have Mary close by her side.

That early morning, she was still a bit unsettled and not feeling her finest. She was grateful she was improving; the pain in her belly was lessening, and her vigor was slightly regained. Mary Neff's elixir had done the trick.

Hannah was frightened for herself and her family. Indian raids were still happening throughout the colony, motivated by the French and the coins they received. Puritans were as disliked by the Catholics as the savages were by the colony. Harmony in New England was a commodity that had a price; neither side had enough coin to secure peace.

"Mary, throw me Master Duston's coat," Hannah asked, no longer whispering. "We need to hide in the woods." The desperation could be heard in her voice.

Mary grabbed the wool coat and tossed it across the bed to her. Hannah grabbed it, quickly put it on while still trying to find something to put on her feet. It had been days since she had worn them, and she could not remember the last time; it was just before the water of the baby came. Mary had the only candle in the room and began looking frantically. Thomas's good shoes, the ones he would wear on Sabbath days, were on a shelf next to the clothing trunk. She hurriedly picked them up and threw them in Hannah's direction; they landed on the disturbed bed.

"Try Master Duston's, I cannot find yours," Mary said.

Hannah was grateful. As she bent down, she grimaced in pain and managed to get the left one on. It was large on her foot, but better than nothing, she thought.

The sound the door made as it was busted open created a sense of demise for them. It was followed by the deafening shriek of the warrior standing in front of them, followed by another carrying a torch burning as bright as the sun.

Hannah screeched, Mary screamed, and baby Martha wailed like a banshee; their chance of escape was not conceivable. The back door was next to be breached, broken down by another savage, with skin as dark as a blackberry in summer. It took but a second, but their fate was now in someone else's hands and not their own.

The warrior standing in front of Mary was naked and covered in a deep color of blue, almost black. His hair was long and shiny, with piercing eyes that seemed to glow against his blackened face. Was this The Devil? Is this what Satan would look like on the day of her reckoning? Mary was frightened for her soul and that of the baby in her arms.

The Indian approached her without breaking his stare; the look in his eyes was soulless, void of compassion or empathy. He reached for her, and she pulled back. He then grabbed a fist full of hair and pulled her with the force of a demon, and dragged them out the front door. She held tight to baby Martha who was crying during the altercation.

Hannah watched what was happening and did not know which direction to turn. The second savage with the torch tossed it into the corner of the great room, setting fire to the wall. Now it was Hannah's turn to see what fate would bring her. Fire was the most feared disaster in the colony, Indian raids notwithstanding.

The flames from the fire started to ignite the basket of dried corn next to the hearth. The blaze continued to climb up the wall, and smoke started to fill the great room. Just as quickly as the warrior started the fire, he began to ransack the house. Overturning baskets and crockery, looking for anything that he could find useful. More arrived and began taking household items out the front door, which was rendered off its hinges when they battered it down.

As this was happening, Hannah stood firm; she decided that she was not going to meet her maker that morning, and fear would not overcome her. She needed to find Mary and the baby; their fate was troubling.

She finished putting on Thomas's coat, leaving it unbuttoned. On a peg next to her bed, she grabbed a skirt and pulled it on over her sleeping garment. The other shoe had not made it onto her foot. She stood there, eye to eye with her intruders as another entered her home.

Hannah was a formidable woman, built broad and tall. Any weakness she might have had from the birth of Martha was gone, and her inner strength surfaced. There were now six warriors in her home, snatching things and bundling them in a portion of linen she had been making. They had ripped it from her loom.

The flames were growing higher, and the room would soon be engulfed. She was sure that if they wanted her dead, she would have been slain already. One warrior dressed in leggings made of animal hide approached her with a hatchet in hand, one that was clearly not made by him. Hannah could see the cast iron and that smooth handle, the dried blood, and the bits of hair worried her. An instrument of The Devil, no doubt a gift from their master's, the French, she thought.

He made a guttural sound, nothing she recognized as a language, and motioned her to move towards the front door. He was not allowing her to do anything; he grabbed her arm; pulled her from behind the bed, and pushed her hard. Her right foot bare, she stepped outside onto the ice-cold ground; the pain from the cold was like a knife penetrating the sole of her foot. She grimaced and held in her gasps of pain. She was content to find Mary and the baby alive and standing next to their captors.

Hannah looked in the direction of the Marsh Garrison. Neither Thomas, nor the children, were anywhere in sight. There was only the bloody body of a savage lying on the ground near the entrance to the house. She had hoped they all had made it to the safety of the garrison.

There was another sound of a musket; the noise rolled down the hillside, falling on the Duston home. Both Mary and Hanna looked to Pecker's Hill. They had no idea what was happening up there and who had fired the shot. Hannah knew Thomas was a keen marksman; his time in the militia would surely have benefited him.

The gunshot did not go undetected by the Indians, and a sense of urgency soon became apparent on their blackened faces. The older one that stood next to Mary, dressed in skins, seemed to be in some sort of authority;

his face was painted like the others, but showed a sign of concern. He said something in their tongue, and the others approached the two women and pushed them in the direction of the river.

They had survived the onslaught of the invaders, and it seemed the savages were taking them as captives. Hannah found this to be true; she had heard all the stories of the Abenaki and the alliance they made with the French. She feared that her fate was now dismal.

Hannah could feel the blunt end of a Tomahawk being jabbed into the middle of her back as they forced her and her nurse across the cold ground in the direction of the river. She managed to look over her shoulder in the direction of the house. The fleeing Indians had bundles of their belongings wrapped in the bed linens and were carrying them over their shoulders. They were stealing anything they thought would be useful for where they were heading. The Tomahawk jabbing in her back drove deeper at that moment, nearly knocking her to the ground. With only one shoe, her balance was compromised. The pain in her belly was now not as severe as the pain in her back. Struggling to keep up with Mary and the baby that were being pushed on ahead of her was difficult with one lone shoe.

Another gunshot was heard, coming from the direction of the garrison. Mary had also heard it and glanced back at Hannah; their eyes met, but for a second. Silently, without words, they both instinctively thought that was a good sign; perchance the militia had arrived.

The Indians were now all heading back into the forest from where they came. They were walking single file across the pasture, the older one leading the charge. The second gunshot had them picking up the pace, pushing the women along. The women walked close to each other, only giving glances to communicate. Mary had kept hold of the baby tightly to her body, trying to keep her quiet and share her warmth. Hannah was having a difficult time walking along the uneven ground with only one shoe.

The air was warming as they dragged themselves along the field next to the river. The apple orchard would be coming into view. The thought of the trees and their blossoms in a few weeks was a needed distraction for Hannah. Thomas had planted that orchard the first year of their marriage, and it had yielded plentifully.

Mary was the eldest and had found it difficult to trek as fast as the others; her age and the baby were slowing her stride. Two of the younger Indians, who were not weighed down by clothing, sprinted past her, waving their tomahawks fiercely in the air. That had startled her, and she tripped and fell to the ground. She managed not to drop poor Martha, who let out a wail that rivaled the savages war cry.

Hannah rushed forward to help her friend back on her feet, taking the baby from her. Martha continued to cry; there was no preventing Martha from her only expression of fear. Hannah held her hand over her new baby's mouth, preventing it from crying.

Mary got back on her feet and turned to take the baby from Hannah. Martha was used to her nurse and the comfort the midwife could provide. Hannah also knew that carrying the baby while still struggling to walk would make it more difficult. Dropping Martha was something they dreaded; they knew it would be the end for the infant.

The orchard was bigger than Mary had remembered, and the sun was finally below the horizon. The tree line ahead and the dense forest beyond would bring another set of complications. She had no idea where these devils of the woods were taking them.

Hannah had found her stride by not thinking about her shoeless foot or the discomfort of childbirth. Survival was the only thing on her mind. Her thoughts took her back to her home and her children, wondering where they might be.

Puritan women, by design, were heartier and stronger than most. The church's expectation of them was being a servant to their husband; relations were a duty, and as often as his desires required. The benefit of children in the eyes of the Lord was truly the only reason for such acts of human frailty. Anything else was pure carnal and the work of The Devil. Baby Martha was an unexpected joy that the Duston house received. Hannah believed Martha was a gift from God, but she also knew it was a result of Thomas's appetite and his need to satisfy it was at times insatiable.

Baby Martha was not having the disruption in her life that morning. Her only defense was to communicate her displeasure by crying; the wailing that came from the infant's lungs could surely be heard across the orchard.

The older warrior had stopped, stepped aside, and waited for Mary and the baby to reach him. He was not pleased with the events of the morning and was now going to have to solve them. He showed no remorse in the raid, the killing, and the plunder of the homes on the outskirts of Haverhill. The Whiteman was taking his people's land, emptying their forest of wildlife, and bringing disease to their families. He knew that they had to be stopped, and at what cost, he did not care.

He could hear the baby crying; it was an uncontrollable sound, the child was a distraction, and it needed to be eradicated. Mary caught up to the savage, and without hesitation, he wrenched the infant from her arms. This was a shameful act, one that showed no remorse.

Mary screamed, the baby wailed, and the Indian unwrapped the Baby Martha, tossing the swaddling to the ground. Hannah ran up to that horrifying scene with shock and disbelief in her eyes. She tried to grab the baby back when the savage behind her used the tomahawk to push her to the ground. She fell face-first to the cold ground. What happened next, she did not believe with her own eyes.

A shriek of almost laughter escaped the older savage's mouth as he took the infant by its ankles and swung it around his head like he was wielding an axe. His solution to the problem was fixed in mere seconds. He slammed the baby into the apple tree that was next to him. Poor baby Martha made not a sound, and the air became still, just as he had hoped. Without another thought, the tiny corpse was tossed into some snow that had not yet melted. Her blood slowly oozed out of her little body, staining the snow in a crimson color of death.

"No!" Mary Neff screamed at the savage.

It was too late; it was over. Martha was now on her way to heaven. Mary sobbed out of remorse and fear, a combination that had deadly consequences. Hannah stood up, looking at the result of the cruel task; she had not witnessed it firsthand, but the result was just as devastating to her.

The Indian who perpetrated the deed was clearly now identified as the leader in the minds of his captives. He had taken the life of a blameless child with not a second thought; it was for his own safeguarding, and that of his people. He was aware that the crying infant would have alerted the white men to their location. He had lost more of his own that morning; justification is another reason to act without retribution. He never looked at the body; he only knew there was no sound. He turned from his brutal act and continued to the edge of the forest, where they could go undetected in the woods.

Mary felt that the end was near, and secretly hoped her own would come soon. The image of the recent event burned into her memory and into her soul; it ached for forgiveness. Hannah stood next to Mary and tried to comfort her with an embrace, something that was not done amongst non-family members. Mary was close enough in her mind that she did not care. Her friend cried as silently as possible.

Hannah did not cry; she felt her body become en-raged as her heart pounded, causing her face to feel flushed. The sensation reminded her of the day on the Boston Common, and later learned that her blood was nearing the boiling point, an affliction she had only read about. Anger and rage overwhelmed her in an ava-lanche of emotion. Looking down at her dead child, she had thought of the other children she had lost, and once again questioned the motivation of her God that she was required to revere.

There was nothing to be done, the body alone, its lifelessness, now surrounded by stained snow. No time to mourn, no time to bury. A silent prayer was all Mary could do; Hannah abstained from any prayer. In their world of Puritan faith, it was unclear if baby Martha, being unbaptized, would go to heaven. Having been born with the original sin from Adam, it would have been cleansed at her baptism. She had hoped God's grace would be extended to poor Martha, as it is written in the good book.

It was but a moment when Hannah felt the jab of the tomahawk once again, this time with less force than previously. The Indian who knocked her to the ground may have shown a slight sign of sympathy towards the infant's mother; in his world, cruelty was not to be disregarded. In all manner of society, the end outweighs the means. Abenaki or Puritan, this too can be the truth.

The sense of urgency was now the greatest, with the sun up and the orchard in full light; haste was needed to distance them from the exploits they rendered that morning. They needed to continue on their trek into the dark forest, home of The Devil and the captors. Hannah and Mary trudged along with only uncertainty.

EIGHT

By the time the war party and their two captives reached the forest's edge, a wave of dread had already overtaken Hannah and Mary. They felt cast aside by their maker, the very one they prayed to so often, the same one they would sit through hours of sermons for each Sunday at the meeting house. Where was their almighty now, in their hour of need? Would they not have been forsaken, or forced to endure such cruelty from these savages? Disillusioned and cold, they walked in a trance-like state following whom they understood to be the sachem. A murdering one at that, but one of authority.

Baby Martha lay dead back in the orchard, all alone, awaiting to be discovered by someone, or worse, something. It was not uncommon for wild animals to smell the flesh and examine its origins. The fury of nature is as unforgiving and unpredictable as an early morning Indian raid.

Hannah had no idea what had happened to her children or her husband. Fearing the same fate Martha received, her only wish was that they were shown more mercy than that of her baby. She feared the worst. It was her personal torment of not knowing her family's out-come that fueled her rage.

Before leaving the orchard, Hannah took one last look back in the direction of the settlement. There were several plumes of dark smoke across the horizon; each was a neighbor's home or their barn. Destruction was the theme that early morning. It was at that point that she knew the attack was well coordinated, and there was no doubt in her mind that more savages were close by.

The thick underbrush was void of any snow; the hem-locks were a kind of insulation for the ground. The path was well-worn, with roots exposed along with rocks, making the walk troublesome. Hannah recognized the path from her countless walks in the area; she would walk along and mull over her thoughts. These paths fol-lowed the river northwest, but she had no idea where they would end up.

Mary was still in front of her, their single file being pushed along at breakneck speed, creating as much dis-tance between them and their horrific deeds as needed. Hannah had resigned herself to one foot in front of the other; she feared one misplaced step would be the end of her. Her bare foot now numb from the cold and bleed-ing, she dared not stop to tend to it for fear of a blow to the back of her head.

"Mary, ye be well?" Hannah asked quietly.

"Oh, Goody Duston," she replied. "I'm so sorry about Baby Martha."

"You did all that you could, Goodwife Neff." Hannah tried to ease her pain.

The pain Mary felt was so disturbing that she thought she should stop and let them have her scalp. It was her scalp that they wanted, she was sure of it.

Scalps were, in fact, a commodity that was collected and a price paid on each by the French. It was common knowledge that Governor General Frontenac of New France had placed a bounty on the scalps of the English. Whether Puritan or heretic, he did not make a distinction; a dead Englishman was a good one.

Most Puritans knew this to be true; a scalp of a man was worth twice as much as a woman's or a child's. The Indians were keen enough to take the stronger captives alive and scalp the weaker. They used this tactic to increase their coin. Women and children, if they lived the ordeal of traversing the wilderness, could be sold into slavery in the North. The French settlers were always eager to take an English settler off the hands of the Abenaki. The reputation of their hard work and good obedience made their servitude more tolerable and easier for their keepers.

"Where ye think they are taking us?" Mary asked without turning around.

"Canada," Hannah answered. "It be a long journey, and we will be sold to the French, I make no mistake of that fact."

Mary thought, Canada? She had only heard of this place in the far reaches of the north. Quebec was also home to the Jesuits, though she had never seen one. They were missionaries who lived alongside these demons, teaching the ways of the Catholics. Those black-robed priests were part of the troubles, teaching them to pray, using beads they called rosaries. Mary had seen a couple in Haverhill years back. They were friendly enough and came south in their bark canoes to trade fur and fish for useful items like pewter plates and pots for cooking. As the wars escalated between the English and the French, the trade stopped.

"Mary, ease your mind free," Hannah told her, "we will be triumphant, I am sure." Hannah was doing her best to see the light at the end of that very dark tunnel.

There were eight warriors, the sachem, and the two white women. As they started to climb the rise away from the river, they entered territory that was unfamiliar to Hannah. The river had always reassured Hannah that following it would take her home, back to Haverhill. Now she was no longer aware of her surroundings.

It seemed they were being forced through the wilderness with such haste that perhaps the militia was following them to gain their release. Thomas, if he had made it through the morning, would have rallied the men in a search party. He was a past constable and a member of the militia from the previous war; he knew his way around the forest.

They reached the top of the rise, and the dense hemlock wood abruptly stopped, and they walked into a field. It was at a higher elevation, away from the river and the village. There were areas in the field still covered in snow; the spring thaw had not melted the drift caused by the winter winds. The sachem raised his right hand, and the warriors stopped. He then made a noise with his mouth that mimicked a seagull; it sounded exactly like the cry of the hungry birds along the river.

The sound was returned from over the crest of the hill; there were others from the raiding party waiting.

Hannah was nudged again, and Mary saw and heeded the warning; up the hill they went. The snow was not deep but crusty and at times difficult to walk on. Mary tried to follow the steps of the older warrior, but his gate did not match hers, and she struggled. Hannah, with her bare foot, noticed she was now bleeding. The crusty snow acted like a sharp blade on her foot that was already tender and raw.

The party followed the sound of the other bird call; they were getting close, and neither of the captives knew what to expect. Hannah could make out a gathering of others under a large tree where the ground was void of any snow. They were all from the village. There were many, most of whom she recognized from the day of the Sabbath. She grabbed Mary's skirt to encourage her to look up and not at the ground. Goodwife Neff would have made an acquaintance with all of them.

Hannah Bradley, a neighbor not a mile from the Duston farm, was there, along with twelve others. Goody Swan was there looking worn and torn, her apron covered in mud and her underskirts showing. She was the grandmother of Timothy, who was accused of Elizabeth's unwanted pregnancy so long ago. There were others, along with Joseph Ladd; there was Goody Brown and her three children standing next to their mother, the youngest crying inconsolably.

They approached the group, and their sachem spoke to the older warrior who clearly seemed to be in charge. The one word that she understood in their tongue was Bampico. The older Indian dressed in deer skin leggings with a necklace of teeth and shells around his neck was called Bampico. He too had skin dyed blueish black from the paste of dried berries, with black, long hair, and tied in a braid, it was shiny like metal. He motioned for the other warriors to come closer, speaking with authority and directness. They listened to his instructions.

Two of them, naked as the day they arrived on earth, retrieved some leather leggings and a breechcloth from one of the sacks they were carrying. They seemed to be preparing for something. The others circled their captives and motioned for them to sit down.

They had ransacked many homes by the look of the sacks they carried, Bampico spoke, and soon the other captors started to dress in the garments they carried. The sacks themselves were nothing more than bundles of bedding pulled from their homes, tied at their corners. They were awkward and cumbersome to carry great distances.

Hannah and Mary sat on the cold ground and watched their captors. They were preparing for something, dressing their bare bodies in clothing suited for colder temperatures. Their master started opening the sacks and redistributing the stolen items, making them less bulky. There were pots, clothing, pewter plates, and utensils from the kitchen, including knives. He then proceeded to give their captives something to carry; the ones that appeared stronger got the heavier of the blunder. He did spare the children of Goody Brown; they did not receive a load to carry.

The first two warriors to get dressed were children themselves. They appeared, through their stained bodies, to be younger and quite fit. Bampico handed one the French rifle, and the other had a bow and quiver. Like the deer running through the forest, these warriors ran with ease over the crest of the hill and in the direction from which they came. The crusty snow that the Puritans labored over went unnoticed by them. A search party was needed to determine if the militia was in pursuit.

With one motion from Bampico, the others followed. Now dressed for the journey, they started to rally the captives; most had something to carry. Both Hannah and Mary had escaped that task; being the end of the line, there was no more that needed to be carried. They began to follow one another, doing their best to be in a single file.

They continued down the ravine, across the snowfield in the opposite direction from the sun that was to their backs. The March sky was turning gray with clouds; the fear of a late snowstorm would surely be their end. With so many now trudging through the snow, the trail they made would be easy for anyone to follow. Bampico insisted they move faster, and each of the warriors nudged their captives with either their hands or tomahawks, which they carried.

The tall pine forest was directly ahead; it was foreboding to all of them, especially the children. The Reverend always told them that The Devil lurked in the forest and that the savages were part of his domain. That morning, all of them agreed with the Reverend; if they saw him the next day, they would never question his preaching again.

The column of walkers slowed slightly; a distraction, up ahead, had caused them to stop and look at something. Sounds of gasps and looks of shock caused a commotion. The children screamed, but the Indians were not distracted and pushed them along. Hannah had welcomed the slowed pace; her foot was now unbearable to walk on, and she was not sure she could go on. Lying down in the snow to wait for the blow of the tomahawk would be a relief, but her resolve was stronger than the pain she was enduring.

Mary was directly ahead of Hannah and saw the distraction first. She tried not to look, but after what had happened that morning, nothing compared to the dead body of an infant. Lying to her right in the snow was a man, his bloody corpse motionless; he had been scalped and gutted like a deer. The entrails from his stomach spread across the white of the snow like a crimson tapestry of violence. Mary's hand instinctively covered her mouth, preventing her from screaming.

"Mary, what is it?" Hannah asked her.

Mary could not say a word, for the body that lay there had shocked her system. Hannah took a pause and surveyed the corpse as she passed slowly; what savagery these heathens had in the arsenal of evil, she thought. He might have been there for some time; perhaps he was a hunter who stumbled upon the war party and paid the price severely. He was unrecognizable due to the amount of blood and disfigurement caused by the scalping.

Hannah finally looked away and went back to concentrate on her footing while moving ahead slowly. Distancing herself from the poor man was what she needed to do. Mary continued ahead of her, slowly trying to forget the scene.

They were almost out of the field; the walking was becoming less arduous but equally painful for Hannah. Her foot had no relief from the cold and pain. It was at that moment that she felt a slight sensation as if someone had touched her side. It was not a forceful push but a gentler nudge; it did not startle her, but made her curious.

Hannah turned to her left, and there next to her, so close she could smell him, was a warrior she had not seen before, from the other raiding party, she reckoned. He was smaller than the others and clearly younger. His face was stained, and he had a full tunic on with a raccoon fur wrap. There was something about him that made him different. Hannah could not figure out what he wanted with her.

Without a spoken word, the savage looked directly at Hannah and placed something in her left hand. He was close enough to her that no one else noticed what it was, and as soon as she took it, he drifted off back to where he came from in the rear of the column. She looked down at what she was given. It was with disbelief that she saw, covered with blood, a shoe, a man's shoe, and it was the right one. The warrior must have taken it off the poor soul she had just passed.

Hannah thought it was a sign from someone more powerful than she; when she was about to give up, providence was bestowed upon her. She slipped into the pocket of Thomas's wool field coat, which she was wearing. At the right moment, it would make its way to her foot without anyone taking notice.

Still, there was something about the warrior; he did not have the same demeanor in his eyes; they were not void of feeling. She had sensed some familiarity in them. She tried to work out her feelings while keeping up with Mary. It came to her as they left the field; his eyes were blue, and he was not one of them.

NINE

The day dragged on. It had been hours since they left the orchard. Hannah and Mary struggled through the snow and the mud in silence; the horrific scene from earlier that morning continued to be embedded in both their minds. They said nothing to one another, and out of fear of the club, they pressed on.

The sky had grown dark with clouds, casting a sense of foreboding over the column of settlers as they were being forced deeper and deeper into the woods. The forest was nothing like Hannah had seen; the pines were taller than any mast sail of any of the ships she had seen in Salem harbor. She had always wanted to board one of those wooden vessels and sail on the ocean, a privilege that only a few managed to do. Perhaps, if she makes it through this day, a sail to another part of the world would heal her broken heart.

The path was barely visible to the settlers; it was becoming narrower and harder to plot their footing. They were walking up a slope, and the lower branches of the pine trees were devoid of needles and life. All about them were branches gray and dry, their life cut off from the lack of sunshine. It was exactly what Reverend Wolf had preached back in Haverhill, the Devil's Foley.

"Take heed when entering the forest," Wolf would tell the congregation. "Wickedness abounds; The Devil could be lurking behind any tree."

The mind does play games, especially when one is fearful of one's own demise. Death and evil had filled that day; The Devil had arrived in their village and taken them away to his domain. These were the thoughts of the captives on their forced march.

Mary was worried about Hannah and her foot; it had amazed her that she was able to continue walking with only one shoe. Her friend was strong; she had accepted that. The birth of baby Martha did take its toll on her body, and being the eleventh child was in its own right a miracle; blessed by the good Lord.

"Hannah, how can you go on?" Mary asked as she used both her hands to climb over a small granite rock that was unavoidable.

"Mary, let us not forget what these savages did," she answered.

Rage filled her voice; revenge was what Hannah sought now. The task of gaining freedom from her captors and vengeance on them was all she wanted. Her life was now not worth living without knowing the fate of her family, and the tragedy of baby Martha only fueled her body to continue. Deliverance from these savages and retribution consumed her. Her mind raced as she stared at the footsteps in the snow before her, her thoughts unbroken, one step after the other.

"Goody Mary," She nudged her. "Look at what the Lord has delivered to me."

Mary turned to see what she had concealed in her pocket, expressing bewilderment was her expression. Hannah had lifted a portion of the leather shoe out to show her, and whispered that a young warrior had brought it to her; it was from the dead man in the snow field.

"You must put it on before your foot is more bruised," Mary told her.

Hannah nodded and told her she would as soon as the moment was right; she did not want to cause a distraction and tempt the sachem to be displeased with her or her benefactor. The Indian that passed it to her was surely a white boy, no older than her own Thomas, she told her.

"I had felt a strange mood when he looked into my eyes," Hannah explained. "They were blue, as blue as any Englishman."

The words had not escaped her mouth when she felt the sturdy jab of the tomahawk handle, her master; the killer of her baby was not pleased that they were talking. English, the tongue they spoke, he knew but a few words, and that frustrated the warrior.

In silence, they returned to their drudgery of walking. Hannah plotted the best time to rescue her foot; the shoe would be a welcome relief. That was not the only ailment she was feeling; her breasts, filled with milk, needed to be released. The pressure of a day without feeding her baby was causing her pain, a pain she feared was getting worse. Her breasts were becoming engorged, filled with milk that was ready to be released.

They had reached the top of the slope, and the trail started to descend in a more gradual slope. That had pleased Hannah; it was also void of snow and mud, making the trek easier. The light ahead that she saw was sure to be a ravine or maybe a clearing. Coming into view, she could see, in fact, that the pines had stopped, and the white birch revealed themselves along with a small stream. Those ahead of her stopped at the stream, huddled together without knowing what the next instruction would be.

Bampico lifted his arms, a rifle in one hand and a tomahawk in the other. He said something in his language and lowered his arms. He was telling everyone to sit. The others looked about for a dry patch of land to rest their bodies on, one void of mud. Hannah and Mary were in the rear of the captive party, followed by only a few warriors.

"Partake in the water," was the message from behind. "It will do you good."

The blue-eyed Indian was back and was encouraging Hannah and Mary to seize the moment of opportunity. They did not need to be told twice and kneeled next to the brook. They used both of their hands to create a cup to scoop the icy water up to drink. Never did water taste so good, they thought; they drank as fast as God allowed, not knowing how long they would stay.

The others looked in their direction and took the same action. All of them dropped to the ground and began to drink from the fresh water. Its nourishment was much needed after hours of tramping through the wilderness. The bundles some carried were more burdensome than they had felt before, especially for the women.

Bampico surveyed what had just happened: the white people all drinking from the stream. A sight that had reminded him of a story the Jesuits taught him so long ago. It was centered around the river Jordan and crossing through the wilderness into the promised land, the waterway that marked the boundary of a place for new beginnings.

He also drank from the stream, and his men followed. The day was coming to an end, and he was aware that nightfall would be soon; the place of rest during the darkness was not far now. He opened the deerskin pouch tied to his leggings, brought out a rosary, a gift from the priest back at the Jesuit mission in Canada.

Hannah saw what was happening, as did the other settlers. Some of the Indians made their way to Bampico to create a circle. Those who did dropped to their knees in front of their sachem; he knew that it was time to pray. The Abenaki were called the people of the Dawn. Prayers would happen at sunrise; that morning, they were otherwise engaged in another ritual of sorts, and their prayers had to wait until then.

Bampico had been converted by the Jesuits many years before, after leaving his village. He was of the *Penacook*, a smaller tribe that lived near the great river where he was now taking the band of warriors and captives.

Methitabel Corliss, one of the oldest of the captives, a church elder, spoke softly to the group of Puritans to encourage them to stand and pray for their salvation as well. The savages that had been converted to Catholicism surely would understand their own need to worship. Corliss started the prayer softly; he intended to seek forgiveness for their sinfulness, asking Jesus Christ, their savior, for some guidance during this time of need.

"Grant us, your Holy Spirit, guidance and deliver us on the path of righteousness," he spoke calmly and directly with his head bowed. "Let your mercy and grace be the beacon that we follow to our freedom and salvation, Amen."

The others followed with a soft, "Amen." They did not want to distract the praying Indians, for fear of a reprisal against them. Hannah had listened to the elder Corliss, but used that time wisely. She retrieved the shoe from her pocket and placed it next to the water. She then sat down on a fallen log and put her right foot into the cold water. It caused her body to cringe; she had hoped the cold water would diminish the pain from the bruising.

"Hannah, take this to dry your foot." Mary joined her on the ground. She also thought the prayer was the perfect time for Hannah.

Her foot had seen better days; the color of the skin was gray; the toes were blackened, with no feeling, which was troublesome to both women. The bottom of her sole was raw, with exposed flesh, but little blood, which was a Godsend. Hannah took the swatch of linen from her nurse and dried her foot, cleaning away any of the caked-on dirt that was then washed downstream.

Mary picked up the dead man's shoe and tried to wash away the blood that stained it. The cold water did little to remove the dried blood; she wished there was something else she could do to ease the pain for her friend.

"Be not worried, the stain of his blood is the reminder to me of their savagery," Hannah told her. "Let us not forget this day, for vengeance and our quest for freedom will be upon us."

Mary Neff was a practical woman, one who had seen many troubles in her fifty-one years on God's earth; that day had to be the hardest ever in her memory. Not the loss of her husband, or even when the threat of a witch-craft allegation came. Those events failed in comparison to the sound of baby Martha's head smashing against the apple tree.

"Goodwife Duston, I admire your strength and forti-tude. I hope ye can share it with me."

The Indian prayer was coming to an end. Bampico had used the rosary as his vessel to show his devoutness. The Jesuits had taught those who were converted to say their prayers in the Algonquian tongue, which they themselves also learned. The teaching of the priests, con-trary to what Reverend Cotton Mather had the Puritans believe, was not Frenchification, but was to be as close to the Catholics' ways as possible.

The shoe surprisingly fit as well as Thomas's had on the other foot. She washed the piece of linen as best she could and handed it back to Mary. They took a few more mouthfuls of water before standing up; both felt refreshed slightly and looked at the group, which started to walk upstream over the ridge beyond.

It was but a moment after they started when one of the children of Goody Brown, her oldest girl, broke from the column. She dropped her bundle and ran in the op-posite direction from where they were all going; her es-cape from captivity was not planned well.

Bampico turned back to watch the girl struggle to create a distance from Hannah's Master, saw what was happening, and laughed aloud. His demeanor had not changed, and it was another opportunity to remind the settlers that their fate was not their own. He shrieked with a deafening howl and ran with ease down the stream in pursuit of the girl.

She had not gotten very far downstream when she tripped and fell face-first into the ferns that were starting to grow during the warming days. The sachem jumped on her back, and in one motion, the tomahawk came down, bludgeoning her to a fast death. Blood spurted out of the hole the weapon created in her skull, staining his deerskin leggings even more. He quickly retrieved the blade that was tied around his waist, stood up, and stepped on her neck and took her scalp with ease. In one motion, her hair was removed more easily than gutting a deer. The entire incident lasted but a few seconds. The girl got the freedom she desired, and the sachem another scalp for his collection, increasing his coin.

The settlers watched in horror and with disbelief that any God-fearing person could act this way without remorse. Catholics or Protestants, were they not to believe that all life is sacred? Perhaps Cotton Mather was right that the savages were just that, and no amount of conversion would sway them from their true calling, which was pure evil.

Bampico had no expression on his face. He turned and pushed John Clement hard with the barrel of his rifle. Clement did not have to be asked twice; with the bundle in hand, he walked up the incline, not knowing where he was going.

The sky above threatened that rain would soon arrive; the clouds had grown darker just as the mood of the settlers had. It was a trying day, and soon it would be dark; would they not stop soon for the night? Many were thinking just that.

As if it were planned, the sound of the gulls was heard once again. Hannah knew it was from the warriors. They were far from the water's edge, no doubt, at least a dozen miles from Haverhill. She had walked many miles in her life. Before they had a horse or even oxen, it was the only way to travel in the early days. She had observed distances from the movement of the sun, but that day the clouds had hidden it.

The cry of the gulls grew louder; the two warriors who had left earlier had now returned. With ease like that of the deer with the white tail, they ran past the captives, only to stop when they reached Bampico. The settlers, though, did not stop. Whatever the warriors were telling their war party leader, it would not stop their trek.

Bampico's face had shown signs that he was more relaxed, less concerned. The warriors returning after nearly a day of running through the forest, and their return only meant one thing. There was no militia coming; the village of Haverhill had its hands full with dousing the fires and burying the dead.

They reached a point where the brook had another tributary going off, in a more westerly direction; it was there that Bampico pushed them in that direction. The downhill slope, so slight, was once again welcomed by the settlers. They came upon another hemlock grove where the brook formed a naturally small pond. There were downed trees, and a thick canopy of tall pine trees to shield them from the weather. Bampico stopped and raised his rifle for one last time. He made the signal to his warriors. They had reached the end of the day.

Hannah was so happy that they stopped, and at the same time so hungry. It had been many hours without food, and she was starting to feel the worst for wear. Mary was starving as well but felt hopeless with nothing they could do.

It was then that one of the Indians retrieved a deer sack that was behind one of the many granite rocks in the area. They had been in that location before; there were remnants of a fire as well. That had been their camp; they knew exactly where they were.

Their captives paid no attention to the settlers at that point; they did not bind them or try to restrain them in any manner. After what had happened to the poor Brown girl, they all knew better. The reality of the violence was their jailer.

There was a dry area next to another fallen tree. It was there that Hannah decided to sit down to rest; far enough away from where the Indians were gathering wood for a fire, and close enough to hopefully feel it's warmth.

The young Englishman turned Indian was close by; he had seemed to keep an eye out for her and Goody Neff. It comforted Hannah in a small way, and she wanted to know more about the lad. How did he come to be amongst these heathens?

"Hannah, may I look at your foot?" Mary asked.

She nodded and allowed her nurse to take the bloody shoe off; the pain that it caused was excruciating to her. She held her breath as a portion of the skin of her heel stuck to the leather of the shoe.

"I'm so sorry, the pain must be so unpleasant. I will try to be as gentle as possible."

Mary took the linen scrap and went down to the water and soaked it. Hannah was sitting against a fallen pine tree, trying to ease her mind and her foot. The linen felt good against her skin as she washed it. Hannah was pleased that the toes were regaining some color, but the worst was the raw flesh; the open sore needed a poultice to prevent infection and to ease the pain.

"Hannah, I think this will help," Mary told her. "It was in my apron pocket all this time."

It was the dried Goldenrod that she had made a poultice from for Hannah's pain in her belly. She could do the same for her foot, anything to try. Mary forged near the water's edge for stones. She needed to grind the weed into a powder to make a paste with the water from the stream. It would have to help; they were convinced of it.

"Let me help," The voice came from behind the fallen tree.

Both were startled as they saw the English captives on the other side of the place where the fire was being built. Turning around, there knelt the young boy who had handed her the shoe earlier in the day.

They did not answer him, and he proceeded to take the rocks from Mary and the dried weed from Hannah; he knew exactly what to do. Both women were at first doubtful of his actions, but a sense of ease, almost familiarity, came over them both. Using both the stones, the goldenrod was reduced to a fine powder in no time. Mary took the linen that was dripping with water and slowly squeezed it onto the larger stone that held the pounded weed.

"My name is Samuel," He spoke as he used his index finger to mix the water with the powder.

"I come from Worcester," he continued without looking up.

"I am Goody Neff, and this is Goodwife Duston," Mary told him. "You know we are from Haverhill."

The boy nodded; he did not speak much, but had told them he was taken over a year ago from the home of his mother when he was thirteen years old. In the beginning, he was so frightened and fearful for his life. But over time, his master had shown him things that he did not show the others; there had been a kindred spirit between them. Bampico was his master and was from the north, where the great river Merrimac began, the region near the lakes.

"How did it come to be that you know the ways of these savages?" Hannah asked.

Mary gave Hannah a look that only an elder could give someone. Hannah knew that her choice of words might have put off young Samuel. He did not look up or even acknowledge her question, only continued to make the poultice.

"It is ready," he told them.

Mary rested Hannah's foot on her lap, and Samuel held the rock for her. Her fingers smudged the paste over her heel and her toes. She applied it everywhere she could; she wanted to use all the poultice, as there was no way to store it.

"Here, let me," The boy said and took the wet linen and wrapped it around her ankle and heel tightly. "This will keep the swelling down and keep it clean." Both women were so grateful for his help, and that they found had found an ally in their captors. He was a true sign from God, they thought; perhaps they one day could return the good deed.

"I must return to my master; he will soon miss me," Samuel told them. "Here, take this, eat it slowly, and drink from the stream."

As quietly as he appeared, he slipped over the fallen tree and returned to the other warriors. The fire they had built was beginning to roar; it lit the underbrush below the tree canopy, as well as propelling heat out in all directions. Bampico and Hannah's master stood near the flames as the others started emptying the sacks to access the plunder from that morning's raid.

"What is it, what is in the pouch?" Mary asked as she slowly laced up the shoe for Hannah's right foot.

Hannah opened the pouch, and it was full of a cake or bread. She broke a piece and tasted it. She confirmed it to be a mixture of dried corn made into a dough and fried. She remembered the traders years ago offered her some, which was called *Nokechick*.

"Mary, here," Hannah said. "Do as he said, eat it slowly."

The *Nokechick* was indeed a hard chew; the women sat there eating small bites at a time. The taste was foreign to them, but it was satisfying after an entire day without anything in their stomachs. They were grateful and felt a bit guilty, not to mention what was happening with the others. They both wondered if the others had been given something to eat.

The days' turmoil of events was catching up to them; never in their lives have they felt so emotionally and physically drained. The day was truly a journey, one that they did not know the outcome of.

They both sat in silence, recounting the day and the events. Hannah could not forget about the book the Reverend Rolfe had lent her after her return to Haverhill following her sister's execution. *The Pilgrim's Progress* came to her at the time when she questioned her faith and her Puritan beliefs; it had been a powerful read for her. That day, she had been one of the characters from a novel; she, too, walked through the valley of death in search of her own salvation.

The fire caused the hemlock boughs to cast shadows onto the group; it created a forbidden dance of nature in the middle of the wilderness. Hannah stared off into the woods, watching the movement, letting sleep overtake her.

TEN

The burning embers of the previous night's fire glowed in the early morning light. An occasional pop or crack of the remaining pine branches created a sound that reminded all that they were still there. It was another day in the wilderness that was upon them. The light of dawn was creeping through the skeletal branches of the tall pines high above them.

Hannah, with her eyes closed, not fully awake, could hear the crackle of the dying blaze and the murmur of the native tongue of her captors. The song of the robin could be heard; it was an assurance that the weather was changing, and warmer days were to come. The crow with its "caw, caw" had interrupted the morning symphony; it was alerting others that perhaps food scraps could be retrieved by its flock. A murder of crows is an omen, one she dared not think about.

She slowly opened her eyes; the scene was exactly as she had left it the night before, when sleep overtook her worn and bruised body. Hannah was grateful that her foot was feeling better; the poultice had helped. Goody Neff had once again helped her through a troubling time.

Hannah stirred slowly; the ground was not very for-giving to her thirty-nine-year-old body. Her slumber was unlike anything she had felt before; the feather bed she was accustomed to was just a cherished memory. Standing up, she reached to support herself from the fallen tree that had supported her through the night. The pain in her belly had reached her back, but it paled in comparison to what she was feeling in her engorged breasts. Her body wanted to feed her baby, a task that could not happen.

The warriors were now kneeling in front of their sachem. Bampico was holding the rosary and quiet-ly speaking a prayer to his minion. Never in Hannah's world had she seen such a sight, praying Indians. It was a strange apparition that she had now witnessed twice. Bampico was devoted, something she could not com-prehend by watching his actions. He finished the prayer and put the Rosary back into the pouch that was tied to his waist. The sachem made a gesture with his hands, followed by the sign of the cross.

The group stood up, now all with some sort of dress, their nakedness mostly covered, their stained faces now fading. They turned from their leader and started to go about their morning duties. The two that had broken away and returned to her village the day before were dressed in full deerskin, a tunic, leggings, and moccasins that reached up their calves and were tied with strips of hide. One still carried the rifle and the other a bow and quiver. After a nod of approval, they vanished into the forest.

"Goody Neff, you must wake," Hannah said as she leaned down to nudge her.

Mary Neff did not stir, did not make a sound. Hannah gasped. Had the good Lord taken her friend in the night? She was sure that Mary was dead. Her mind, as it always did, raced ahead to the days to come; she knew her own would be numbered without Neff.

"Mary, wake thee from your slumber, it is time," She nudged her again, this time with more force.

Mary groaned and snorted a bit; she was alive. Hannah felt a sudden sense of relief. Her nurse had slept through the night, never waking; her body had needed rest; like herself, she had been emotionally spent and physically drained. Hannah reached down and pulled her to her feet. Mary, half-awake, was grateful that, in fact, she was not dead.

"Hannah, tis morning already?" She asked.

Neff, at times, could be humorous, a trait with the Puritans that was a rare commodity. She was a bit disheveled, her skirt still wet along the bottom, encrusted in mud. The blood from Hannah's foot had made a stain in the center of her apron; it was a reminder of the previous day's turmoil.

"I must make water, Hannah," Mary told her friend.

They both looked about the campsite for a place of privacy, something the eyes would not see. Even in captivity, they worried about what the others would think and what they might say. They walked away from the fire and into the underbrush of the hemlock. Not a set of eyes could see through the evergreen branches.

They each turned so their backs were to one another and lifted their skirts. They pulled down their undergarments and squatted; it was not an easy task. They were next to a small patch of snow, which only added to the challenge. Their urine was much warmer than the air, creating steam as it rose from the ground and escaped from under their garments. As quickly as they started, they finished; each grabbed a handful of snow to clean their privates. Mary gave notice to the grimace on Hannah's face as she rearranged her clothing; she could tell that she was in pain.

"Hannah, what be your trouble?" She asked. "Has your foot worsened?"

"Oh, Goody Neff, the burden I feel with the loss of Martha has now entered my bosom."

Hannah explained that her breasts were filled with milk that had not been released. The pain was growing worse, and she did not know what to do. She was very at ease telling her this trouble; their friendship transcended anything she had felt with Thomas or even her mother. Women could create a bond that would stand the challenges of time and any predicament that they could encounter, which she knew to be true. This situation with her milk was something that had not made it into Mary's thoughts. If a newborn had died in the village, she would seek out another newborn; there would always be a hungry infant that could help. There were other ways to assist a mother that she had done in the past, but without her herbs, she had to come up with another remedy.

They walked back to the site, and both had wondered what the day would bring. They could tell by the savage's lack of concern; no one was coming for them. The Indians were packing up the stolen items from the village and readying themselves to continue the forced march.

"Hannah, I have an idea," Mary told her.

She rushed back to where they relieved themselves and came back with handfuls of snow. It had been her thought that the cold from the snow would reduce the pain and swelling that she was feeling. Mary put the snow on top of the fallen tree, trying not to spill onto the ground. She wanted it as clean as possible.

"Help me, Hannah, we need to bind them." She told her.

Mary lifted her skirt and tried with her might to rip a strip of fabric from one of her under skirts. It had been the only one not soiled. Hannah held the fabric with both hands and tugged on it. It was not a task that came easily, but the fabric that Mary herself loomed gave way, and then the tearing part came easily. A strip of white flax linen tore off her petticoat.

"Take your coat off, and your smock," Mary instructed. "I will bind your bosom; it will help."

Hannah did not think twice, eyes or not. She had no part in petty gossip; her determination to survive was more apparent than the day before. She disrobed as quickly as she could, trying not to gain attention from the Indians; she gained no pleasure from more altercations with the savages.

The cold air on her exposed breasts did make them feel better, Hannah thought. Mary and her ingenuity were helping her once again. The strip of fabric was wrapped around her breasts with tightly packed snow in between the layers. The piece of linen flax was only able to go around twice, covering her enlarged bosoms. Mary tied it off as tight as possible. The snow would eventually melt, but the cold, wet fabric would continue to help soothe the pain by taking down the swelling.

Hannah dressed as quickly as possible, never looking in the direction of the others. She did not care, nor worry about the others. The situation was at its gravest, and her only thought was to return to Haverhill.

"Skunk cabbage," Mary said, "yes, skunk cabbage."

Hannah was confused; skunk cabbage was the rottenest-smelling plant that she had known, and never would she go near it. Goody Neff explained that sometimes the leaves of a cabbage would also be bound against the breast to dry the mother's milk. Skunk cabbage was used for other ailments; it would be worth the chance if they could find some growing nearby.

Samuel, their new friend, had approached them from the other side of the campsite. He inquired about Hannah's foot and how they fared the night. He spoke softly with concern and authenticity. The women were fortunate to find an ally amongst the savages to help them during their ordeal.

"Here, take these," Samuel told them. "Hungry, you must be. Save them for later when the pain of an empty stomach is the worst."

"What are they?" Hannah asked.

Both women took what appeared to be roots of a tree; they looked like small potatoes. They were about the size of an egg and felt slightly warmed as if they had been cooked. They had been cleaned with no sign of soil on them.

"They call them Penacook in their language," he told the women.

They were a tuberous root that the Abenaki ate mostly during the winter months when food was dwindling. Pulled from the ground, they would cut the other roots away and wash the soil from them. On a stone next to the fire, they would be roasted, which softened them, and when they cooled, they could be eaten. Samuel told the women that his master had taught him a great deal about their ways and what the forest had to offer.

"Thank you, Samuel, your kindness knows not a boundary," Hannah told him.

They stuffed the warm root into their pockets. They desperately wanted to eat them right then, but heeded the advice from the young warrior. He also alerted the women that they would be moving from their current place in a short time. It would be best to be ready when his master makes the command to the others.

The thought of another day in the wilderness only brought discouragement to all the captives. They had not been accustomed to such physical abuse to their bodies; it was only second to the visible cruelty that they witnessed and had to endure in their memories.

The group of captives was rallying into a formation of sorts. The sacks and bundles had been tied back up; that was the signal for those who carried them to pick them up. Bampico let out a call of whoop-whoop, which caused everyone to be alert. It was time to move.

His voice carried through the morning air with ease; his command also alerted the crows that roost high in the pines to swoop down to scavenge what they could from the nomadic party.

ELEVEN

It was nearly the middle of the day, and the sun was finally out and high in the sky. The heat that radiated on their backs felt like a blessing from above for the settlers as they trudged up the snow field. The shadow that the captives cast onto pure white snow created a column of ghost-like figures that were making haste to their doom. It was a dismal sight at best.

Hannah and Mary were no longer at the end of the group; Samuel, the young Englishman, was keeping a keen eye on them and directed them closer to his master, Bampico. His reason for doing so was unclear to them; except that his kindred spirit to the older women might remind him of his own mother, and that of his grandmother, whom he had seen neither in nearly two years.

Bampico paid no real attention to the captives or cared if they lived or died. This had not been his first raid on the white settlers, nor would he doubt his last. Years before, he had learned the ways of the English after leaving his own village; he lived with a family who treated him well and tried to teach him the Puritan way, something he greatly hated. He left them after learning their language as best he could. He continued his way further north to New France, a land where his people were not looked down upon, but where they were embraced by the French.

When he arrived at St. Francis, a village in the far north, he was among his people. The Algonquin and their smaller bands lived along the rivers and waterways from New Hampshire to the wilderness of Canada. He did not have to struggle to communicate; they spoke the same language he did. His tribe was Penacook and lived along the great river they called the Merrimac, each village about a day's paddle away from one another.

For Bampico, the journey that day had reminded him of his long walk through the wilderness on his own a few years before. That was a rite of passage for the young warrior to the Saint Francis Mission, which was in Quebec, in a place called Pierreville. He had heard about the place where the Abenaki and Penacook lived amongst the French traders and the Jesuits. He wanted to learn as much as he could. His desire to stop the English from taking his people's land and hunting in their woods was his driving force.

During his time with the Society of Jesus, he learned their ways and the power of the rosary; daily prayer was something that was instilled in him, and that task was his offering for the salvation of his soul. The English and their Puritan ways were contrary to the Catholics, both in the new world and the old. When Governor General Frontenac offered a payment on the scalp of the English pilgrims from the south, Bampico knew that would be his mission.

The English had brought many to the shores south of them, one sailing ship after another; they besieged the south. To those of them who called the land theirs, there was no escape except for heading north.

It was an invasion of the white man, and they had encroached upon his ancestral land with no regard for the Great Spirit. Disease had come, years before, wiping out villages all through the land. The Indians were diminished in great numbers.

He had heard talk of the tribes called Narragansett and Wampanoags, who tried to make peace, but it did not last. When word from across the great pond came, their troubles from the old world, for some reason, continued to their shores. He knew the white men were never going to see eye to eye; perhaps that had been God's will. Bampico was glad he had met the priests and learned the way of the Jesuits; at least they had learned his language.

Bampico was now far ahead of the group; he was looking for the wood of the white trees. He knew once he reached the birch forest, it would be only another day before they would be upon the great river. The snow field was nearly gone, melted from the warming days. Bampico was not fooled by the Great Spirit or even his new God; a snow could come without warning. If that were to happen, their journey would be slowed.

The captives were but a mixture of the old and the young, all English and all called Puritans. He did not have an affinity to any of them; they were English, Protestant, and worth coin back in Canada. A child or a woman was worth the same amount to Frontenac; unless they were of good hardiness and would be desirable as a house slave, then coin would be more, something the sachem liked. The scalp of a man, who brought the most, was less trouble to navigate through the north woods to New France.

He stopped long enough to survey the land ahead. He was far enough ahead that the others would continue their march before catching up to him. Using his hand to shield his eyes from the sun, he saw the mountain off in the distance; it was high enough to see great distances on clear days. The distinct shape had reminded him of the crotch of a tree. He had always remembered that because his village was another crotch where the great river Merrimac was created.

Hannah was now carrying a deerskin sack, something that was given to her from Samuel; he did not want Bampico to see that he had shown the women favor. She stopped briefly and dropped the sack, something one did not normally do; she needed snow for two reasons. She bent down and grabbed two fistfuls and shoved them into the space where her bosoms met. Mary Neff had been accurate; it soothed them.

She felt the jab from her master's tomahawk; he was a cruel one and a baby killer. Hannah turned and stood there, not moving. Defiance was written on her face, and vengeance shone in her eyes. Without breaking his glare of disdain, she bent down and scooped up another handful of snow and shoved it into her mouth. It tasted good, and the nourishment it gave once it melted was what she needed. She picked up the sack of thievery and continued in the direction of the rest.

Her master ran past her; he was watching her, for she was the largest of the group and the one to show the most contempt. He ran past Samuel and onto Bampico, who waited for him to catch up. Hannah watched from afar but realized that they disagreed on the direction they would be heading. She did not need to hear their voices or understand their language; Bampico was in charge, and her master only needed to follow.

"Hannah, why do you act so disobediently to him?" Mary asked, referring to her master.

Hannah could not speak for the snow had not completely melted in her mouth, so she did not turn her head and kept walking. Goody Mary was concerned that the fate of Hannah would be like all the others they had left on the side of the trail. Mary had been spared a sack to carry; she was nearly the oldest of the captives, and years of healing and midwifery had softened her; she was not the woman she had once been.

The snow melted enough for Hannah to speak to her friend; she wanted to be clear on her message and communicate her intent without causing notice. She did not turn her head when she replied to Mary.

"Mary, you ask why I am contrary to these savages," she started her tirade. "They came into my world and destroyed every part of my happiness that I knew. Without remorse, my baby is dead, my home burned to the ground, and my family, no doubt, as well dead. Disobedience is all I have left."

Mary knew the rage in her voice would only be outdone by her actions, given the opportunity. Hannah was a strong-willed woman, and now that she was feeling better, her resolve strengthened.

"I fear that you bring discourse to yourself," Mary said. "I fear you as well will end up on the way side with your scalp removed."

Hannah did not reply to her but kept walking; her focus remained on one foot in front of the other. They had now passed the point where her master and Bampico were at odds. The direction now was west, her body casting a shadow to her right.

Mary reached into her apron pocket to grab the last of the groundnuts she was given. Samuel had been correct; eating them slowly had eased the pain in her empty stomach. Hannah had already eaten her ration of nuts that was given to her; she was feeling the hunger and wished she had heeded the young Englishman's advice.

Their walk continued for a few more hours; there had been no rest for them. Bampico and her master pushed the captives to near breaking point. They had cleared the snow field; their walking had become less strenuous. The forest of White Birch had fallen leaves that had been packed down by the winter's snow and which now covered the trail. There were hundreds in the grove, Hannah thought, and for a brief moment, she had forgotten her ordeal and admired the beauty of the land, for it was a magnificent sight that had shown itself to her. It gave a sense of comfort and peace walking past them; their bark as bright as the snow field they just traversed.

The day had to be coming to an end; the captives were now tripping and dropping the sacks that they were carrying along with their burdens. Bampico had noticed that for the last hour, the sun was fading as fast as his captives. The progress of the afternoon was slow despite the fact that the terrain was easier. He was aware that until he had gotten the stolen items to their destination, he must do his best not to eliminate any more of them. His role was not to act as a slave master.

The afternoon was not wasted on Hannah, with her much-improved foot, along with her breasts less troublesome; she had time to think about all that had happened and how she would resolve it. A plan needed to be formed, one that would be beneficial to Mary and her new friend, Samuel, if he so chose.

In 1675, over twenty years' prior, Mary Rowlandson of Lancaster, a village in the western area of the colony, had experienced almost the exact situation as Hannah and Mary. Rowlandson, like Hannah, was formidable and very capable, a true Puritan and believer in the Almighty. Hannah was very acquainted with her story, for she had written an account of her time with the savages. The book was readily available throughout the colony. Hannah had read it and was captivated by her story.

Hannah had loved to read, one of the few privileges, as a woman, that she was allowed. Puritan women had many roles: to procreate, please their husbands, raise their children, and teach them The Bible. All of these tasks Goodwife Hannah embraced, and after reading The Bible, she enjoyed other writings that were sanctioned in the community by the pastor of the town council.

Mary Rowlandson's narrative of her captivity was written by her own hand, with every detail of her eleven weeks in captivity in a version of hell told. The situation was only over after a ransom of twenty pounds was paid by her husband, and then she was released. Hannah could not imagine what eleven weeks of this would feel like. Thinking the worst, and with no husband to pay for her release, she had to take matters into her own hands and do something, and fast.

Deep in thought, Hannah had not realized that the sun was gaining on the horizon and that they had stopped moving. She stumbled onto Elijah Tuttle and tripped over the sack he had dropped onto the ground.

"Goodwife Duston," Tuttle said. "You be ok?"

Hannah was slightly embarrassed by the mishap and stood up quickly, picking her sack up and placing it near Bampico, who was standing nearby. The day was over, and, hopefully, a night of rest with a fire to warm their souls would be upon them.

TWELVE

"Shall we pray?" asked Goody Neff. "We should give thanks that the dawn is upon us, and we are alive."

Hannah stood up from her dry spot on the ground where she had spent the long, cold night covered in branches of hemlock to keep her warm. Mary was already standing there looking down at her friend. They bowed their heads and grabbed each other's hands. They had been through so much as friends; they were as one. Mary whispered a prayer, one that Hannah was not familiar with; she paid it no mind. Her plan was coming into fruition: God may or may not play a part in it, she thought.

"We offer ourselves to you, Lord, guide us with strength so that were remain your faithful servants away from these sinners, we pray to you. Amen," Mary finished.

Hannah whispered Amen; she was feeling that if God was as benevolent as her friend had prayed, then surely, he would approve of her plan. She had read parts of Old Testament, and was reminded, again, of the book of Exodus and the verse that had been written: *an eye for an eye*. Those five words haunted her since the morning back in Haverhill.

The smoldering coals of the fire emitted a trail of smoke with the distinct odor of cooked animal flesh. It could still be smelled through the campsite, and it caused hunger pains for the captives who were denied the roasted doe. It had been a long and revealing night for Hannah and Mary; the morning light gave them a glimmer of hope, along with a sense of failure if the right situation did not present itself for her scheme to be implemented.

The morning air chilled the women, and the others were still huddled together in smaller groups, all trying to sleep despite the rising sun. They were trying to retain as much of their body heat as possible. The group had looked smaller to Hannah, as if someone was missing; the number of Puritans she counted had in fact presented one less soul. It was still early, and the Indians had not stirred; they, too, were as exhausted as their captives.

The campsite proved be the most comfortable yet during their ordeal. It had been a night of activity, one that would not be forgotten. Hannah sat back down after the prayer and thought long and hard about the previous night.

The young scouts who had returned from a day of stalking had returned with a small doe; they laid the carcass across a large rock and gutted it; the entrails fell to the ground. The hide was removed with precision, and the raw flesh was cut into strips.

The captives sat on the ground on the other side of the small stream and watched the Indians as they all scurried about creating the site for another long night.

It was during that time that Hannah gathered that they were unguarded, no warriors were about, not even her master. The two scouts that were flaying the deer across the way paid the Puritans no mind.

Escape was first to come to mind for her, an unrealistic venture at that point. The wilderness was vast and harsh; it was their jailer. The time was not prudent for her plan. Sitting on the ground and resting, she felt her strength returning. Mary had knelt by the nearby stream and was soaking another strip of fabric from her undergarment. Hannah removed her shoe slowly; the pain was better, just not completely gone.

"Place ye foot here," Mary instructed her.

The stain of blood was still there from Hannah's foot on her apron. Mary unwrapped the fabric as gently as possible. The poultice was working; she was convinced of that. The new skin would be tender and easily pulled from the wounds, something she did not want to happen.

"It feels better," Hannah said. "Your magic is working."

The word magic had always frightened Goody Neff; it was associated with the sorcery and the troubles in Salem. She still shuddered at the thought of being accused of witchcraft; she had thanked the good Reverend for coming to her side in defense of such nonsense.

"Not magic, but God's will, Hannah; he will deliver us from these servants of The Devil."

Hannah tried to smile; the removal of the linen was painful. She had hoped that her friend was right, that the almighty was watching and was also waiting for the right time, just as she was. Her foot was much improved; most of the color had returned, and the blisters of skin were a rosy color, a sign of healing. Mary cleaned her foot with the wet fabric and rewrapped it with the new dry linen, which she had ripped off earlier.

The sun was setting, and the daylight fading, when five warriors returned with arms full of squaw wood. They were dead branches, either picked from the ground or easily broken off from the pine trees. That task was usually reserved for the warrior's female counterparts.

Hannah, along with Mary and the others, watched as they stacked the branches high. The amount of wood gathered would last the night. One of them had removed the bark of the birch; it was light as paper and would be easily ignited. Another warrior knelt at the base of the pile. He had two pieces of wood that he laid on the ground. He used both his hands and rotated a dry stick back and forth; the friction caused heat, followed by a spark. Their method worked, and the bark was set on fire. Hannah had heard of this technique, but until that night she had not witnessed it.

The other Indians returned and began emptying the sacks again; this time, they were dividing the stolen goods, as if distributing them amongst each other. They had a system, it appeared, and would each share in the pillage. A copper pot was produced, as well as other items. Hannah recognized the fabric from her loom; it had taken her weeks to weave it, and it had been ripped from her home. The sight of her hard work only caused her dismay.

Samuel had approached the group and given them some sticks. The Puritans had no idea what they were to do with them. He motioned them to get up and follow him. He walked along the stream edge looking for the right plant. The cowslip, along with the fiddleheads, were emerging from their winter slumber. Green and tender, they would easily make a soup. It took but a minute for them to catch on, and soon each had pulled the roots up, snapped off the tubers, and filled their pockets with fiddleheads. Starvation and desperation, when combined, created an efficient work ethic.

Hannah looked back in the direction of the fire, which was ablaze, burning the dead wood as fast as the wall in her cabin. Fire represented the element that they could not live without, but it also reminded her of the depths of hell. It surely was a contrary image for her.

The other Indians paid no mind to Samuel and his helping the captives; they had made themselves busy with the task at hand. The venison was being cut into strips and skewered on long saplings to be cooked on the fire. Each of the warriors was anxious to fill their bellies; the meat would be a welcome taste after days of Nokechick and groundnuts.

Samuel signaled the group to return to the stream with what they foraged. He knelt at the side of the stream and washed what he had found, and the others followed his example.

He got up and went to the open sacks and produced a bottle of rum, which he had taken from one of the houses in the village. He had waited for the right time to present it to his master, Bampico. He handed the bottle to the sachem, the bottle full and the cork not compromised; the warrior let out a hoot that could be heard through the forest.

The young Englishman left the group and grabbed the large copper pot from the pile. He crossed back over the stream and filled it with water. He was going to make a soup of the ferns and tubers they had gathered. The Puritans were in amazement that this young man was showing them some compassion, something they thought those savages were void of. After he placed the undergrowth in the cold water, he went to the fire and placed the pot on a stone next to the flames.

The group sat back down as close to the fire as possible without giving notice to the Indians who were passing the bottle between them. Not all Puritans approved of drinking distilled spirits. Rum was something for the men to enjoy, and ale was always available in the taverns. Drunkenness and public display of vulgarity that followed the consumption were something they all frowned upon.

Hannah noticed that the others from Haverhill were watching what was happening, especially mindful of the young blue-eyed Indian who had been so helpful. She decided that they should know why he was such a help to them all, and she walked nearer to the dwindling group.

"He is but from Worcester," she told. "Taken over a year ago and made one of them."

"He is English?" Hannah Bradley asked.

"Yes, the same age as my Thomas," she continued. "Stolen in the middle of the night, he says, never to see his family again, tis be sad."

Hannah Bradley knew there was something about the young man; he was more than helpful; he was a savior to them. The others all listened with great interest. Dread overcame them like a dark cloud, each thinking the same.

The sun had set, and the fire had grown as robustly. The Indians had started to gorge themselves on the meat. It was now cooked enough to eat. With each sapling, they cleaned another strip of meat that was to be cooked. The small doe was soon reduced to a skeletal version of its former being.

Using a branch, the helpful Indian picked up the copper pot that had been boiling for some time and brought it to the group. Their faces were gaunt and lifeless in the glow of the fire, and Samuel knew the soup would help. He had only hoped that there would be enough. He sat down, squatting next to the steaming liquid. He then filled a pewter tankard that was in one of the sacks; he knew they would share the use of it to drink the liquid after the ferns and tubers were removed with their fingers.

Mary Neff caught young Samuel's eyes and gave him a look of approval, one she had given her grandson many times. He returned to his people, letting the captives enjoy what offering he could provide.

The captives sat on the cold ground around the pot and pulled the fiddleheads out and ate them with caution, as they were still very hot. The soup had been a lifesaver as well as a renewal of their faith. After the last drop of liquid was passed between them, and the pot was empty, they all stood up.

A prayer of thanksgiving was offered from Hannah Bradley, and they all agreed it was the right thing to do. Bradley had been as devoted to the faith as most of them; she wanted her Lord to hear her prayer, and her raised voice did not go unnoticed by Bampico. He watched for the side of the stream with a strip of meat he was eating with one hand and the bottle of rum in the other.

When the prayer was finished and with something in their stomachs, they returned to their spots to settle in for the night. Goodwife Duston and Goody Neff broke away and retreated to their spot near the stream. Samuel returned to them and picked up the empty copper pot and tankard. He was going to return it to the pile of stolen items when Hannah spoke.

"Thank ye, Master Samuel, tis was helpful to my friends," Hannah told him.

"Ye only wish there would be more that I could do," he replied.

Hannah and Mary were sitting next to each other, and she patted the ground next to her and encouraged Samuel to sit. He did without fear of reprisal from his master, who was enjoying the meat and the spirits. His mood was a lively one.

"There is something," Hannah whispered. "I seek the knowledge of a warrior."

Mary was all too aware of Hannah's mind and how it worked. She was convinced her friend was plotting something. She leaned in and listened intently, watching the face of the young English boy for signs of camaraderie or for a look of displeasure. He nodded his head and shrugged a couple of times, and when Hannah finished, he met her eyes as he had the very first time when he passed her the shoe, he had given his approval.

They were in such deep conversation that they had not noticed Bampico approaching from where he stood next to the fire. The sound he made as he walked through the stream, the water sloshing about, indicated that the rum had done its job; the sachem was feeling more relaxed and bolder. Samuel jumped to his feet and helped

Mary stand. The gesture of kindness from his young warrior was very curious to him. He did not mention it and only approached Hannah.

"Woman, you know not where we are taking you?" Bampico said in his version of English.

Hannah and Mary were shocked and amazed that he had spoken the same as them. How had that been overlooked by them? This sachem knew English and possibly French; it had been a great surprise to both of them.

"No, we know not where," she answered with her voice guarded, so as not to make offense.

Bampico stood so close to her that she could smell the rum on his breath mixed with the cooked meat that he just devoured. His body was still clothed in deer skin leggings, which were soaked, and a robe made of what she had figured to be a moose hide. The smell his body emitted was foul, rank, and offensive to the captives.

"Far beyond my village in Penacook on the great river," he told her. "It will be Quebec."

Hannah and Mary both felt that their fate was exactly how they imagined it would be: days of wandering north through the forest, crossing streams, freezing from the unsettled weather, and starving. With only groundnuts to eat, surely, they would perish, Mary thought. It was worse than death; how could their God sanction such a travesty?

"Tell me, white woman," Bampico continued. "Say what a price your husband would pay for your return to where you came?"

Hannah continued to be dumbfounded by his grasp of English, which rendered her somewhat speechless. Her mind took her back to the book by Mary Rowlandson, and she recalled the amount to be twenty pounds that her husband had paid.

"Twenty pounds," she blurted it out with confidence.

That was a lot of money, and she had hoped it would entice him to keep her alive so that one day she would see her beloved husband. Bampico's face revealed exactly what was expected; he felt that twenty pounds was a fair price for her. It was more than he would get from a French family. He took a pull from the bottle of rum, which was nearly empty.

"Tis my good fortune when that happens," he told her.

Bampico was not finished with her; he wanted to tell her more. The foul story that he spoke was as distressing to her as the baby Martha being smashed against the apple tree. He reminded her that her home was burned to the ground, nothing but an ashen cellar hole remained, and her children, all of them, were dead.

Martha felt flushed, the fire in her soul was erupting like the first morning. She wanted to sit down; she wanted to run in the forest so that one of the savages would follow and club her to death. The pain of losing Martha and now the rest of them was all too much for her.

"Ye husband ran to the house on the hill, never stopping," he told her.

Rage, defiance, and revenge overwhelmed her before he spoke those words. She stood straight and looked him in his eyes, holding back any motherly emotion that she had. Hannah was not about to let even a tear fall on her cheek. Their eyes were locked in a duel of captor and captive; there would be no peaceful outcome on either of their sides.

The rum bottle now empty, Bampico tossed it into the woods. He was feeling a sense of consummation; she would not give her master any more trouble, he thought. He turned and waded back across the stream. Hannah fell to her knees, sobbing as any good mother would have.

"Hannah, my heart breaks for you," Mary said, joining her on the ground. "Let us pray for their souls."

"I cannot pray my faith has been contested too many times of late," Hannah said.

Goody Mary was still going to pray for the souls; she as well had had a loss. The Duston children had all been delivered by her, and she raised them alongside Hannah. They all were good servants of the Lord; they deserved so much more in life than to be cut down by savages. She prayed, on her knees next to Hannah, silently.

Samuel was standing there the entire time, listening to his master speak to poor Hannah with such disregard for her feelings. It was very clear to him, at that moment, that his time wandering the forest with these savages was over. He would heed Hannah's request and follow the plan she had devised. He knew not what to say to her and only rested his hand on her shoulder. Her sobbing had stopped, and she looked up; the time had come, it was written on her face.

Samuel was totally at odds with the world he was in and the world that he had been taken from. He was straddling a fence and feared he would soon fall off. He crossed the stream and caught up with his master. They exchanged a few words and continued to the fire.

Hannah dried her tears with the hem of her sleeve as best she could. She watched Samuel and The Devil as they spoke to each other at the fire. Bampico was clearly affected by the rum; his drunkenness was apparent.

From a distance, Hannah could make out that Samuel was asking him something. She hoped it was the question that she wanted her new friend to ask his master. Bampico's hands were moving in strange directions, motioning to Samuel in a silent pantomime. He appeared to be joyful in his expression and was not worried by it. She watched as The Devil picked up a tomahawk and demonstrated its use. He swung it around his head in a slow and calculated move and then stopped when it reached the height of his head. Letting the weapon fall to the ground, he pointed to Samuel's head, touching his temple with his finger.

Hannah felt a sudden rush as if she just learned all the answers to the question in her Bible. Samuel had done his job; by the one act of alliance they had spoken volumes for what was to come. She closed her eyes and meditated in her silent resolve.

"Hannah, open your eyes, it's time." Mary Neff's words were never truer.

"I must have fallen back asleep," Hannah said and stood up.

The war party had finally awakened; the rum had caused them all to sleep longer than perhaps they should. The deerskin sacks were retied, and captives picked up their assigned bundle and walked into the forest, Bampico leading the charge.

Samuel rushed over, fearing something had gone wrong, and Hannah was not well. It was not the right time, she felt that they all needed to be ready, for her plan to work. Mary started walking, and Hannah followed with Samuel next to her. She was pleased that the young Englishman was next to her, for liberation would soon be at hand.

THIRTEEN

The captives were all losing any sense of time and space. They were unsure if it had been a week or a month since they were forced on their death march north. Their intended destination was just a village in Canada, but they had no idea where it was. The terrain that they covered was that of open fields, groves of pine, and countless waterways. They forded brooks, waded through streams, and avoided bogs; the land was as unforgiving as their captors. Each day they were prodded and pushed for hours until their collective masters had made sufficient gains on each of their missions; only then would they stop for the night.

The Puritans were looking more and more like the prisoners Hannah had seen when she visited her sister at the Gaol in Boston. Their clothes were torn, stained in mud, blood, and their own excrement. Their faces gaunt and hollow, malnutrition and exhaustion were a deadly combination. With each step, the deerskin sacks seemed to grow in weight, and as the day wore on, they would stumble and drop them. That caused Hannah's master to show his anger, his true nature. It did not take a great deal for his face to go from disdain to displeasure.

Hannah Bradley was near the front of the column and dropped the parcel she was carrying that morning; the knot was loosened, and the contents spilled onto the open ground. Bampico, who was leading the charge, turned when he heard the sound of the pewter plates hitting the ground and splashing into the mucky water. He snapped his head back; he was also tired, and the slightest provocation would anger him. He shot a glare back at the baby killer, his eyes as gray as the sky and lifeless like the bog that they were trying to skirt. He raised his right arm, the tomahawk in full view for all to see. The message was received by his second in command.

Goodwife Duston's master saw his sachem; the signal he gave was to set an example for the others. Hannah Bradley was on her hands and knees, collecting the contents and trying her best to stuff them back in the sack. On her hands and knees, she reached into the stagnant water, feeling for the metal plate that fell into the abyss.

The child behind her gave notice with the sound of the splashing. The sachem came bounding along the water's edge on all fours towards Goody Bradley. The cold water was soaking her clothes. A blood-curdling scream came from one of the youngest, something her mother, Goody Brown, was all too familiar with. The warrior had raised his war club, ready to show the others the ultimate price to pay for their failure.

The scream did not go undetected by the others, and they turned to watch first-hand the fate of one of their own. The savage stopped at his intended victim and quickly lowered his weapon as fast as he had raised it. Goody Bradley looked up, terrified, and was ready to meet her maker. She knew that her life had no value to those servants of The Devil, except to act as a carrier of her own stolen property and the benefit of coin for their souls.

The encounter was brief, but long enough for the others to stop and catch their breath. It was an unfortunate incident for Bradley, but the others took advantage of the respite to rest as she readjusted her sack, which was covered in mud, and her own clothing was soaked.

"Hannah, I'm feeling weak," Mary Neff told her. "I have not eaten today, and I fear I will faint."

"Here, take mine," her friend said.

Hannah handed her a fistful of roasted groundnuts that she had put into her pocket the night before. She did not mind giving Mary whatever she had; their bond grew stronger every day of their captivity. Where Goody Neff stopped, Hannah started. She knew that without Mary Neff, she herself would have perished days before.

Mary put a nut into her mouth and the others into her apron pocket. They would have to last until they stopped for the night, when they could forage for more. Samuel had always been nearby with a watchful eye; he would help them when they stopped for the day. She was thankful for the young Englishman.

Hannah turned back and took a step forward. She felt grateful that the sack she carried every day was manageable, the weight of an armload of cord wood. Her foot was nearly healed, the wrapping dry and free of her blood. Mary insisted she keep it wrapped since she never had any socks on. The snow on her breasts reduced the swelling and the production of her milk. They were tender but did not cause her distraction. One step in front of the other was still her focus, her daily meditation.

Deep in thought, the visual of her master ready to strike Goody Bradley had sickened her. He was the work of Satan; she was convinced of it. He had raised his war club high, ready to strike; he knew the fear of death was a great motivator for them during these desperate times. Hannah wondered if he ever feared his own mortality, and when it did happen, would he burn in some version of Hades for his kind, or would his newfound belief accept him? Hannah was plagued with these thoughts as her steadfastness was needed to see her plan through.

It was another few hours until they rested as they walked west, Hannah thought; the sky had clouded over, and she was not sure the direction they were headed. She was just glad it was downhill, a small blessing that they were all grateful for. She could not see through the dense forest and wondered what lay ahead for them.

Bampico looked past the trail they were on. He saw that it was lighter; the wood was coming to an end. The darkest of the forest would be over. He was certain the river was just ahead. The mighty river that he had once called home would be a welcome sight.

His people, the Penacook, had lived along the Merrimac for many generations peacefully. Their land was abundant with game, the waters rich with fish, and the soil fertile for growing.

It was a time before the white man had arrived, a time before disease and war. Their great Chief, years before Bampico's time, made a treaty with the English for land; he was called Passaconaway, and he was a great sachem. It had been the English that changed everything for his people; they had all but gone onto the Great Spirit from the diseases the white man brought. The treaty that Passaconaway had made his mark on allowed harmony between the different people, giving them a portion of land for their settlement. The agreement was soon broken, the white man cheated the natives; after that, war followed. The Penacook, those that did not die during those times, moved further up the river trying to survive. They took refuge with another tribe, the Wabanaki, who had welcomed them.

The sachem had increased his speed and ran along the worn trail. He wanted his reunion with the river all to himself. He would give thanks to both the Great Spirit and his new God that the Jesuits taught him. The river's edge was just beyond the great, large oak tree to the north; a few more minutes, he thought, and he would see it.

His departure from the group did not go unnoticed by Samuel, who maneuvered past the others to the front of the line. If there was trouble ahead, he wanted to do what he could to prevent more discourse.

"What do you think is happening?" Goody Neff questioned.

"I am as perplexed as you," Hannah answered. "We will discover the trouble in no time, that is certain."

Bampico was out of view from Samuel, and the others followed him. The two warriors who had been the hunters ran past the young English boy in the same direction as his master. There was something ahead that caused them to speed their step; he himself was curious.

The sight of the river came into full view for Samuel shortly after the scouts passed him. He knew the river well but had not recognized it from the trail they were on. His master had taught him to respect the Merrimac, for it was once the center of his people's world.

It was a welcome sight for them all, as the captives filed onto the shoreline, they dropped their bundles and knelt to use their hands to drink the cold water. It was refreshing and nurturing; it could not have come at a better time.

Bampico was at the water's edge looking north; he was in search of something, or someone. The two scouts had stripped naked, leaving their stained deer skin coverings on a dry patch of land. They hooted and yelled, splashing about, washing the stench of death and exhaustion off sinewy bodies.

Hannah's master walked past the group and continued along the shoreline, passing even Bampico. He surveyed the area and continued; he was looking for something as well. The river was placid, gray in color, reflecting the sky above. There was a good amount of rocks and large boulders that had settled along the shore as the river meandered to the west, just north of where he stood.

The river was like a snake in his mind, long and winding, sometimes peaceful and other times unforgiving, never stopping for a moment; it would bite you. It followed the landscape as if it flowed south to the great sea, passing the remnants of deserted villages of the Abenaki and of days gone by. He, too, was happy to see it, for it was the place he would meet the others.

The Puritans had drunk their fill of water, and Mary finished the last of the groundnuts. It was time to give thanks. She gave Hannah a look, and the others grew near. The group of captives had dwindled to only ten, eleven if young Samuel was included. They lowered their head, and Goody Nurse proceeded to speak softly, always giving thanks for their salvation and guidance through their time in bondage. Her reference to the Old Testament could not have been more appropriate.

"We thank ye for the grace of the almighty, Amen." Mary finished.

Hannah heard a whistle; it was a signal the Indians had also used. Bampico was upstream. He raised his other hand, the one with the musket in it. That alerted the others to follow him. Samuel told the group to pick their bundles and continue along the water's edge.

The sound of the water's current as it passed over the rocks was heard, and there was a collective fear among the captives that they would have to cross over the rushing river. The water always caused great concern amongst them; being able to swim was not something they had aspired to. For those old enough to remember, water and witchcraft were something that also went together back in the old world. The dunking test had never made it to Salem, and they all hoped it would never.

Hannah's master returned to the group. He spoke to Samuel in his language, and the boy made a gesture for them to walk up the grassy embankment in the direction of Bampico. It was only a few rods away from the edge of the river where the sachem wanted to stop for the day. It appeared to them that they were to meet others.

Like every other day during this ordeal, the Puritans dropped the sacks where they were instructed and sat down. The tiredness they felt was like a disease with no cure. They could treat it with scraps of meat the Indians left behind on the discarded saplings or the groundnuts they foraged daily. The constant discomfort of a slow starvation was one they did not wish upon their own enemies.

The other warriors were off in the woods doing what they always did, looking for wood for the fire or some unsuspecting game to kill to add to their evening meal. They were hungry as well, tired tramping through the forest, with a destination far away.

Samuel knew daylight would soon be gone, and it was time to forage the river's edge for something they all could eat. The weather had proved to be useful for some plants; a warm early spring would always yield something to find of nature's harvest.

"Goody Hannah," Samuel said. "Gather, Goody Mary, and follow me."

Samuel instructed the others to look for groundnuts and fiddleheads, which were also abundant at the edge of the water. He signaled to Hannah and Mary to follow him. He was sure there would be wild leeks in the area. The three of them walked back down to the river's edge in search of them. He had described the plant as having the same leaves as the lily of the valley, which were noxious.

"There," Samuel pointed.

Next to a wash, where the embankment that at one time met the rising river, an area filled with growth. The sun had worked its magic, for the area was facing due south. It was a small curve in the river; the soil was a collective mixture of nutrients washed into the bend. Cat-o'-nine tails, groundnut tubers, and the elusive leafy wild leek had grown. The womenfolk bent over and started to pluck the plants out by handfuls, first the groundnuts, then the leeks, and the cat-o'-nine tails, which had been a new revelation to them.

Samuel took his knife out that was stuck in his waist under his leggings and cut the roots from the tubers as best he could. He was pleased with the find; all these items could make a hearty stew. He hoped that his fellow warriors would find some game, and they would share some of the meat with the Puritans.

The late afternoon passed without incident, a true blessing for the captives. Samuel had organized the bounty from their foraging and assembled the stew. The wild leeks were a new taste for them, one that he assured them would add an onion flavor to the hot broth.

Hannah Bradley had taken her wet clothes off and placed them on a makeshift line next to the fire. Goody Duston had loaned her Thomas's coat until her clothes dried the best they could. There was time for rest and prayer before they shared the stew.

The Puritan society practiced prayer often; their frequent show of devotion was at all times of the day. They believed that prayer was essential to connect with their Lord God. They would pray as a family, as a group, or alone; it was expected. They were never sure where the eyes were and who would judge them. That afternoon they needed to express their gratitude for the food they would receive and that they had made it through another day on earth.

Hannah and Mary left the prayer group and looked for their spot to call their own. Close enough to the fire, but far enough away so they could talk in private. There was much to discuss.

"Hannah, how be your bosoms?" Goody Neff asked her.

"They be fine, the milk has dried a bit," Hannah told her. "I will keep them bound; it feels better."

Mary and Hannah used their feet to clear the spot on the ground free of fallen branches and rocks. The earth can be very unforgiving to sleep upon; it was apparent they knew their destination was many days away.

"Mary, the time is near," she told her.

Hannah was about to review the plan with her when the sound of footsteps was heard approaching them. Young Samuel and her master, the baby killer, were walking in their direction. Both of the women stood up and became steadfast, trying not to be intimidated by his presence.

He was about five feet away, and the stench from his body engulfed the air they were breathing. It was fouler than a dead animal left to rot after the crows had had their way with the carcass. It astounded them that Samuel was not bothered by it; after nearly two years with the savages, one gets desensitized to many things; smell and death went hand in hand.

"Good wife Duston," Samuel said. "And Goody Neff, your master Mato wants me to help him."

Both the women looked at each other; the baby killer, their master, as called Mato. It was clearly a name that was not heard in those past days.

"Mato," Hannah said. "What manner of business does present him here to us?"

Mato grunted. He did not know what was said, but he sensed her contempt. That larger white woman was in his language, *chajibikki;* one that was frightening and dangerous. He had used that word when the militia out-numbered his own people during a raid gone foul.

The master was himself as disagreeable and angry as any. Hannah would not show fear. Mary, shorter and older, moved closer to her friend and grabbed her hand. Neither of them knew what this savage wanted with them. Hannah thought maybe Samuel had been pressured to reveal her plan, a fleeting notion she tossed out of her mind.

"Mato wants to tell you both about Quebec and the gauntlet," Samuel told them.

Their master began to speak in his native Wabanaki tongue; it sounded very similar to Bampico when he spoke. Hannah did not know that many of the tribes of the Algonquin territory spoke a similar language; only the way they spoke sounded different to her.

"We are heading to Kanata, where we will be in the newly established village of Saint Francois. It would be there that the ultimate judgment of your white people will be." Samuel was trying to translate as Mato spoke. "The gauntlet awaits you; you will all run the gauntlet."

The gauntlet was something the women had never heard of, and as Samuel began to describe it, their hearts sank into their bellies. Despair once again overwhelmed them, and fear began to consume them. Hannah was not having any part of this; without showing her true feelings, she stood even taller. She would never let the baby killer get the best of her.

Samuel continued to interpret Mato's words. The gauntlet is a test. It is what all the captives are forced to do. They are stripped naked, and the entire village comes out and forms two columns a few feet apart. This is a custom of resilience, for which they will be forced to run through. His people can have sticks, clubs, or their bare hands; each will try to land a blow against your exposed body.

Mato finished his story; he was pleased with himself once again by showing them who was in control. He wanted to break them; if fear did not, then the physical abuse would surely do it. He turned and walked to his own kind, taking the foul smell with him.

Mary sat down. She was now teary-eyed; she felt that she could never withstand the ordeal that had just been told to her. Hannah looked to Samuel for some guidance or an opinion about what he said.

"Goody Duston, it will not come to that," Samuel assured her.

"How ye prevent such cruelty, what more manner of sinfulness could be bestowed?" Hannah asked.

It was obvious to her and Samuel that if they did make it all the way north, the possibility of escape would be harder, if not impossible. Mary was beside herself with distress, hunger, and tiredness; going on much longer would not be in her cards.

"Do not take mind of Mato's evilness," Samuel said. "When the time is near, we have the plan."

Hannah nodded her head and quietly agreed with the young English lad. The plan would work; they had to be patient. God would present them with the correct moment to implement it.

"I must return to my master; he thinks I spend too much favor on ye," Samuel told her. "Take these, eat them with your stew when it is ready."

He passed Hannah a few bits of dried meat that he had in his leather pouch tied around his waist. The meat also had a foul smell to it; something they would overlook when they ate it. Taste was never considered when famine was upon your being.

FOURTEEN

The fire crackled and groaned with each burning branch that was tossed onto it; it cast a beacon of light throughout the campsite and illuminated the water in both directions along the river. The sky had cleared, and the moon rose from the southeast, adding more light along the mighty river.

That night Bampico had instructed his warriors to keep the fire burning throughout the night. With no fear of the English militia, he wanted to signal the others that they had arrived at the bend on the water, a spot where they had met in the past. The time had come for the warriors to return to their own people, taking what share of the plunder they deserved.

It had been a harrowing few nights; the English would not recall them, for in their memories it had been a pure hell. Bampico thought their progress from Haverhill had been slowed by the captives, and he was concerned that the others might have come and gone. He hoped that the result of his actions would pay off once they reached Quebec. The coin he would receive would help him and his family; he knew the war called King Philip's War would be coming to an end. His days of murdering and pillaging the white man were growing short.

"Hannah, I need to sleep," Goody Mary said. "I am weary, and my belly for once is full; or that I am grateful."

"Here, lie next to me, we will warm each other," Hannah told her. "The flames are strangely high this night."

Goody Bradley's clothes were nearly dry, so she dressed in the shadows of the forest. She had returned Thomas's coat to Hannah and gave thanks for her generosity. Good wife Duston used it as a blanket to shield both women from the cold. They had lain atop a collection of evergreen boughs they had gathered earlier to soften their slumber.

Mary was ready for sleep, and she knew it would not take long for her to fall off. Hannah stared intently into the flames, feeling the heat across the encampment to where they sat, nestled in the curve of a granite rock. She could not sleep and was still reliving the story of the gauntlet from earlier in the day. She feared her friend Mary would not survive such a test of physical strength; she surely would persist. The gauntlet was another reminder of the savages and their ways; they truly were servants of The Devil, she thought.

Everyone, it seemed, had reached a breaking point, except Mato, whose foulness only continued to fuel his desire to torment them. The baby killer, as Hannah would always think of him, needed to meet his maker, for his death would ease the pain in her heart. It was an unholy thought, but she would not feel regret for it.

"An eye for an eye," she spoke so only her soul could hear it.

There was no rum left to entice the savages into a frenzy; except for Bampico and the warriors feeding the fire, the others were settled for the night. Mato was not in sight, and Hannah wondered where he might be and what evil deed he was perpetrating.

Then came a quiet snore from Mary's open mouth; it was a reassuring sound to Hannah, one that meant the night had fallen and they both had endured another day. Hannah's eyelids were growing weary; keeping them open had become a chore, and she, too, fell into a deep sleep, her body needing it to heal and reenergize.

Across the way, the moon was high in the horizon, not quite full, casting just enough light for anyone traveling in the forest to find their way. It was now late, and even Bampico had taken to the ground, sleeping next to the fire. The captives and the captors were sleeping harmoniously, a strange event.

"Goodwife Duston," a whispered voice was heard in her ear. "Hannah, I'm here."

Hannah stirred and opened her eyes; she had no idea how long she had been sleeping. She sat up in a straight position and looked about; there was not a person near her, but Mary, who was purring like her cat back in Haverhill.

"Hannah, over here," there was the voice again. "Come this way."

Hannah looked in the direction of the forest's edge. She could not see anyone and wondered who was there. Was there someone in need of her help, she wondered to herself. Without disturbing Mary, she slipped out from under the coat and stood. She was surprised that she did not feel the cold against her body and wondered how the fire had warmed the air so far away. She paid it no mind and slowly walked in the direction of the voice. She reached the edge of the wood and peered through the branches, looking for the source of it.

"This way, Goodwife Duston," it told her. "I am here; I want to lend help to you."

"Who ye be? I cannot see ye." Hannah responded to the voice fearlessly.

She continued walking carefully deeper into the forest, using both her hands to push away the branches from the undergrowth. She stopped when she reached a small clearing and looked about.

"I am Tsienneto, a friend of those in need," the voice told her with the slightest of an Indian accent.

She was perplexed, but not frightened. She had wished that whoever it was, she could find the origin of the voice. It had sounded like an old man, one that she believed to be familiar to her, but how could that be? It was an improbable thought.

"Rest yourself, sit there on the rock," the voice told her. "It is necessary I speak."

Hannah found the rock; it was a small boulder that came to a point. She managed to find a spot to rest. Her curiosity was getting the better of her, and she still wondered why she could not see the origin of the voice or feel the cold night air.

"I am Tsienneto. I have lived in these woods for many moons," it told her. "Long before your people crossed the great waters."

Hannah sorted out the voice to be a man, one who was old and wise. He was comforting to listen to when he spoke; seeing his face was not needed.

Tsienneto is a great advisor to the people who are in need of help. He told her that the death of her baby, Martha, was a shocking event, and her death would be avenged. He would help her because he had foreseen the injustice that she and her family had endured before it happened. He told her that he lived on an enchanted island in the middle of a lake nearby, under the tallest pine tree in the forest.

"Please tell, how did you come to know my dilemma?" She asked him.

"It does not matter; your true strength will deliver you," he said. "The plan will reveal itself."

Just as quickly as she had arrived at the place in the forest, and listened to the unseen, he told her to return to the others.

"It is time for you to yield to your place among the others," Tsienneto told her.

The sound of a musket was fired off in the distance, followed by another in closer range. The group had started to wake. The fire embers are still strong; the heat was felt by the stirring captives. It was daybreak, and the savages were getting ready to leave the campsite; their faces showed emotion that was not of fear, but of relief. The sound of the musket was from an Indian approaching party, not the militia. The moment of hope dissipated as fast as it had appeared.

Mary was the first to stir; she could not believe that she had slept through the night and had awakened before Hannah. Thomas's coat was still draped across them; it created a sense of security for them, a sense that Hannah's husband always gave her and their family.

"Hannah, did you hear that gunshot?" Mary asked.

She stirred and nudged her friend in the ribs, careful not to poke her breasts. Hannah mumbled; it was undetectable to Mary. Hannah sometimes mumbled in her sleep, and Mary never paid it much mind.

"Hannah, we have to make ready for today," Mary told her. "Wake ye, the sun has risen."

Hannah opened her eyes. It took a second to adjust to the morning light. The warriors were breaking camp, and the other captives were readying themselves for another day. Hannah Bradley emerged from behind a large tree as discreetly as possible. She had just relieved herself, a morning ritual everyone does, but attempts to conceal.

"Are ye fine?" Mary asked. "You look perplexed, did ye not sleep?"

Hannah didn't answer. What would she tell her? Last night was a troubled sleep for her, and a voice beckoned her into the forest, one that had no face. Mary would surely think it was the work of The Devil. Hannah could not explain that she thought she spoke to a very old Indian who sounded like a mystic. The witch trials had taught her and her friends not to speak of such things. Hannah questioned whether it had really happened or if it was, in fact, an apparition from a great force. She was still too tired, and her mind was as foggy as the river was that morning.

Samuel was walking in their direction, carrying a sack of goods. They knew it was time. Mary handed Thomas's coat to her and helped put it on. Samuel handed the sack to Hannah; it was noticeably lighter. The Englishman just gave her a look but did not say a word; he turned and headed in the direction of the others.

Mary followed him, and Hannah was in close pursuit. They headed back down towards the riverbank to the trail and turned in the direction where the distant gunshot was heard, north.

FIFTEEN

There was a sense of anxiety that filled the morning air as the captives trekked in a single column near the river's edge. The path was well-worn in comparison to the trail across the wilderness over the past few days. It did not go unnoticed by the few men that were left in the group that the trail was a part of a larger system, perhaps one used for many years. They knew they were not in their domain, a place where few of their kind would dare venture.

The bundles they carried had all been emptied on the ground and rearranged. The night before the Indians had painstakingly reviewed the contents and divided their stolen belongings up, a curious project indeed; the captives thought. The group whispered to each other that the gunshots that they had heard earlier that morning were a signal to another war party. The Puritans had assumed something was going to happen. None of the captives knew their fate that morning.

The water in the mighty river flowed past them, but it remained dark and lifeless, almost black. The sun was doing its best to warm the air, but it had been unsuccessful that morning, feeling the coldest yet. Some of them intently watched the skies for signs; they feared that a snowstorm, if it came, would be a disaster. It would be a sign that their providence had become a reality, and any faith left to their survival would surely dwindle.

While the others were watching the sky for signs of snow, Goodwife Duston watched her surroundings with a clever eye. She wanted to be sure, as they moved north, that there were no other sites where these savages were camped. She, too, thought that the trail, worn and free of obstacles, was used frequently, and if that were true, that would hinder her plan. She had heard the word Merrimac the previous night, and she was immediately aware that the river would be the best scheme to lead them back home.

Hannah carried her new, lighter bundle with ease and more confidence. Her strength was nearly back, and, in her mind, she was ready to be free of her bondage; it was only a matter of time.

"Look there," Mary told her friend.

Hannah was intently watching the other bank of the river as she walked; the other side was less than a few yards away at the bend in the river. They could swim across to gain distance from the savages. She quickly figured that this was not beneficial for her plan. After hearing Mary's statement, she looked forward.

Bampico and her master were high atop a grassy knoll, standing next to a few other Indians who were dressed similarly in matching leathers, their face free of blackened stain. She was sure now that something was about to happen; she was just unclear of what it was.

"Hannah, will we be separated?" Mary asked with panic in her voice.

"Goody Neff, we will show patience," she replied. "Let us not forget our friend Samuel; he is there watching."

At the front of the line, Samuel turned and made eye contact with Hannah. That one sign of solidarity was all she needed. The captives were prodded and poked to walk off the trail and up to where the sachems were standing. Reaching the knoll, Mato motioned for them to drop the bundles. The group stood there in fear. One of the children started to cry, and Goody Brown tried to comfort her daughter as best she could.

The two scouts who had been the runners throughout the ordeal approached the Puritans and began separating them. They forcibly grabbed them one by one, turning them completely around; they were displaying their possessions to the newly arrived warriors. It was apparent that the few who had lived were being placed into smaller groups.

Goodwife Bradley and three others, including the mother and child, were forced across the grassy area to where the two unfamiliar savages were standing. They stood there, their clothing soiled, ripped, and their total beings distressed. Fear was present on their faces; it had been the same look they showed when their neighbors had been dragged from their homes, arrested, and accused of witchcraft. It was a sense of helplessness.

Hannah and Mary were grabbed by their arms and led to the other side where Bampico and Mato stood. Samuel was motioned to also join that group. Mary let out a quiet sigh of relief and thought her God, once again, had shown favor on her and her friend. Nothing good would ever happen in her world if she did not give thanks, either aloud or quietly under her breath. Prayer was her salvation.

The few that remained included John Clement, his son, and the Tuttles, their fate still undisclosed. The warriors motioned for them to sit and wait. Bampico told them that another party from the west was arriving. Bampico told them that they would be heading to the Monadnock, a region west, next to another great river, which he called Kwenitegok.

Hannah Bradley and the others were given sacks to carry; it would have appeared that the stolen items seemed to their captors to be of as much value as the captives. The sachem without a name signaled the warriors who had arrived with him that it was time to leave and continue back north.

Mary and Hannah were feeling wretched; though they knew the others, they were not as close as they could have been. It was no fault of anyone. Puritans were a strange lot, and in the conditions they had been forced to live had created the most challenging environment.

Hannah Bradley, barely twenty-four summers, had also shown the resolve of an older woman. She walked over to Mary Neff and Goodwife Duston, wishing them Godspeed and a safe return. Bradley touched Hannah's arm as a gesture of her generosity and for her strength; Goody Bradley felt that Hannah was the example they all followed. She bowed her head and picked up her sack, walking slowly away, never looking back.

The group had gotten smaller with the departure of the captives, the two scouts, and four warriors. They followed the group in a northerly direction. Each of the members of the group was required to carry something; a bow and quiver for the lucky savage and a filled leather sack for the unlucky, the captives.

Bampico instructed his captives to sit; he wanted the first group to be underway before the next one was to leave. Small bands of warriors are less detected than a large group, though he had no worries of the white man's arrival.

"Where are they taking them?" Hannah asked Samuel.

"For I am not sure where they will end up," he told her. "But I am certain they will be up the river at the crotch where this mighty river begins."

Samuel told his friends that there was a very old settlement of Abenaki not too far up the river. It was a sacred place but only during the spring; when the fish returned, so would the tribe. From there, he thought they would be taken to Maine and further into that part of Kanata.

"Do not worry," he continued, "They have made it this far; they will surely survive."

Mary reached for Hannah's hand and held it tightly. Nothing was said; but only felt. They sat there waiting for commands from one of the two masters now: the baby killer and Bampico. They had hoped Samuel would have some Nokechick or some meat in his pouch; if he had, he did not pass it to them; without breakfast, their stomachs ached for attention.

Bampico was watching the sky; the morning was growing long, and he wanted to start on his own journey. The others could wait there at the bend; it was the easiest place to cross the river to the west. They could ford the river and meet the ones called N'dakinna. Those Abenaki were fierce defenders of the land there; the region was called Monadnock. The white man had not arrived in great numbers in their land.

Bampico motioned for the second group to head to the river's edge. He ran down to meet them to show them the way. Two of the warriors who had been with them the entire time were part of the N'dakinna and could lead them onto the correct trail once they waded across the river. He instructed them to make camp once the sun was gone; their people would be there soon. The warriors agreed; their stoic faces showed no emotion. They nodded and accepted the challenge.

Bampico returned to the grassy knoll and made the signal; it was time to also head to their own destination. The women, along with Samuel, each picked up a sack, which was manageable even for Mary. They returned to the trail they had been on and continued north, with the water to their left.

Hannah looked back and briefly watched the others as they slowly traversed the shallow part of the water; the rocks that had washed into the shallows acted as a bridge of sorts. She wondered what fate was in store for them; it had been the same thought she had had for herself and Mary.

The weather had not improved as they continued north. The wind had increased its force and was coming from a westerly direction. It crossed the frigid waters and gusted in their direction. A storm was coming, and this had been a sure sign.

Bampico was a few yards ahead of the small band, with just Samuel; their number was reduced to only five. That had given Hannah the thought that all was coming together; five was a worthy and manageable number.

They walked for a couple of more hours, never veering off the worn trail, nor far from the river. Mary asked again where they were going, and Hannah shrugged, for she did not know for certain either. Samuel heard her and turned back to tell Goody Neff what he knew.

"It is a scarce place, I have been told," Samuel told her. "It was the summer camp of the great sachem Passaconaway many years ago."

The young English boy had never visited the place and had only heard stories from Bampico, who had heard about it from his father. He told the women what he knew about the place, which was not much. The Abenaki had thought of it as a dwelling where the great spirit would visit and give guidance to the all-powerful sachem, Passaconaway. That was all he knew.

"Is it far from here?" Mary was never short of enquiries.

Samuel told them that they would meet the others, and there would be a tall pine to the west that would be the place of Passaconaway. When the tall pine could be seen, the others would be there with canoes, for they too had to cross the mighty river to his island.

Hannah stopped and reflected on what Samuel had just said. What the young English boy was telling them sounded all too strange to her, but much like the dream she had had the night before.

"Master Samuel, is ye island on a lake?" She asked.

"Nay, Goodwife Duston, it is where the water Contoocook meets the Merrimac," he explained.

"But, what of this tall pine tree you speak of?" It was Hannah's time to be inquisitive.

"The tall pine is near the center of the small island," Samuel told them. It was used as the marker, as it could be seen in many directions. Passaconaway spent the warm time there with his family; many of the Abenaki had visited it. The Great Spirit would often give counsel to the sachem there, as it was told to him.

Hannah was still thinking about her dream and what the voice had said to her in the forest. Was it not a dream, but an apparition created by The Devil to confuse her? The journey had been so long, and her physical being, which was much improved, had seen much hardship. Her mind could be tempting her with something unnatural. She refused to let such thoughts consume her.

Bampico was out of sight now, far ahead of the small group. Mato knew not to interfere with his master; he was looking for the others who were to meet him before crossing to the island.

The sound of the seagull was heard; this time both Mary and Hannah knew it to be Bampico. They were miles and miles from the great water; the seagull would surely be lost. The sound of the gull came again, and they all looked down in the direction of the riverbank.

They carefully climbed down to the water's edge over the eroded shoreline, where an exposed section of sandy beach was free of debris and rocks. Bampico was standing there next to a squaw and a young Indian boy not older than ten, Hannah had guessed.

Bampico gestured for Mato and Samuel to go where the birch bark canoes were tied. He wanted to load them quickly and be on their way. The bundles were placed in the center of each of the canoes. The vessels were massive in length; Hannah figured them to be at least eighteen feet long.

Neither Hannah nor Mary had ever been in one; they were fearful of the device and the Icy water. Samuel was first to get in and gestured for Mary to sit behind him.

She attempted to climb over the side, and when the canoe tipped on the sandy shore, she stumbled and placed her right foot squarely into the river. The squaw behind her let out what sounded like a chuckle and quickly hopped in the canoe like she had at least a thousand times before. Mary quickly got the hang of it and sat next to the bundle. She sat in the center of the canoe with the bundle she carried next to her. The squaw looked at her with disdain in her eyes.

Mato threw his tomahawk into the boat and pushed it with great force before hopping in. He picked up the paddle and steered it away from the shoreline, letting the slow current bring it out to the center of the waterway. Samuel, with his paddle in hand, waited for Mato to signal him to begin to use it. The sachem said something, and the English boy looked to his right; a tall pine majestically appeared, atop a small island. He was now made aware of the direction.

Hannah stood watching the entire scene and was determined not to fall into the river. The young Indian hopped in first and sat in the front. He picked up his paddle immediately. This was not his first crossing. Hannah cautiously and successfully reached the center and quickly sat down, resting her back against the sack she had carried. The Indian boy smiled at Hannah. He had never seen a white woman before.

The canoe was something she had never been in and had not known how they had been constructed or even floated. It appeared to be one large piece of birch bark that was attached to a frame of smaller straps made of another kind of wood. There were laces like a shoe the entire length of the vessel, made of leather, she thought; it was hard to tell how, exactly, it all stayed together and floated.

Bampico gave it a mighty push from the shoreline and jumped in. He had placed his tomahawk and the French musket next to him. His paddling was incredibly strong; the canoe glided across the water with no effort. The young Indian boy in the front was a master at it as well; in no time, they had caught up with the others.

The full view of the tall pine tree came into sight, and she was brought back to the previous night and her dream, if in fact it had been a dream. In her mind, she tried to recollect in detail what the voice told her after giving his name. He had lived on an island in the middle of a lake for many years, next to a tall pine tree. The island was magical, and he could foresee when someone close by needed help. Hannah did not know what to think, except that her plan needed to come into realization, soon, if they were to survive.

Both vessels reached the shore of the island, which sat there overlooking the Merrimac, with a waterway on both sides. There was no doubt that it was the Contoocook that Samuel had told her about, flowing continuously into the Merrimac. They unloaded the supplies, and the young Indian, along with Samuel, tied the canoes to a fallen tree that had landed on the embankment in the water. It was a perfect spot to conceal the canoes between the branches that reached into the water.

Samuel returned to where the supplies were being offloaded; they needed to be carried up a steep section where the sand had been exposed due to erosion. The smell of a campfire was apparent, and the smoke rising above the higher ground was an indication that they were not alone on the island. Mary and the squaw had already started up the embankment, and the loose sand made it a challenge. Goody Neff was struggling, using both hands, trying to grasp exposed roots to pull her to the top. The squaw who was much younger made it to the top with ease. She looked back at the white woman and offered nothing but a sneer and continued, no aid for a woman old enough to be her grandmother.

The young boy picked up a sack and scaled the embankment with ease. After reaching the top, he returned and lent a hand to Goody Neff, pulling her the rest of the way up. Hannah was alone on the shoreline, with only her sack. She contemplated, at that moment, freeing the canoe and heading downriver. Escaping before nightfall was a fleeting thought. Samuel jumped in the sand and ran back down to meet her. Both Bampico and the baby killer were nowhere in sight, having been the first to scale the shoreline.

"Master Samuel," Hannah got his attention. "Can I ask you something?"

"Yes, I welcome it." He replied.

"Have you ever heard of an Indian called Tsienneto?" She asked prudently.

"What a strange question," was his answer. "It is an old legend about a Pawtucket warrior who was a soothsayer; he foretold the coming of the white man, that is all I know," he continued.

"Why do you ask, Goodwife Duston?" He inquired while looking at her strangely.

Hannah did not say a word and started to make her attempt up the embankment.

SIXTEEN

It was not a very large landmass; the island's position was perfect for anyone who feared approaching enemies. Their approaching presence would be made known from a great distance. It was in a triangle shape with the tip jetting out into the Merrimac, where it felt the burden of the rising waters, causing erosion along the shoreline. From the top of the embankment, you could look in both directions of the river, north and south. It was a clear view until the bends of the river prevented it.

Samuel carried the last sack from the edge of the embankment in the direction of the smoke that could be seen rising. The tall pine was somewhat away from the campsite, to the west in the direction of the other river, the Contoocook. It was as he had imagined it, a tall white pine that had grown so high he could not remember seeing one as tall.

Hannah and Mary had already arrived at the site and were sitting next to the fire, watching the others. Along with Bampico and Mato, there were ten others, the young boy from the canoe and the annoyed Squaw. The majority of the group was children, and two others were older women. Hannah watched with much curiosity, trying to sort out what the connection was to her masters.

The fire felt good. Goody Mary was happy to sit there and hoped their time on the island would be long enough to rest and regain her strength. Mary was feeling all of her age and then some; her years were catching up to her, and she feared that more of the same ordeal would be too much for her to endure.

Hannah was not in the same mindset as her friend. She grew stronger each day; the anger and the contempt she felt about those savages had only fueled her. Mato was The Devil himself, and each time she looked at him or smelt his rotten odor, it brought her back to the first day of their captivity. She would often pray in silence to her God, to release her from the memory of poor Martha, her head smashed with her blood staining the snow.

"Eat this," Samuel told them.

He had approached the two next to the fire, and he handed them each a piece of dried meat. By the smell of it, they were convinced it was rancid and would surely make them sick. They looked at each other and bit into the dried venison; the taste was foul as they had thought, but they ate it anyway. They had nearly tasted starvation and did not want a repeat of that.

On the island, there had been an old-looking wigwam or long house next to the fire. Hannah never knew the difference between what the structures were called, nor did she pay them any mind. The place where the savages lived was built of animal hides, hemlock boughs, and bark. There was a curved roof to it, and like the canoe, it was also stitched together. It worked well, keeping out the elements and providing a shelter for them to live. The deer skin hides acted as a door, just a large flap covering the opening, one at each end.

Mato approached the squaw who was attending to the fire. He gave her a sign of affection that was a half-hearted hug, something Hannah thought was strange. Just as that occurred, a young child, a girl of about five years of age, ran out from behind the deer skin flap and grabbed Mato's legs and hugged him, as only one of his own would. That scene infuriated Hannah and only re-inforced her belief that he was evil personified.

Samuel and Bampico brought the sacks near to the fire and untied them. The Indians gathered to watch the reveal of the sacks contents. First came a silver candle-stick, then another; there had been a pewter platter and some iron cooking utensils. There was a spool of spun yarn and the copper bucket they had been using. There were more things than either of the women imagined had been stolen, which saddened Mary Neff and angered Hannah.

The Indian women quickly grabbed the items that were intended for them. More items came out, including a couple of hatchets, some gunpowder, another bottle of rum, and the cloth from Hannah's loom. That one piece of fabric represented hours of labor; her rage continued to swell as items that she recognized were exposed in the daylight.

After the distribution of the loot, they went back to their duties. Bampico produced a pipe that was made of clay, no doubt another stolen object or a trade he made with the French. It was not the normal Abenaki smoking instrument made of soft stone. He filled the small bowl with tobacco from a pouch that was near the squaw and lit it. He smoked as a ritual when he felt that the task at hand was nearly done, and success was evident in his mind.

The entire campsite had seen better days; the wigwam needed repair, and there had been evidence of another long house that had been destroyed by fire or the harsh weather conditions over the years. There had been other signs throughout the area, making it feel remorseful to Hannah; it was an abandoned settlement, with spirits of the dead.

She was convinced that it was where the great sachem, Passaconaway, had lived. She believed the story Samuel had told her earlier. Most legends had an element of truth; it was like the good book that she had read almost every day, for it was only a legend that was written.

Goody Neff felt a drop of rain on her cheek. She looked up, and the sky was dark and menacing; rain was coming. The squaw that was attending the fire also knew the sky would open up and the cold rain, like ice, would fall. She took a pewter plate from the heap of goods on the ground and filled it with fish that she had removed from the hot stones next to the fire.

Bampico motioned for Samuel to gather the goods and put them in the shelter. The English boy ran over to the items and gathered them into his arms as best he could and brought them to the opening in the wigwam.

Bampico did not mind the rain, for it had only been a few drops; he would take heed once it poured. He stood there staring into the fire and enjoying the tobacco he had received from the French trappers.

Mato was corralling the children into the wigwam, for fear the cold rain would make them sick. Spring-time illnesses were forever prevalent amongst the young when the weather changed. Hannah watched and was once again dumbfounded by his actions; they were contrary to what she had witnessed since being taken.

Samuel had almost finished moving the items. He picked up the deer hide sacks and brought them near to where Hannah and Mary sat. They were worried about the rain as well and hoped they would be allowed into the shelter.

"Take these, use them as covering." He told them.

Hannah reached for what she thought was an empty sack and heard a distinctive sound of metal; something inside made of that material made a sound. She reached in and felt the wood handles of two hatchets, the sound created by the collision against each other. Samuel had deliberately neglected to bring them into the shelter with the rest of the things. Hannah quickly concealed the tools under Thomas's coat and covered her and Mary with the sacks. The rain had started.

"I will see what I can find to save the rain from ye," Samuel told the women.

The trees on the island had not fully leafed yet, still bare from the winter past. The fir trees, though, were exceptionally full. He quickly cut a few wide hemlock branches and fashioned them together to make a cano-py of greenery, something he hoped would help. He no-ticed a young sapling not far from the fire, which had grown upright in a straight direction, and it was twice the height of his own.

Hannah and Mary sat and watched as he bent the young tree down and staked it into the ground. He was glad the soil was not frozen. Using the evergreens, he hooked them over the curved shape the sapling created. It was a crude lean too, something that would help his friends through the night. It was close enough to the fire that the heat would ease the cold away from the women through the night.

Bampico was still standing in the rain; he had his pipe in hand, and he was not fazed by the approaching storm. He did watch as his young warrior tried to relieve the discomfort of the two white women. He was unclear of the boy's motives but did not interfere.

"Mary, get in here closer, we will weather this as we have in the past," Hannah instructed.

Mary and Hannah were under the lean-to; it was just sufficient if they huddled together, they could almost be out of the cold rain that was falling. The deer hides were very helpful, and they were most grateful. Mary had not seen the two hatchets that Hannah had hidden under Thomas's coat. When the time was right, she would make Goody Neff aware of the situation.

Bampico finished smoking and emptied the tobacco ash into the fire that was still burning. The flames were still strong and would last most of the night, he reckoned. He did add more of the wood the squaws had collected before their arrival, and the fire swallowed the dry branches instantly. He glanced over to the women, his captives; he gave them not a thought. They would not try to escape; they were nearly broken in body and spirit, just the way he wanted them to be.

"I must join them," Samuel whispered. "Or they might have reason for concern."

"Master Samuel, ye are but a true servant of God," Mary told him.

"Ye not worry, we will do our best not to perish in the dark of night," Hannah added.

Bampico walked to the wigwam and pulled back the deerskin flap to enter. He could smell the fish that Mato's woman had cooked. It was time to eat. Bampico made a whistle sound to alert Samuel to come at that moment.

Inside their shelter, it was dry, with an abundance of fur pelts and baskets with provisions. It was evident that the squaws and children had been there a while, waiting for the arrival of the sachems. There was a small fire in the center of the structure and a hole in the roof where the smoke escaped. The smell of burning wood, stale fish, and body odor was something none of them noticed.

Samuel arrived in the crowded space; there were now thirteen of them in that wigwam. It was tight quarters, but they would make do during the rainstorm. They ate the fish and the Nokechick in silence. The children were happy to see Mato, who was their master as well as the father of the three of them. The others belonged to the squaw who rode in the canoe across the Merrimac and was displeased with Goody Neff.

The chill in the air was like a blade cutting the surface of their exposed skin, the rain became more intense, and the makeshift shelter did its best to keep most of the moisture from the women.

"Goody Neff, it is all coming to fruition," Hannah told her. "The plan is near."

"Are you certain that he will give us freedom or surely death?" Mary questioned.

Hannah sat there under the warmth of the deerskin and felt the ground for the concealed weapons. She slowly pulled one and showed it to her friend. It was now dark; the light of the fire caused the metal of the wet blade to glisten in the firelight. An eerie image at best, it had frightened Mary.

Hannah explained that Samuel had left the hatchets in the sack; they were a gift from their benefactor, one that was greatly appreciated. Samuel was with them and would see the plan through. The time of their escape was fast approaching, with only the two sachems and three squaws, Hannah was convinced it was doable.

"But, I have never killed a person before," Mary told her.

"Nor have I," Hannah responded. "We have to show our strength and overcome these savages; it is the way to gain our freedom."

"What about the children?" Mary asked.

Hannah had not counted on the presence of children when formulating the plan in her mind. Her resolve was unbroken, and the demise of the children would be reality; there was nothing that would deter her from the outcome.

"I think the young boy is a strong one with the paddle," she told her.

The young Indian boy was close to Samuel's age, and she would spare him. He would aid with the course-plotting along the river as they paddled south, back to Haverhill.

"And the rest?" Mary asked.

"Let us not forget the fate of all that was lost these past days in the wilderness," Hannah was becoming angry. "What ye think was the fate of my own children? Ye heard Bampico."

Goody Neff became silent. She did not want to argue with her friend or question her way of thinking. She was right; Bampico had killed the Duston children, and Mato wrenched the baby Martha from her hands. It was an eye for an eye; the good book had said so. "We should try to sleep; we will need all the strength possible in the coming days," Hannah said.

The fire was ablaze and created a glow in the darkness. The rain was creating a mist as it came into contact with the flames, creating a sense of foreboding through the campsite. The women huddled together, reserving their strength and their body heat. The savages were inside the dry longhouse, warm, feasting on fish, with no knowledge of a traitor in their midst.

SEVENTEEN

It had been only a few hours since the dawn light awakened the women who had slept through the night in their makeshift shelter. Their bones ached from the cold, and no amount of deer skins or hemlock branches could prevent it; it had crept in and remained. They shivered until sleep fell upon them, without realizing the rain had stopped.

They woke that morning to a gift from God, a fresh blanket of snow that covered the island like a quilt made with love, hiding all its secrets and ugliness. Goody Neff felt it was a sign from heaven, and thought about the Book of Isaiah, where it was written; *Though your sins are like scarlet, they shall be as white as snow.*

Goodwife Hannah was down at the river's edge trying to fill the copper pot with water; a very thin layer of ice was attempting to form around the small rocks that lined the shoreline. She paused and looked at the water, the light as it refracted off it, lighting her face. Even through the slight movement of the water, she could see a face that had lived a hundred years in those last few days. Hannah was worn, her face soiled with soot and fatigue; this ordeal had to be ending soon, for she feared the amount of her determination was being depleted.

"Ye need help?" Mary Neff yelled down the embankment to Hannah.

Hannah waved; she wanted to assure her friend that she was fine. Mary could not easily make it down to assist her; it was difficult enough with the sand, and the freshly fallen snow would surely send her face-first into the river.

Hannah climbed back up to the campsite, paying close attention to her footing, following her steps she had made on the way down. Mary took the pot from her and walked to the remnant of the previous night's fire and placed it on a stone next to the embers. The coals were still glowing, the heat keeping the light snow that had fallen far away from it.

"The sun will surely melt most of it," Hannah told Mary. "Then we can look for groundnuts."

"And fiddleheads," Mary answered. "I saw some over there before the rain last night."

Mary was pointing in the direction of the tall pine, the beacon for the island, and the one Hannah thought that the voice told her about. If it had been a dream, it had stirred a desire in Hannah to see her plan through. If there was a spirit that lurked in the forest, then he would guide her.

"Good morning, Goodwife Duston," Samuel said,

He approached the fire carrying a load of squaw wood that he had snapped on the nearby pine trees. He dropped them next to Goody Neff and nodded to her. Mary Neff so enjoyed the young English lad, and his help to them was endless.

"Master Samuel?" Mary had questioned. "Do you miss your family?"

Samuel looked at Mary and paused. Then he knelt next to the coals and stirred them with a stick; they grew brighter, the air causing them to flare. He started to place the broken branches into the fire.

"Goody Neff," he started, "it be the truth, I have forgotten my mother's face, and that of my grandmother."

Samuel was remorseful, recalling his family back in Worcester, explaining the time Bampico came in the night and stole him. There had been others, some met the tomahawk on their journey north, and others were taken by French settlers, sold into service. The story he told the women was heart-wrenching to them, and not unlike what they had been experiencing.

"How ye come to be Bampico's?" Hannah asked.

He explained that Bampico's only son died of a strange disease, the one where your face is covered in red blotches, something that had taken many in his village. That had been a few years before, and Samuel had filled the void. He was taken under Bampico's wing and taught their ways, their tongue, and in exchange, his life was not sold into service.

Both of the women listened to him with their own thoughts racing in their minds. Mary knew she was too old to be sold into service; she felt she would not even make it that far north before she, too, felt the blunt stone of the tomahawk on her temple. Hannah refused to think that she would forget the faces of her Thomas or any of her children. It has been every night before she slept, the image of her husband at the door, fear on his face that morning when he alerted her to the Indians.

"I'm so sorry for ye, Samuel," Mary told.

"Are ye ready to free yourself from the bondage of these savages?" Hannah asked.

Samuel nodded, and Mary looked down in the direction of the copper pot and said a quiet prayer that the others could not hear. Hannah was pleased that it was all coming together, and Samuel was as committed as they were.

Bampico and Mato emerged from the wigwam; they were dressed in another layer of deerskin. Their faces all but free of the dark stain, each of them had a weapon in hand. The French rifle for Bampico and a pole axe for Mato. It looked to Hannah that they were ready for a hunt, or it was time for them to enter the kingdom above. She stood tall, her defiance never wavering, especially when her baby killer approached.

Mato said something to Samuel, speaking in a gruff and displeasing manner; he was not very fond of the adopted English boy. He felt that Bampico should not have taken the white man into their world; even though they were from different tribes, Mato had a kinship with Bampico. He did not like sharing. Both the sachems walked past without a glance or acknowledgment that the women were in their presence.

"What did he say?" Hannah wanted to know.

Samuel explained that they were going to look for game, and they needed to ready themselves for the next day's departure. He was to look after the women. "If you tried to flee, I would have to stop you and end your life. He was tired of dragging you both through the wilderness."

Hannah's hair on her neck stood up; the anger she felt was burning deep within her. She had had enough of the way she was treated, especially as a woman. The Puritan life was a hardship in itself; being a woman in that society, amongst the male brethren, was at times equal to her captivity with the savages. It had seemed to Hannah that she had no recognition, no say in her fate, and only subservient to the men that surrounded her. It was time.

Mary looked to Hannah for guidance, for she was the strongest woman she had known. The Emerson family had seen its fair share of turmoil, some unjust and some deserved, starting with The Devil himself, her father, Michael. How her friend had coped with that man and his doings was as bewildering to her as their chance was for survival.

"Pay them no mind's moment," Hannah said and retreated to her makeshift shelter.

She sat down and retrieved one of the hatchets from under the deer skin sacks. Using the blade, she cut a section of her underskirt to rip a strip of fabric off. The strip was then cut in half along with the shirt, ripped up the center in front and in back. Mary noticed what she had done and joined her under the hemlock branches.

"Hannah, what ye doing?" Mary asked.

Hannah created pants from her undergarments, using the strips of cloth to tie around her ankles after she gathered half of the skirt. This had created a better sense of freedom for her; it was not very ladylike, but neither was her plan. Mary approved of her actions and was equally committed to her as was Master Samuel.

The morning passed without incident, and the other squaws tended their duties while watching the children frolic in the snow that was melting as the day grew longer. The squaws were keeping the fire going and keeping an eye on the white women. They were not pleased to be in their presence, and the feeling was mutual.

Mary had put the last of the dried meat from Samuel in the boiling water along with some cornmeal the young Indian boy had given Hannah earlier. Mary's concoction would only be enhanced with some groundnuts; it was her version of a stew. Anything to stave off starvation, but the sachems had no desire to share anything with them.

Samuel had found some nuts and cleaned them in the snow; the dirt from the roots staining the fresh white blanket was disappearing in the sunlight. He used his knife, cut them in half, and dropped them into the boiling water.

One of the squaws spoke to him, the one from the canoe who watched Mary fall. Her tone and body mannerisms were those of Bampico's earlier. Hannah watched the interactions of the squaw and her new friend; she did not ask what was said, it had been written all over her face, and she, as well, did not approve of them.

The morning turned into afternoon light, the day had passed, the soup had been eaten, and the children were in the wigwam. The squaws were waiting for the return of the sachems; they stood waiting to dress whatever the forest allowed them to have to eat.

The men returned with two rabbits tied along their waist over their breeches. The white of the animal's fur stained with fresh blood; soon they would be ready to feed the hungry Indians. The two older Indian women ran over to the sachems and untied the dead animals. It was a matter of minutes: the rabbits were laid on a rock, gutted, and strung up on a branch to remove their fur.

Bampico and Mato dropped their weapons, the rifle leaning against the wigwam opening and the bow against the woodpile. Bampico went into the wigwam and returned in a split second. In one hand he had two pipes and in the other a full bottle of rum. It was a long day in search of game; he had wanted a doe and settled for a couple of hares.

The children ran out to greet Mato with sounds of glee, happy to see he had returned. He returned the emotion as best he could; even the evilest of men can muster a moment of happiness; the sachem did his best.

The men both sat down on the ground next to the fire, the soil dry and warm from a day of sunshine and the heat of the fire. Bampico leaned against the rock and stuffed one pipe with tobacco and handed it to Mato, who sat down to join him. Bampico lit his own pipe from a burning stick he pulled from the fire and handed it to his friend, who repeated the task. They sat in silence, enjoying the effect of the tobacco.

Hannah and Mary had been sitting in their shelter eating their soup, which was not very tasty to them. They have grown accustomed to the offerings of the forest; it has kept them alive, and for that they were grateful. The smell of the tobacco wafted across the campsite, and the women enjoyed the smell. It was an uncomfortable reminder of days passed when Mary's husband and Hannah's father would share a smoke after returning from the meeting house, where only men were allowed to gather on those days of village business.

Samuel had helped the squaws with the rabbits, putting a skewer through the center of the gutted animals. Then he used a large stone to anchor the sapling branch over the fire. The squaws took over, and he joined the sachems on the other side.

"Master Bampico," Samuel spoke in English, something he never did. "Tell me, what is the taste like of that?"

Samuel saw the bottle of rum leaning against the rock next to him. He motioned for him to pass it. Bampico was puzzled by his request. Samuel had not shown any interest in the white man's spirits before, and that had amused him. Mato was enjoying the smoke and watching his woman as she turned the meat over, the little fat from the rabbit splatted into the flames, creating a crackling sound.

Bampico picked up the bottle and pulled the cork from it. He handed it to the young English lad whom he considered almost a son. Samuel put the bottle to his nose and smelled the amber liquid; it did not offend him. He raised the bottle and took a drink from it. The taste was not so bad, but the burning sensation caused him to cough uncontrollably, and his eyes had grown wide with tears.

Bampico laughed and took the bottle from him. Samuel got up to find some snow that had not melted to fill his mouth. The coldness calmed his burning tongue. Both sachems now were laughing, as were the squaws tending the cooking.

Samuel went and sat with the Goody Neff and Hannah. He felt his mission was accomplished. The bottle was open, and the mood had turned more joyful. It would be only a matter of time for their masters to succumb to the effects of the spirits.

The sun had now faded before the tall pine tree; the campsite was cast into dusk, and darkness would soon follow. The rabbits were enjoyed, as was the rum. Both masters passed the bottle between them as they ate and spoke in their tongue, telling tales of their endeavors. Like most men, drunkenness leads to being self-serving, boastful, and boosts one's ego. It was no different with men of the village and their captors; at times, both cut from the same cloth.

The temperature had fallen as fast as the sun behind the horizon. The three squaws and the children had retired to the wigwam, where another fire was burning, keeping them warm. Hannah and Mary sat across from the wigwam, plotting their move. Samuel had retrieved the pole axe that was near his master on the ground. Neither of the sachems took any notice of his actions.

The fire was creating light that caused shadows to dance in the air; they landed on the underbrush that surrounded them. Mary thought it reminded her of the flames of hell, something she feared with her whole heart. Samuel quietly sat next to Hannah on the ground, the pole axe in reach. Hannah placed the hatchets between her and Mary; the wait had begun.

The flap of the wigwam opened, and Mato's woman appeared and walked to him. She sat down on the ground next to him. It appeared that she was there for a while, having brought out the hide of an animal to cover herself. Her master did not mind; the rum had taken hold of his mood, and nothing would bother him.

Bampico stood up and walked to the edge of the campsite and untied his breeches. He made water like a horse, melting a hole in the snow faster than the sun could. He let out a sigh; the rum had truly taken over his body. He turned to return to the fire and stumbled onto the ground. Mato let up a hoot and laughed as he raised the nearly empty bottle to his lips.

Bampico sat back down. He had never felt as he did at that moment; the rum he consumed was the most he had ever tasted. He liked the feeling. And with no concern for his surroundings, he grabbed the bottle from Mato and drank the last of it in one long swig.

Mato laughed, and Bampico threw the empty bottle into the fire. Both Indians were displaying drunkenness, a condition the Puritans frowned upon. It was a mortal sin to be intoxicated for the eyes to see; they would always report back to the town's elders. Spirits or ale were allowed in moderation amongst them.

They watched and waited. That night, the good Puritan women, held in captivity, graciously approved of such reckless conduct.

EIGHTEEN

Hannah stood up, her body aching from the cold and damp earth that was her prison. She longed to be back in her feather bed in Haverhill with her husband close by and her baby, Martha, in her arms. She knew that neither of those things would happen; the sleeping demons across the campsite had seen to that. It was her time to destroy any of their desires.

"Mary, it's time," Hannah leaned over and whispered to her friend.

Mary had fallen asleep while watching the cavorting of the savages across the way. She tried her best to stay alert, but she had fallen asleep, and she hoped that Hannah was not upset and the plan not wrecked.

"Where is Samuel?" Mary asked.

Hannah helped her friend to stand up; she was removing Thomas's coat. She explained that Samuel had snuck into the wigwam to be sure they were all asleep. "The plan for their freedom would happen in seconds," she explained.

"We all must be ready, Goody Neff," Hannah stated.

Mary was ready in her mind, but not her body. She was shaking with fear; her uncontrollable nervousness was getting the best of her, and she tried to stop the trembling of her hands.

"This is not the time, we have to strike," Hannah said, grabbing her hands, squeezing them tightly.

Samuel arrived back at where the women stood and confirmed there was no activity in the wigwam; they were all sound asleep. From where they stood, they had a clear view of their captors and one squaw, all sleeping like the others. The rum had done its duty. Hannah would never look at a bottle again without the memory of Bampico falling to the ground.

Hannah told Mary to remove her shawl and apron; she could put them back on after. Samuel picked up the poleax and stood waiting for the signal. He had removed his leather tunic and was bare-chested like a true warrior; he was ready to strike.

Hannah bent down and picked up the hatchets and handed one to Mary. Hannah had been ready for this for many days. Vengeance and freedom were within her reach; it was now or never.

The three of them had spoken many times about the plan and never had really thought it would present itself as easily as it had that night. They crept slowly and quietly around the fire; it continued to burn, lighting the way. They reached the three sleeping savages, Bampico flat on his back; his snoring was a tell-tale sign that he would not wake easily. Mato was close by, lying on his side, always making noises as he had passed out from his inexperience with the rum made from molasses. The baby killer's woman was next to him, on her side, wrapped in a fur blanket made of a bearskin. The three did not speak a word with their mouths; it would have to be in their eyes.

Hannah, with her hatchet gripped firmly, stood over Mato. She felt no fear, no remorse. Years of working the fields side by side with Thomas, chopping wood, and carrying her children had prepared her for that task. Strong like a man, her husband would often tease her, but she never took offense.

Mary stood next to the squaw, the shaking in her hands had stopped. Her only thought was that she had to be strong enough to hold the hatchet, preventing it from slipping through her grip too soon. She had resigned herself that an eye for an eye was the only way to gain her freedom. She was ready and waited for the signal.

Samuel looked down on his sleeping master and thought of all the pain he had brought upon him. It outweighed any favor that Bampico might have shown the young English boy. He stood so that Bampico's head was between his legs, and with his two hands he gripped his master's poleax high over his head.

Hannah saw how Samuel held the poleax, and she followed his example; two hands with all the rage she had stored up would be all she would need to take the life of this savage. Mary had already used her other hand to grasp the handle of her hatchet. They were ready.

Hannah looked to the others and gave a glare so frightening that The Devil himself would run back into the forest. Mary received the signal as Samuel had, and in unison, the plan began.

There is a distinct sound that is created when the metal of the blade comes into contact with a human skull; it is not unlike a crack of thunder heard on a hot summer night, just after a lightning bolt lit the sky.

The lesson that Bampico had given to Samuel only days before had proven worthy of his skills as a teacher. The temple was the target and the most vulnerable spot for the deed at hand.

Samuel, with all his might, rendered his master dead with one drop of the poleax; blood spurted out of the hole in the side of his head, splattering across his face. Samuel tasted his master's blood as it dripped into his own mouth. His skull was crushed and disfigured beyond recognition. Bampico lay there with his life of crimson red slowly spilling onto the ground.

Mary stood between the other two; she had kneeled over the squaw and raised the hatchet at the same time as the others. She felt more in control closer to her victim's head; a missed strike by her was not an acceptable part of the plan. With both hands tightly gripped around the handle, the hatchet fell in one motion, and it connected precisely with the soft temple of her head. The position of the sleeping squaw made it easy. The Indian never made a sound, and Mary had surprised herself at how quick and easy it was to take a life.

Hannah did not see what was happening to the others; her eyes were fixated on the drunken savage who had murdered her baby in cold blood and was likely responsible for the death of her entire family. He received exactly what he had deserved. Hannah did not have to sit down to aim her hatchet; she envisioned a piece of dried oak that needed splitting. The blade severed Mato's skull nearly in two. After the first blow came another and then another. Hannah was on the verge of losing control of the plan. Her blood boiled, and the blood of her baby's killer covered her clothing and her face. She was disgusted with her victim and elated that he was no more.

As fast as the blows had fallen in unison, it was over. The carnage would tell a tale in the daylight, but that would have to wait until then. Mary stood, her hands dripping in the squaw's blood, her face speckled in red splatters; she started for the wigwam. She knew the plan and was on the move; there were others that night who would meet their fate.

Samuel, with the poleaxe in hand, was in close pursuit, followed by Hannah. Samuel knew where they would be sleeping; the squaws would be the first to feel the strong arm of death, followed by all the children. Hannah wanted to show mercy to the young boy who had shown her favor earlier; he would be spared. This had all been a part of the plan.

The sound of the cracking skulls had, in fact, woken the oldest of the two squaws, who, in her slumber, was trying to get up when Mary appeared in the darkness, the smoldering embers of the fire inside the wigwam barely emitted enough light for her to see her prey. The hatchet came crashing down on the squaw, missing her head and landing on her shoulder, the blade cutting her skin deep. The woman screamed, waking some of the others. Mary raised her weapon again and brought it down firmly; it hit the earth and not the Indian woman.

Samuel had already entered the wigwam and bludgeoned the other squaw who had not awakened, just as his master hadn't. One swing of the poleaxe, and she was finished.

The scream from the old woman came nearly at the same time as Hannah entered the shelter. Her eyes had adjusted quickly, and she made her way to the children. Some were still asleep. The hatchet fell over and over in the darkness. She connected with one sleeping Indian child after another, their blood splattering her face; it had gotten into her eyes, and it clouded her vision. She kept swinging, the blade falling in vengeance.

She only had the images of her own children dead in the snowbank back in Haverhill; she felt no remorse for her actions. These savages would learn to kill just as their elders had; one dead child is one less warrior. She truly felt divine vengeance at that instant.

Samuel was making his way down the longhouse. He knew that others were still alive and that they needed to be eliminated; any one of them that escaped could alert the others further north at the crotch where the river started. That would impede their escape.

Hannah was swinging her hatchet, crushing the tiny skulls of the children she could see. The younger boy whom she wanted to spare was awakened and stood in the darkness, watching his family being obliterated by a mad white woman.

Hannah motioned for him to stay there. As that was happening, Mary was still trying to finish the job with the older squaw; she had screamed again and pushed Mary to the ground. The wigwam was in a state of frenzy, and now whoever was left alive was aware of the carnage that was happening.

The old woman ran past Mary and out into the night. Mary struggled to her feet and went out to find her. Her escape could not happen. One child, the oldest of the girls, stood and faced Hannah. The hatchet came down and missed the young Indian. She quickly ran out into the night from the opening at the other end.

Hannah ran after her; the young squaw ran around the front in the direction of the fire and the river. The sight the young girl saw stunned her. Her mother lay in the light of the fire, covered in blood, next to Mato; they were all dead. The squaw stopped and screamed. This was not a sight any child should see, even one born into a murderous family.

The youngster that Hannah had thought to be ten years of age did not feel the blow of the hatchet; she never even saw it coming. As she stood there screaming at the sight that was presented to her, the blade entered the back of her head, and she instantly fell face-first to the ground. Hannah stood behind her, looking down at the body that was rendered motionless.

Hannah scarcely recognized the woman she became; the taste of blood that drizzled into her mouth was both disgusting and liberating to her. This feeling was as intoxicating as the rum that the savages drank. It was a sensation of control she had never felt in her lifetime; it was giving her control of her own destiny, one free of any manly jurisdiction.

Her next thought was of the young boy; she ran back into the wigwam to claim her young captive. He was nowhere to be found; he, as well, escaped through the back door, the deerskin flap still showing movement from his hurried departure.

"Hannah, Samuel," screamed Mary. "She went into the woods."

Mary was in the back of the wigwam, not far from the back entrance. Her friend was flustered because the old squaw outmaneuvered her and ran into the darkness. Samuel, who was also close by, ran in the direction of her footprints. There were but a few; most of the snow had melted during the day.

"Mary, fear not, young Samuel will find her," Hannah told her. "She will not disrupt us."

Hannah was still clutching the hatchet, and Mary was as well. Her bloody hands dripping with the life of the savages she just murdered. The stench of it all was causing her stomach to turn and her senses to be on high alert.

"Let's go back to the fire," Hannah said, in a breathy voice.

Mary started to cry; her tears trickled down to help wash the blood from her eyes, and she could not stop. She felt the pain of remorse, the thought of the children in the wigwam all dead, their blood mixing with all the others into one mass of child bloody flesh, innocent perhaps and undeserving of their fate.

"Goody Neff, enough. Take thee heed of thou self forthwith," Hannah demanded.

Mary tried her best to pull herself together. She used the sleeve of her top to wipe her tears and blood away from her face. Hannah stood there, hatchet in hand, with blood in her hair, on her face, and the bodice of her undergarment, covered like that of a butcher. That frightened Mary as much as the sight of the dead girl face down, which had reminded her of what she had witnessed on the trail in the snow field.

"Make no repentance for your actions on this night," Hannah told her sternly.

Mary did not answer; she dropped the hatchet and fell to her knees next to the fire. A silent prayer was offered to her God on behalf of them all; it was the least she could do. Samuel came running around the back of the wigwam, poleaxe in hand, along with a look of desperation on his face.

"Goodwife Duston, they are gone. I cannot find them in the darkness," he told her.

Hannah did not panic; the old woman was injured, and the blow Mary had given her would have killed any English woman of the same age. The Indian boy was crafty, and she had recognized that. He could escape, but in what direction would he go?

Samuel sat down on the ground next to Mary; he, too, was exhausted. He felt as drained as he had after the raid on Haverhill; killing was never part of his life until he was taken by Bampico. He was glad the sachem was dead, and more glad that he had inflicted the blow that did it. Not a moment of repentance would he feel.

"If he makes it," Samuel told them, "he would go north to where the two rivers make one."

The crotch was the beginning of the Merrimac, where there was also a settlement of a small band of Abenaki. Bampico's woman lived there, and that is where the first group was being taken, the one that included Hannah Bradley.

"How long?" Hannah asked frantically. "How long will it take them to get upriver?"

The river is like a serpent, it winds in a pattern of the snake, the trail follows the edge with no straight direction. Samuel also explained that they would have to cross the river at one point to reach the settlement.

"At least a day," he ended his thoughts.

Hannah took a deep breath and sat down to join her accomplices. The plan was in motion, and they needed to see it through. She was grateful to be made aware that perhaps they would have a full day on any Indian party seeking retribution for their deeds.

The light of the day would soon be coming up; it was futile to try to do anything in the darkness. They agreed and soon found themselves trying to rest; they would have to reserve as much strength as they could if they were to escape by canoe.

Mary had stopped crying and tried to close her eyes; her heart had returned to a normal beat, and the feeling that she would explode had passed. Samuel was still in shock as he stared into the fire; the images of what they had done were ingrained in his memory. Hannah got up and took the empty copper pot that was next to the fire and walked to the edge of the site. She stopped once she found some fresh snow and filled the vessel.

"Here, use this to clean yourselves," she instructed. "When the sun comes, we will go to the river and wash as best we can."

They each took a handful of the snow and smeared it onto their faces. The blood had started to dry, making it harder to remove. Their hands, which were crimson, were starting to show their true color. The snow acted as a physical prayer absolving them of their deeds; it had felt good to them.

The sun was breaking the horizon to the east, where the river flowed. It was time to act, for with the daylight comes another set of problems; they need to make haste.

They were like a well-rehearsed play of actors, each knowing what their role was. Hannah stood up, retrieved the French rifle, some powder, and shot. She picked up Thomas's coat and her apron. Mary reacted in the same swiftness. There had been some meal, and Nokechick she saw in a basket that the old squaw had put in the wigwam. Samuel picked up the hatchets, along with the fur blanket covering Mato's woman.

The pile of supplies grew at the edge of the embankment. They wanted to make their way down the sandy side of it to where the canoes were hidden. The plan was for Samuel to go first, and Hannah would toss the supplies they collected down to him. Mary would go next, sitting down and slowly sliding to the bottom. It all seemed to be going to plan.

Hannah had not shown any fear throughout the night; her resolve was steadfast, and the embankment, as steep as it was, proved not to be a challenge to her. They were all assembled next to the water, the canoes just a few feet away; they were happy to see both of them. No one had tried to take the canoes; the old squaw was in no shape to use a paddle against the current.

"Hannah, here take one," Samuel said, handing her a blood-stained hatchet.

They both hurried to the canoes, releasing one from the tree that it was tied to. Samuel guided it down to Mary, who would fill it, as he and Hannah scuttled the one that remained tied. Each took their hatchet and chopped holes along the side and in the bottom. That canoe would surely sink in no time if it were put into water; they both had reckoned.

Back at the canoe, they placed the hatchets on the bottom next to the supplies. Mary had completed her part of the plan; all the supplies were placed in the center of the canoe along with herself, who had carefully climbed in without falling into the river.

Hannah was next to climb in. She waded into the water and easily climbed over the side to be in the front of the vessel. Samuel passed the loaded musket to Mary, who then passed it to Hannah; she carefully leaned it next to her, easily reached. She picked a paddle and planted it into the shallow water, preventing the canoe from being taken away with the current until Samuel was securely in it. He was in the back, taking the lead with the most navigating experience.

"We are nearly there," Mary announced. "Praise be."

Samuel used his paddle effortlessly and shoved the end of the canoe from the shoreline. The canoe floated slowly with the current and turned miraculously, heading south. Hannah had known to wait for Samuel's instruction before she began to paddle in the water.

She watched as they drifted downriver; the island of such misery was slowly becoming smaller. The current had been stronger, she thought, than when they arrived. Samuel whistled to signal it was time for her to steer the canoe with her paddle into the center of the river.

It was at that moment that she felt flushed. The anxiety of the past few hours had her forgetting the part of the plan she had not shared with her friends.

"We have to go back," Hannah screamed.

NINETEEN

The wind had pushed the canoe from the island further to the western shoreline; the current was stronger, and the river deeper. Hannah had dropped her paddle in the water, trying to slow their progress from the scene of such carnage. She managed to steer the canoe in an eastern direction, but it was still being taken downriver.

"Samuel, we have to go back," Hannah screamed again.

Samuel was confused by her request and looked at Goody Neff. Mary thought they had done what they needed; escape downriver as fast as they could be Hannah's plan.

"Help me," Hannah pleaded.

Whatever Goodwife Duston had forgotten, it was obviously very apparent to her and her fellow escapees that it was of the utmost importance to her. Samuel was in the bow of the vessel, and without questioning her motive, he dropped his paddle into the water on the opposite side of the direction she wanted to go. He knew he had to guide the canoe slowly; the current could easily swamp it, rendering the end of her plan.

Hannah quickly got the gist of how the paddle would maneuver the front of the canoe where she kneeled. With the little strength she had left from the night before, she stroked as fast as she could. The wooden paddle barely completed its duty when she lifted it and did the same on the other side. The freezing water flew haphazardly, landing on Goody Neff's backside. The speed they were going frightened Mary; it was only her second time in such a vessel.

They were only a few yards now from the shoreline; the embankment was easily within their reach, Hannah thought. Samuel soon discovered the current that was pushing them downstream and it had slowed, allowing him to help her. The gap between them and the land had closed. Samuel grabbed the tether from the bow and jumped into the water. He was just a step away from dry land. He pulled with all his might; the front of the canoe sliced into the sand.

Hannah did not say a word and quickly moved past Mary and the supplies in the center of the canoe. She did not acknowledge her friends and scrambled up the embankment in the direction of the campsite. Mary watched from her position on her hands and knees, crawling in a state of frenzy. Samuel looked for a tree to tie off the canoe. She reached the top and turned back.

"Samuel, stay there," She said firmly. "Be ready to push off on my return."

The site of their previous activities the night before was now in full view. The sun was up; there was no concealing what they had done. Hannah stopped for just a moment to catch her breath; the paddling and the climb up the hill to where she stood had depleted any reserves of energy she had left.

Time was not on her side; she was aware of that. Satisfied her breathing was under control, she hurriedly approached the still-smoldering fire. She did not dare look directly at the bodies that were lifeless and no longer emitting any sign of heat into the morning air. They were cold, and the blood that had spilled onto the ground had stopped flowing. It was now thick and had darkened in the cold air.

As quickly as the task had taken to end their lives, the task she needed to do had to be as fast. Hannah ran past the fallen Indian girl who was face-first on the ground, her open skull displaying parts of her brain, something that went unnoticed in the darkness. Goody Duston could not look at her; she was on a mission for her baby killer's knife.

Mato was still on his side, the exact position she had ingrained into her memory. The wound the hatchet made was squarely in the middle of his temple; it had been the fatal blow. The knife she was in search of was exactly where it had been since that morning of the raid. Hannah knelt and pulled the blade from his waist belt that held his leggings to his body. It had splattered blood on it, his own mixed with that of her friends, she thought. It was befitting to her that such an instrument of pain would be used on its owner.

Hannah stood, went around the body, and placed her foot on Mato's neck. She heard a slight crack as her full body weight pressed down on it. With her left hand, she grabbed a fistful of his greasy hair and pulled. His head reared back, and the skin on his forehead became taut.

His eyes were open and were still as black and cold in death as they were in life.

With a quick slash of his own knife, she sliced the front of the hairline, which cut straight across. She was pleased that the blood did not spurt out and was amazed at how little there was of it. The act of scalping was more difficult than she had planned on. With her left hand full of hair, she yanked with all her strength. The scalp would not come off the top of the savage's head.

A blood-curdling scream that was a mixture of rage and frustration escaped her lungs. She screamed again and thrust the blade into the gash on his forehead. The knife went back and forth in the manner the squaws used to skin the rabbit that she had watched so intently. The force of her pulling on his hair had sent her toppling backwards when the hair was finally torn from the top of his head.

She landed squarely on her backside, the scalp in her left hand and the knife in her right. For a second, she lay there taking notice of the horrendous sight. She rolled onto her side and vomited; the little remnant of the food in her stomach oozed out of her mouth. The second time the urge came, nothing came up. Her stomach and her soul were both empty.

Hannah had figured out quickly to let the blade of the knife do the work; she did not have to exert so much force to remove the scalp. She got up on her feet and tossed his scalp near the edge of the fire. She moved to his squaw, who was almost in the same position as Mato had been. With her foot on her neck and a fistful of her hair, she sliced once, then again and again. She had it down to three swipes of the blade, each time going deeper, separating the scalp from the skin of the face.

Her hand was covered in blood, just enough that her grip on the knife would be compromised. She tried to wipe it off on the squaw's leather tunic. It helped. The second scalp landed next to Mato's, a mass of black hair and flesh.

Bampico was next. He was on his back, looking directly at the sky, his eyes must have opened just as the hatchet connected with his forehead. His skull was smashed like a pumpkin; fragments of bone, mixed with brain, would make scalping more difficult, his hairline not as visible. Hannah placed her foot on his throat. The pressure made his eyes bulge bigger, and his body attempted to get a better look at his fate.

The knife worked its usefulness, taking a few more strokes to remove the long black braid along with the skin that attached it to the top of his head. The pile of trophies was growing; they were evidence of her actions, affirming to herself and anyone who would inquire that she had taken control.

Hannah would not look back at her work; she moved quickly into the wigwam. The light from the smoke hole lit the interior; it was something out of the depths of Hades. The blood of the Indians was everywhere, on the sides of the shelter, across the ground, and covering the blankets and furs they had been sleeping in. Their fallen bodies lay in a blood mass, entangled and broken, where one child ended, it was hard to determine where the other started.

She started with the squaw, which had been the most identifiable and closest to the entrance. Her head was still in clear view. With the knife in her hand, she made the first cut; her scalp was easily removed, not like the others.

She turned and looked further into the longhouse; the smell of blood and flesh filled her nostrils. It was like the barn back in Haverhill, when she would help Thomas dress a stag. Butchering the carcass of an animal was oddly similar to her actions that morning, something she did not want to accept.

Next to the squaw was that same piece of cloth that Bampico had shown as his trophy. Hannah's cloth lay next to the dead woman. That alone was a sign to justify what she was doing. The memory of her spending hours weaving it next to the hearth in the great room was always a pleasant time with her family. Now that cloth would hold the scalps of her perpetrator's family, a befitting stroke of irony.

She pulled the cloth from under the squaw's corpse; it had just a bit of her blood on it. The scalp in her hand was placed in the center of the fabric. The moccasins that the squaw wore looked dryer and were without a doubt a better fit for her than her husband's boots and the poor, dead man's boot that Samuel had taken from him along the trail. Without a second thought, she removed her mismatched shoes and forced the moccasins onto her own. They were snug on her feet; they would stretch, she was sure.

It was a hard decision for her, but she knew the children had to also be a part of her collection. It was something she took no pleasure in, as well as no remorse; it had to be done. An eye for an eye was part of her mission.

Hannah found the youngest of the children, and the scalp removal was effortless. She moved down the line.

The children were all in proximity of each other, and she refused to think about her actions, which would come later. A time for reflection would no doubt cause her extreme pain.

Had that been all of them? That question arose when she reached the end of the pile of corpses; she counted six scalps altogether as she placed them on the fabric. Her memory of the young boy who seemed to have disappeared into the darkness, and the old squaw whom Mary had bludgeoned with her hatchet, had both escaped the reign of bloodshed.

Hannah had no time to think about the others; she knew that getting back to the canoe had to happen quickly. Outside of the wigwam, Hannah picked up the three scalps from the ground and put them with the others in the broadcloth.

There had been one body left to disfigure. She approached the young squaw, her body not far from the others; it was Hannah's last victim and one she dreaded to scalp. The young girl reminded her of her Hannah, at that age, tall and slender with boundless energy. If she had been a little faster, the girl might have made it down to the canoes; her escape would have been inevitable, but her end, like the others, was in seconds, as was the removal of her scalp.

The evidence joined the others, and Hannah took the cloth and rolled it into a pouch, tying off the ends, preventing the scalps from falling out. She counted ten in total; they would prove to her community what had happened. It is common knowledge that such actions, by women, do not happen.

Hannah ran across to the edge of the island and looked down. Samuel had the rifle in hand, keeping an eye on the direction of the river. Mary was in the canoe, her head resting in her hands. Exhaustion was painful, and sleep was needed by them all.

Samuel noticed Hannah at the top of the rise and signaled for her to hurry. They had been there less than an hour, which was too long in his mind. He watched her as she slid down the sand on her backside with a parcel in her hands. She had carried it with great caution, and he wondered what was inside the cloth.

"Hannah, we must go," Samuel told her.

She did not disagree and swiftly climbed into the canoe, over the pile of supplies and Mary. In the bow now, she felt she had a better grasp of the paddling and piloting of the craft. Samuel untied the rope and tossed it into the canoe, and placed the rifle leaning against the thwart piece in the center. He shoved it off and jumped in with ease.

"Hannah, ye was so worried,' Mary spoke. "Tell me what troubled you. Why did ye return?"

Goodwife Duston did not say a word; she placed the makeshift sack next to the heap of supplies. Mary did notice the blood stain on the fabric; it appeared to be coming from inside. She paid it no mind; sleep was the only thing she thought of, and she feared it would not be forthcoming.

The canoe was back in the river's current in seconds. Samuel, in the back, used his paddle to guide it through the turbulent waters to the center of the river. Hannah knew Samuel knew what he was doing; she had done the same thing not one hour before. When the time was right, Samuel whistled to gain her attention. She grabbed the paddle and gripped it like a hatchet. It was now her second device for survival.

The water was high, it was now late March, and the snows were melting, and soon the rains would come. The river, in that direction, was a strange sight for Hannah; she had only known it from the direction where she was abducted.

The island was now behind them, and the competing currents of the two rivers had dissolved into one, making both their tasks with the paddles easier. On both sides of the river, there were wide open spaces of grassy fields that were no doubt flooded when the waters flowed higher. The hills that surrounded them were gentler, rounded as if softened from the great Gods Samuel had spoken about.

The entire view was pleasant to Hannah; she was also too delirious with exhaustion to appreciate it thoroughly. She was hungry; rage and vengeance had caused a hunger in her belly that was reminiscent of the time in the forest.

"Mary, have we not something to eat?" She asked.

Mary handed her a sack of Nokechick. It was one of the few things that they grabbed earlier in the day with the other supplies. Hannah was grateful and broke a piece off and put it in her mouth. Samuel was focused on paddling and hoped Hannah would do the same. He wanted to gain as much distance from the island as possible. He was also worried that they could be seen in either direction; if a war party spotted them, it would not take much to stop them.

"Mary, try to rest, you need to sleep," Hannah told her.

With that, Mary made herself comfortable and leaned against the various supplies they had gathered. She took one of the fur blankets and draped it across her body; the warmth it provided had caused her to overlook the wretched smell. She closed her eyes.

Hannah looked back in the direction of Samuel and watched his strokes of the paddle. She was a fast learner and knew that to keep the canoe straight, her actions needed to be opposite to his. After a few minutes, she raised her paddle and, with all the force she could muster, she plunged it into the river and began to paddle. Her strokes were deep and meaningful to the mission.

Samuel felt a sudden thrust forward of the canoe and was pleased that Hannah had started. The river could be their salvation, a watery byway back to where the women were abducted, Haverhill. It would be from there that he would make his way to Worcester to find his family. He had missed his mother dearly and hoped she was in good health.

Mary had fallen asleep; it had not taken much for her to succumb to slumber; it was badly needed on all their parts. Hannah took to paddling in the same way she had been forced to walk for hours, one foot in front of the other, one stroke after another. Her mind controlled the task, and emotions would not get the best of her.

The river was wide and free of strong currents; they had successfully kept the canoe upright and moving in a direction towards home. Neither Samuel nor Hannah was aware of where they were or how far they had floated. It was now out of their hands, and they both resigned themselves to fate.

For Hannah, her fate was in the voice in the forest; her dream was still as vivid as it had been when woken that bitterly cold morning. Her thoughts were to Tsien-neto, whomever he might be.

TWENTY

Samuel watched Hannah as her movements began to slow; her paddling was less intense. The rage that was visible on her face was slowly fading; he thought it was a sign that she had found some peace in her actions. The wooden blade was just scratching the surface of the water, making the slightest cut. The canoe continued its journey; the current had been doing most of the work, and he had only to steer it from where he sat at the stern.

It had not been a full day since the blood had been spilled on the island, rendering all but two of the savages dead. Samuel was still very leery of a war party that might approach them from further up the river. The Abenaki site that he knew to be the closest had not been that far north at the crotch. The young boy who had disappeared into the night could have found his way to them, alerting the others of their escape. The old squaw that Mary had attempted to kill was badly injured; she would have had a harder time in the wilderness.

Samuel was glad that the plan was working up to that moment; it had been many months since Bampico dragged him from one village to another, attempting to make him his son. He had bided his time and learned what he had to from his master; like the English women in the front of the canoe, survival was their motivation as well.

Goody Neff was sound asleep. It had been some time, and the current was soothing to her and rocked her like a baby. Sleep, she had thought earlier, would cure her of the images of her deeds; the blood that oozed out of the squaw's head was the last thing she saw before slumber overtook her.

Hannah was tired; her body ached from exhaustion, and her arms and hands were sore from the stress of the hatchet and then the knife. Her hands were ragged, the skin worn nearly off from the rough handle of the paddle. The task had taken its toll on her body and her mind; her focus had to be on making it back to Haverhill. The insecurity of what her fate would be was now the driving force. If what the sachem said was true, then all would be lost to her, her family, and her home. She looked back at the bloody, stained fabric pouch. The reward on the scalps she received would be their justification; it would come directly after revenge in her mind.

The Governor of Massachusetts Bay Colony had placed a bounty on the scalps of Abenaki or any other native savage who threatened their community. Since all the troubles with the previous wars, the status quo has continued during the current conflict. Hannah had not known the exact amount that she could receive; the court would decide based on the age and gender of the victim. Hannah thought whatever it was would help her pick up the pieces of the life she once knew.

The river had been a Godsend; the current fostered their escape with a steady push in the correct direction.

The sun was now overhead, and Hannah estimated that it had been nearly five hours since they had lost sight of the island.

"Goodwife Duston," Samuel spoke, trying not to wake Mary. "Why did we return to the island?" He asked.

Hannah had been waiting for that question; she thought she had prepared an answer that would ease both of her friends' minds. She was aware that her answer would not be an easy one. She rested the paddle next to her and turned to speak to him.

"Ye not familiar with what being a woman is like, Master Samuel." Hannah answered. "What I did was for proof that my freedom was worth more than the lives of my captors."

Samuel had a difficult time trying to understand her words; he, too, was a captive, stolen from his family in the middle of the night, forced to endure one hardship after another. Why did Goodwife Duston need to prove that?

"I took ye scalps; they are there," She pointed to the knotted cloth. "Good women are taught to be obedient and pious."

Hannah knew that the young English boy was not aware of the frustration of the women in his community. She wanted to tell him of her sister Elizabeth and the tragic tale of her life. She had been forced by the will of men stronger than her and paid the ultimate price. Elizabeth, for fear of being shunned again for something she had no control over, took her story all the way to the gallows. There was nothing in Hannah's mind that would ease the pain she felt for her younger sibling. Sometimes, truth can be a substitute for control; once you establish it, control is yours for the taking.

It was fine that he did not grasp the words that she was saying; it mattered not. The ten scalps would be the testament of her taking control of the situation and fetch much-needed coin to restart the life that had been shattered less than a month before.

They both took a pause from the conversation when they noticed Mary was starting to stir. She had heard their voices and slowly awoke. She was feeling as refreshed as expected. Her body ached as well, sleeping cramped in the canoe, covered with a bear blanket, and the foul smell of blood on her clothing only made it more unpleasant.

Mary sat up and pushed away the bear fur. She looked at her hands; they were still stained in blood. Her fingers were sore from the grip of the hatchet, and her apron looked as if she had butchered a deer. Tears began to appear in the old woman's eyes, and remorse filled her senses.

Hannah was watching her friend slowly dissolve into despair, which had been something she could not allow herself to feel. She looked about the pile of supplies and saw the copper pot that had been so useful during their ordeal.

"Mary, pass me that pot," she instructed her.

Hannah took the vessel and held the handle tight as she lowered it into the river, filling nearly full. The water was indeed freezing, she thought, and the weight when it was full surprised her. Using both hands, she placed the pitcher between herself and Mary. She lifted her apron and ripped another section off her makeshift pantaloons.

The fabric only had a small amount of blood splatter on it.

"Here, Goody Neff, wash thee self," she told her.

Mary did not try to conceal the tears on her face; she was ashamed and wanted her and her God to see it. She took the cloth, soaked it in the water, and started with her face. It had felt good; the dried blood came off, and with every soaking, the frigid water began to turn crimson. It was a visual reminder of what happened; one she did not want to see.

"Pay it no mind," Hannah told her. "I will refresh it."

The women took their time cleaning what they could from their faces, hands, and hair. The blood-stained clothing would have to wait; they were certain they would destroy them all. They would take great pleasure in tossing it all into the fire, casting the garments into hell. A befitting end, Mary thought.

"Hannah," Mary said. "We should pray."

Mary was still trying to cope with it all, and prayer for her was a much-needed diversion for her own forgiveness from her God. She quoted a verse from the Book of John. As Jesus had washed the feet of his disciples, it was an act of spiritual cleansing and forgiveness. Mary had hope that they, too, would find their own forgiveness within themselves.

Hannah felt better; the blood was removed, and her temperament as well had changed. Returning to the island was also a start for Mary, and a chance to move forward. The bounty on the scalps would help them both regain their lives. The court surely would forgive her and Mary; it would be the first step towards redemption.

Mary insisted that Hannah rest and started to move towards the front of the canoe carefully, as her friend took her spot in the middle. Hannah was pleased that it was still warm from where Mary had been nestled. It did not take long once she closed her eyes.

Samuel had watched the women during their washing and hoped he could do the same soon. He did not understand the need for prayer; he could not recall the last time he prayed, but out of respect, he bowed his head when Goody Neff spoke her words.

He had kept the vessel on course, avoiding any debris or rocks that might have been present. The river was getting wider, and the current slightly stronger, which did not go unnoticed by Mary. She was paddling as best she could, watching Samuel and trying to match his strokes. Hannah did not stir.

The rushed noise of the water as it pushed against the canoe flowed over the rocks that had started to appear along the edge. It was too loud for any real conversation. They paddled in silence, each of them buried in thought, hoping to reach their destination soon.

Samuel had only heard about the river from his master; he had never been on it since he was taken. The story of Passaconaway was a legend and one the Abenaki would repeat often, each time slightly exaggerated, he thought. Bampico told him of a great fishing place south of the island, which he had called *Amoskeag*. It had been where all his people would come to fish when the water was high, and the salmon would be plentiful. The great falls were well known throughout the settlements.

He paddled from the back; they were making great progress, but he feared the approaching falls. With no idea where *Amoskeag* was, he knew he had to be vigilant for them. He was confident that the river itself would reveal them in enough time for the three of them to react. There could be no missteps, for the canoe and themselves could not survive a disastrous encounter with the fury of the river.

The day was coming to an end, the sun was down, and twilight drifted over the horizon and descended on the river. Hannah had stirred and sat up. She was amazed that she had slept and felt alert. Mary was in the front, keeping a steady hand on the paddle, and Samuel looked as if he was in a trance, with an expression of exhaustion.

"Master Samuel, come here, rest," Hannah told him.

He was not in disagreement with her. He laid the paddle onto the strapping that he was kneeling on and crawled to the center. The canoe tipped slightly, which caused the water to slosh and spill over the gunwale. It had been just enough to soak Hannah's moccasins.

Samuel leaned against the supplies and took a position under the blanket. He needed to rest. He wanted to tell Hannah about the falls, but he did not want to worry her. He had convinced himself that they were nowhere near them. He would sleep only a brief spell; the slightest odd movement of the vessel and he would wake, he told himself.

Hannah was happy to see the moon rise over the distant horizon; it was nearly full as the light shone onto the water. She could see what lay ahead as she paddled. Mary was in the bow and was watching intently. They watched the shoreline for any sign of life, a smoldering fire, a canoe tied or a fishing weir strung up in their path.

It was prudent for them to remain alert to any distractions that would disrupt the journey

The two women did not speak; the river had become eerily quiet. The current slowed, and the water appeared to be shallower. Hannah noticed the number of rocks that had started to appear on each side of the riverbank; they appeared in the moonlight like dead bodies floating, clustered together, creating a barrier for the water to flow through.

On the western side of the river, there was a sharp bend to the left as the river flowed. It was an unnatural turn; one she had figured would turn to the east. The cluster rocks were getting closer as they floated in the near darkness around the curve, narrowly colliding with them. She had signaled Mary to stop paddling while she used her paddle as a rudder and guided the canoe.

Mary had thought she should wake Samuel but waited for Hannah to decide that. Hannah was in control of the situation at that point, just as she had been the past few days. Her paddle made an excellent steering device, and the rocks slowly passed by her side. They floated around the bend of the river; Hannah kept the canoe as close to the center as possible. Running aground in the shallows could be as bad for them as slamming into a rock.

They both took a deep breath and began to paddle again. The river opened back up; it was wider once again, and the current regained its speed. There were dead pine trees on both sides of them, like ghostly figures emerging from the water on the shoreline. It was a line of silhouetted trunks that the moonlight unveiled, void of any signs of life. It was as if the entire river shifted over time and slowly drowned the trees. They had reminded Mary how she and the other captives must have looked as they marched in the wilderness.

They had lost all sense of time; if it had not been for the clear sky, the movement of the moon would have gone unnoticed. The nights were still long in March, but thankfully not as long as the dead of winter. Longer days meant it would be time to plant the fields, in anticipation of a bountiful harvest. With every stroke she made, Hannah was mulling over what was to come.

It had been hours, and both women had done their duty and not fallen asleep or scuttled the canoe. Hannah had eaten the last of the Nokechick that was in the pocket of Thomas's coat and was beginning to feel the pain of hunger once again. Mary looked to the east, over the horizon, for the light of another day was beginning to show. The river, without showing its course, was back flowing south at a more rapid rate.

Hannah had felt the strength of the water; the canoe jostled just a bit more. The current had started to become angry, and it did not like the canoe on its back. The light of day did not show anything unusual ahead in their path, but below the surface, it might have been showing something different. The canoe tipped to the right, Hannah doing her best to lean to keep it upright. The water breached the gunwale and soaked poor Samuel whilst he slept. The frigid water was like a frozen slap in his face, awakening him in the same violent manner.

"The falls," he screamed. "We must be coming close to the falls."

TWENTY-ONE

Samuel nearly stood up in the canoe when the sense of panic engulfed his body. He used both his hands on each side of the gunwale to support himself and steady the canoe. The sound of the rushing water was growing louder and louder as they floated downstream.

"Samuel, what are we to do?" Hannah screamed.

"Steer us to the shore," He yelled back. "Goody Mary."

He pointed to the east side of the river for Hannah to direct the canoe. Mary turned when she heard her name. Samuel motioned for her to hand him the paddle. He grabbed it and plunged it into the water. He was in the middle of the long canoe, and it did not help Hannah's efforts from the stern.

"Switch with me," Samuel yelled to Mary.

The canoe rocked in both directions as they struggled past each other, changing positions. He looked back at Hannah to be sure the paddle was in the correct spot to change their course. He had had no idea how far the actual falls were, but judging from the sound, it would be a matter of minutes before they went over, swamping the canoe and bringing sudden death, he was sure of it.

The rocks were coming into view as Hannah held the paddle steadfast in the water. Samuel was paddling with such vigor that it was actually working; he saw the rocks to his right, and directly ahead was an area where he thought he could breach the vessel.

Mary was frightened; her inability to swim and the fear of drowning had her in a state. She was kneeling in the center and holding on to both sides of the canoe as firmly as possible. Her hands hurt, the strain and the icy water numbing them; she was not sure how long her grip would last.

Hannah began to paddle, never letting up; the canoe had been steered sideways across the river. The current had become rapids, and more rocks were visible in the early morning light. The current splashed up on the side of the canoe; they had started to take on water. If the canoe filled too much, it would surely overturn, sending them and the contents downstream.

"Goodwife Hannah," Samuel screamed. "Steer for that rock."

That had confused her, but she was aware Master Samuel had far more experience than she. She stopped paddling and dragged the paddle; the front of the canoe turned slightly, and it was now deadheaded for the rock. Samuel continued with his strokes; they had gained speed as they crossed the water. The rock was less than ten feet away, slowly closing to the shoreline. Samuel had taken into mind the speed of the current and the position of the canoe; if he had been correct, the canoe would pass the rock and slice into the shore where he could jump out and secure it to one of the many trees that were down along the rocky edge.

"Now, paddle as fast as you can," he screamed.

The canoe narrowly missed the rocky outcropping and hit the edge of the land with an abrupt halt, sending Mary into the front of the canoe. Samuel had the tether in hand; he leaped into the water and climbed up onto the shore. He had to secure it fast, or the current would cause the stern to swing around and over the falls with both women in it. Hannah tried to use her paddle to secure it to the ground under the canoe, but the water was too deep. They were both at the mercy of Samuel and his talents.

Samuel did not think the water was that deep so close to the shore. He was surprised that it was almost over his head, the water so cold he thought for sure it was the dead of winter. He struggled all but a second and then resurfaced. He reached for a branch that was attached to a fallen tree and grabbed hold, never dropping the rope in his other hand. He pulled himself up and tugged on the rope. It took all his strength to keep it from flowing further downstream, but he could not pull it closer. The weight of the women and the supplies was more than he could handle.

Mary knew that she had to get out of the canoe, or surely, they would perish in a watery grave. The rope the boy had would be her savior or her noose. Her clothes at that point were soaking wet; the weight of them made any movement more strenuous. Mary knew she had no time to remove them. She grabbed onto the rope as she crawled over the bow, holding it with both hands. She was now in the water, and her feet were frantically trying to make a connection with solid ground.

Samuel saw what Mary had done and, in an instant, lashed the rope securely around the trunk of the tree, preventing the canoe from moving. Samuel waded into the water and grabbed her, preventing her from slipping under the frigid water.

Hannah was in a panic. From the back of the canoe, she watched the scene unfold. Acting on her instincts, she threw the paddle into the center, where Mary had been, and began to crawl to the front. With each hand on either side of the gunwale, she used her weight to keep the canoe from tipping more; it had helped, but the water continued to spill over the sides, filling it.

Samuel had pulled Mary to the edge of the water, where the sand was, and she was able to crawl out and onto the small embankment. The river did not get the best of her, she thought, and collapsed, grateful it was dry land.

Hannah was over the bow and into the water; she held the rope as her feet easily found footing; her height was nearly a foot taller than Samuel and Goody Neff. Samuel returned to the water, and together they pulled on the rope. The nearly empty canoe glided across the short distance onto the shore, exactly where he wanted it to land.

Mary was panting, trying to catch her breath. There was a pain she felt in her chest, and she feared more malice would come to her that morning. Hannah waded across to where she was sitting and helped her to remove her wet clothes, down to her undershirt. The morning air had not warmed at all. Mary began to shiver. Hannah sat next to her and tried to warm her friend with her own body heat.

Samuel had pulled the canoe far enough off the water that he had no fear it would float away. The supplies in the center of the canoe were spared; the water had not penetrated the deer skin sacks. He grabbed the bear blanket that was only wet on the edge and helped Hannah clothe Goody Neff in it. Mary felt better, and her breathing had started to slow.

They were all exhausted, soaked, and feeling the cold as they had never felt before. Hannah was a strong woman and had managed to overcome the obstacles that were presented to her during her captivity, but she feared this challenge might have been her last.

"Master Samuel," Hannah said with deep breaths. "What ye think will become of us?"

For such a young man, he had proved himself worthy beyond measure; of the three of them, he had shown the most resolve. He had been living for nearly two years in the forest among the savages, a miracle that a boy of his age managed to survive.

"We must portage the canoe around the Amoskeag and continue." He was not going to give up.

He stood up and surveyed the land. He knew that there must be a way around: a trail that the Indians would use, for they could not breach the falls either. He went back to the canoe, recovered another animal hide blanket, and gave it to Hannah. The two women were feeling a bit helpless at that point and watched as the young Englishman went off into the woods.

The canoe rested on the shore, tied securely to the fallen tree. The back end was still in the water; it rocked with the rhythm of the undercurrent. Hannah was cold, but she knew sitting there shivering was not helping.

She removed Thomas's coat and draped it onto the rock, then did the same with Mary's outer garments. The sun would be at its best soon, and perhaps it would begin the drying process.

The canoe had taken enough water to make a nuisance, but not enough to prevent their mission. Hannah took the supplies out and placed them above where Mary was sitting. Returning to the canoe, she removed the paddles and the pouch with the scalps in it. The cloth was soaked along with the scalps. She put the paddles on the land and removed the scalps, the water had caused the blood to run again; it was a ghastly sight. One by one, she counted ten, they were all there. She then lined them up on another rock with the hopes the sun would dry them.

Neither of them feared a war party; it had been a day and a half, and the terror of reprisal from the Abenaki was dimming. That had given them comfort while they rested and regrouped. Samuel came from around the collection of rocks with good news. He had found a trail, one that had been used for many years, maybe as far back as the great sachem himself, Passaconaway.

"We need to empty the canoe and carry it," he explained. "We should not linger very long; our freedom is at hand."

Their clothes were wet, and their mood remained dampened. Samuel was right; the only answer was to keep moving. Samuel went to the supplies and pulled out some dried meat. It was enough to stave off their hunger, at least until they could join the river once again. He took it upon himself to gather the supplies and start for the trail; his youthful energy and determination were admired by the women. They watched as he walked the shoreline and disappeared into the forest, carrying the bundles. The boy knew exactly what to do.

Hannah had hoped their clothes and the scalps would have dried more; she would just have to make do. Without hesitation, Mary stood and dressed in her cold, damp clothes, as Hannah placed her trophies back into the fabric.

Both women worked together and managed to pull the birch bark canoe further up on land. It had amazed them how light the vessel was when it was empty. Hannah had thought how ingenious the savages were in constructing such a durable and useful thing. They had each grabbed an end and turned it over. The water flowed out onto the ground.

Samuel appeared a little out of breath, but he was not deterred by his own tiredness. They had reckoned that the canoe needed to be carried down around the falls following the trail. Hannah felt confident she could take the back end if Samuel led the way with the front. Mary would pick up the remaining supplies and blankets and would follow. It was another plan that came to fruition.

The trail around the falls had been used by many warriors and fishermen; it was well-worn and free of debris and undergrowth. It took a lot less effort carrying the canoe on dry land than it did fighting the rapids with fear of impending death close at hand.

They did not speak and slowly made their way down to the bottom of the falls, where the supplies had lain. Once they got to the bottom, they dropped the canoe and looked back up the river, taking in the full view of the Amoskeag. They could now see that the falls were wide and quite overpowering. They had never seen such an array of rocks, ledges, and long overflows and pools of turbulent waters all in one spot. It was at that moment that Hannah had second-guessed her own mortal abilities; it displayed the turbulent side of God's work. They would surely have perished if they had gone over the falls. It was a humbling sight for her.

"Goodwife Duston," Samuel interrupted her brief meditation. "We cannot stay; we have the light."

She turned and helped Mary load the supplies back into the canoe. She took the pouch of scalps and placed them inside one of the deerskin pouches; she did not want to lose sight of them. Samuel laid the paddles out at each end and placed the rifle next to him. He motioned for Hannah to get in the front and for Mary to get in the middle. He pushed the canoe out into the river before jumping in himself.

The numerous waterfalls had created a mist of freezing water that they pushed their way through, paddling with determination. The spray stung their faces, causing pain similar to that when one has worked in the fields and has caught the full day's sun.

Once they were back on course, in the center of the river and in full sun, they relaxed. The current had slowed to a pace that was not so frenetic, as it had been above the falls.

Samuel should have been frozen, but his conditioning over months of being exposed to the elements had hardened him. He was paddling slowly, letting the current guide them, while continuing to keep an eye out for adversaries.

They glided past a deserted campsite, which was strangely like the one they had camped in on the island. The Abenaki were nomadic since the English moved north, forcing them deeper into the wilderness. They would return to fish or hunt, but with their numbers diminished, it was safer for them to be making their permanent villages further north.

Mary was bitter; she was shivering and doing her best not to be a nuisance to the others. Hannah was cold, wet, and annoyed. She dropped the paddle in the water with what vigor she had left.

"We need to stop," Hannah told Samuel. "It will be nightfall in a few hours, and the cold will surrender us."

Samuel agreed and told her that in one hour, they would have put a greater distance between them and the falls and be closer to the end. Hannah nodded and hoped Mary understood. The river was once again wide and slowly moving. Their paddling was creating the body heat they needed to ward off the cold.

The hour had passed, and the sun was moving in the opposite direction in the sky. They floated around one bend to the east and another back to the west; the direction of the mighty Merrimac was not so straightforward any longer. It was uncharted territory for them all.

Up ahead was a small body of water, to her right. Hannah could see it, and it was concealed by the overhanging limbs of the hemlocks that had grown near the edge. It appeared to be a small inlet, maybe a brook or small tributary from a larger source.

"There," Hannah said to gain their attention, as she pointed to the brook.

Samuel agreed and nodded his head. He was exhausted. It crossed his mind that the undergrowth would conceal a fire, if they could even start one. His flint and stone were somewhere in the sack with the other supplies.

They got closer to the spot, and Samuel steered the vessel into the small waterway. It was, in fact, very secluded and camouflaged from the river. They paddled slowly; all eyes were on the shoreline when it was in view, looking for a spot where they could warm themselves. The trees were thick on both sides, preventing them from seeing what was further upstream.

"Do you smell that?" Hannah asked.

She was the first to smell smoke; a campfire was close by. Even Mary had smelled the wood burning, the smoke drifting down the brook. Had they paddled right into the hands of the Indians, were they trapped in a battle, in some sort of purgatory? Mary had rejected that thought as fast as it came to mind. Catholics preached damnation and purgatory; their salvation would be achieved by faith.

"It's getting stronger," Samuel whispered. "We should head back to the river."

They agreed and were equally disappointed. Samuel turned the canoe slowly and as quietly as possible. No one spoke a word, for fear of exposure. The fire was no doubt a band of warriors fishing in those waters.

The canoe turned and was headed down the brook in the direction from whence they came. Mary was the first to see him and let out a gasp of fright, something she had done often. It was an uncontrollable reaction she had.

There, hidden among the hemlock, stood a white man, fishing weir in hand, and a musket leaned next to him against a tree. His wiry white hair and pale skin identified him as one of their own, an Englishman without a doubt.

The three of them were speechless, frozen in that moment by the cold and the sight in front of them.

TWENTY-TWO

It had been many days since Mary had felt this warm; the heat from the stone hearth was more than enough to cause the pain in her joints to ease. She sat there on a wooden bench wrapped in a dry blanket, where she could see all that was happening in the tiny cabin. She was still in awe of what had happened earlier: the three of them, weary and close to being frozen to death, in need of shelter, and stumbling onto such hospitality. Goody Neff was convinced that it was another sign of God's providence.

John Lovewell, a fit man, the same age as Goodwife Hannah, had opened his home to them. He had been the first to make a signal of welcome to them, once they spotted each other in the dense hemlocks. He waved the weary party closer and assisted them by securing the canoe next to his, in a concealed spot along the brook. Hannah had been apprehensive at first, but Goody Mary was desperate; she needed to be warmed and was the first out of the canoe. Samuel brought the gun, carried their sack of provisions, and followed all of them in the direction of his home.

The cabin was just a short distance away, just above the shoreline. The structure was made using very large pine trees, notched, with the logs sealed with river clay. He had two leaded glass windows on either side of the heavy front door, like his mooring; the cabin was also secluded from any view from the water. Perfectly perched on the side of a hill, it cut into the earth for protection on two sides. The roof was covered in sod, and ferns, and saplings had taken root, which only added to the camouflage. The structure was ready for all the elements of nature and hidden from the ones man had created.

The wood fire that had alerted them to Mr. Lovewell's presence was now in full blaze after loading a piece of dry oak onto the existing coals. The popping sound the wood made as it crackled was a comfort to them all that they were making progress on the return to their own homes.

"I came here to Dunstable in 1683 with my father and brother," Lovewell told them. "It was many a year ago."

John sat on a bench at the only table in the cabin, and he had a tankard of cider that he was enjoying. Hannah and Samuel were directly across from him, slowly eating a bowl of porridge, which was thick and creamy, a combination of corn and oatmeal. It was so hot that steam rose off the bowl in their hands, something they did not mind. Lovewell was telling how he came to be in such a place.

"There, that's all of it," Anna said. "It won't be too long before the underclothes are dry; the others will be shortly after."

John's wife, a sturdy woman, ladled a bowl of steamy gruel into the clay bowl and sat down next to her husband. Anna had met John the day of his arrival in her town, and it was not long after that that they were married. John and his father were Tanners back in Lynn; Dunstable was a fresh start for them, and he never looked back.

"We do not see many folks like ye," he said, "This still can be a dangerous place."

Over the years, John Lovewell had shown cordiality for anyone in need; he paid no mind if they were white or Indian. He had learned over the years not to pry; his story needed to be told first, for theirs would no doubt come out in time and in their own words.

"Wife, those trout smell good," he told Anna.

In a cast-iron pan that rested on a metal grate, the smell of bacon fat and fish was slowly sizzling; the aroma was pleasing to the hungry travelers. Anna got up and used a flat wooden spoon to turn the brown trout over, cooking them evenly.

"Goodwife Lovewell," Hannah spoke. "We are much indebted, for dry clothes and a full belly are a blessing to us; our journey had been quite a torment."

Anna acknowledged her with a smile. She was a practical woman and was equally as cautious as Hannah. Without passing judgment, she, like her husband, would wait for their story to come forth.

"'Tis a cold night, Providence brought you here," Anna told her.

The fish was served on wooden boards, worn and stained from many meals. The best use of their fingers was to remove the heads of the fish and separate the skin from the cooked pink flesh. Mary and Hannah waited for the fish to cool before attempting. Young Samuel did not hesitate; he used both his hands to hold the fish and bit into the skin, savoring the taste of the entire fish. The others watched as he attacked the meal.

John drank the cider and intently watched them eat. They had disrobed and were wrapped in blankets that Anna pulled from the chest next to their bed. The soiled clothes, which were soaked from the river, and had blood stains and mud, were hanging behind them in an attempt to dry. It would take a little time, but he was convinced the heat from the fire would render them wearable. He had been most curious with the young English boy's attire, deerskin leggings, and a tunic; had it been a disguise, he wondered?

"Master Lovewell," Mary had made the first move. "We abide in Haverhill, near the Merrimac. Our journey has been most treacherous; one we did not choose to take."

It was only a matter of moments before they told the family Lovewell of what happened. Goody Mary had been more than emotional when she recited the story of baby Martha's death. Tears rolled down her cheeks; the salt she tasted from them was just another reminder of that morning next to the apple tree.

"Goody Neff," Hannah interjected. "Ye cannot take the blame; it was that savage Mato, a baby killer."

Anna's face displayed total despair and such empathy for both women that the Abenaki can show such savageries to the innocent. She got up and climbed the short ladder to the sleeping loft. She needed a visual verification that her son, John, nearly six years old, was fine. She had heard him stir during Goodwife Duston's tale.

"The tribes had aligned themselves with Frontenac; it was a pact with The Devil himself," Lovewell commented.

"It did not stop there," Mary blurted.

Hannah decided to resume the story that Mary had started. After the abduction and the days of walking, with many of the others dead on the trail, her story began to be more intense. Hannah's eyes, unlike Mary's, did not fill with tears. They filled with anger, and some leftover rage that was deep-seated in her.

Telling the story aloud was a liberating feeling for Hannah, one she could retell without fear of judgment. It was for their survival that the events happened. She would show no remorse when asked and would use wrath to make her point.

Samuel listened and did not say a word. It was Hannah who spoke of this story, telling Master Lovewell that after months of Samuel's own captivity, they together agreed to help one another to liberation, one that came with a cost.

John listened; it truly was a horrifying story on so many levels. He was glad his wife had gone to check on young John; for her to hear, it would upset her sleep for months. The bloody clothing, the Indian garments, and the French rifle all came together. His opinion was one of justification for their acts. He was a God-fearing man, and he knew parts of The Bible. An eye for an eye was his utmost thought.

"Goodwife Hannah, I must ask," John said. "The scalps, how many in total?"

She was ready for the question, one she had to be familiar with to tell on their return. She explained how, after leaving the island, she had a sudden need to return.

The more gruesome details she had not even shared with Samuel or Mary.

"Tell me ye reason, surely your escape would be at risk?" His curiosity was stimulated.

"Master Lovewell, my intention is not to offend," she said.

Hannah went on to explain that no one would believe their story; it was too tragic a tale. In her community, women had a role, one that is often dismissed by the church elders and some husbands. They were, at best, the property of the men; their duties were clearly made known from such a young age by their mothers, who were taught by theirs. Having no say in their own destiny was nothing more than a form of control over them by men who used the veil of religious doctrine, which promoted such teachings.

Her acts against her captors were a statement of freedom, freedom from control by savages. The outcome in the end achieved a sense of vengeance and ultimately revenge, something she took no pride in. The savages had come into her world; she had not come into theirs.

Anna had climbed down the ladder with young John in her arms; she could not hear the words of Goodwife Duston. She had agreed with most of what she said and felt a kinship of sorts for her taking the matter into her own hands. Every day Anna lived in fear of Indian raids, or worse, unfriendly Frenchmen who would force themselves into their world.

"The scalps, can I see them?" Master Lovewell asked.

Hannah went to the cabin door and pulled out the damp fabric, the blood and the water from the river had mixed, dyeing it a rose color. She placed it on the table and slowly loosened the knots. The fabric lay open, and the heap of hair, skin, and bloody flesh was in full view for him to see. Having only imagined what the actual trophy looked like, his curiosity was piqued because he had only seen the other side, the result of a scalping.

"That's enough, John," Anna said. "Your son need not see such things."

"Tis a violent world here; he best learn of it when he can," her husband rebutted.

Hannah quickly closed the fabric, tying the ends together firmly. She would not take them out again until she presented them for reward to be paid. No one needed to see such a blatant display of defiance. She tossed the pouch back with the other supplies in the sack.

"You are welcome to spend the night," Lovewell told them. "But that is the safest time on the river."

He explained that the Indians he had made acquaintance with were peaceful; they would come when the salmon and shad ran upstream. It was on the river between the Amoskeag and the Pawtucket, where, at times, it was plentiful with fish. At either of the two sets of falls, he would see both Penacook and Abenaki fishing. But the times had changed, King William's war was still raging, and everyone had to be watchful.

"We should dress and leave after the sun goes down," Young Samuel finally spoke.

They had agreed, that the rest, the warmth, and their food had served them well; it was time to return to the Merrimac. The good fortune of meeting would not be forgotten; for in their prayers, they would hold them tight.

They waited for the darkest part of the night to return. The clothes that were hanging were almost dry; the little dampness that lingered was something they all had grown accustomed to. Goody Neff was the first to dress. Hannah held the blanket to conceal her naked body as she dressed. Mary had done the same for Hannah, but the truth was, she did not care.

Samuel busied himself dressing, with no notice of who could see him. In the summer months, he was often naked with the other warriors with whom he lived. He wondered if that time would ever vanish from his memory as his mother's image had. That thought made him sad.

The sun had been down for a couple of hours, and Mary had helped Anna with picking up and wiping the trenches clean. Hannah organized the supplies so Samuel and Master Lovewell could carry them down to the canoe.

The women said their goodbyes to Anna and young John; they were equally sad to say goodbye, as they were happy to be even closer to Haverhill. The moonlight helped them as they made their way back down the path. Samuel was already on the stern waiting for them.

"Goody Neff," John said. "May God's grace guide you along the Merrimac to the place you desire."

She thanked him once again, and Hannah said her pleasantries. With Mary securely in the center of the vessel, Hannah turned to Master Lovewell and whispered to him. She did not want Goody Neff to hear her question.

"Master Lovewell, hast thou any account of the savage Tsienneto?" She quietly asked.

"A passing question, to be sure. He is but a story," he whispered. "For what reason did ye make such a query?"

Hannah took a pause. She did not want to tell Master Lovewell of her strange encounter. Thinking that it had been a dream satisfied her. Haverhill was out there somewhere on the horizon; that would be her focus.

"No matter, it is not worth the talk," she replied. "We had best be on our way; the river doth await us."

Hannah climbed into the bow, never looking directly back at him. Master Lovewell untied the tether and gently pushed them back in the brook in the direction of the river.

No one said a word; the stillness of the night was only outmatched by the darkness. It had engulfed them; the dense forest that surrounded them prevented any light from above from shining through. Samuel used the paddle to turn the canoe about slowly. They did not want to bring any attention to them.

With John's help, they had estimated that they had about six hours before the sun would rise. The river between the Lovewell cabin and Pawtucket, where the next series of falls would be, would be quiet, John had told them. The waters should cause them no interruptions, but at the falls, they would need to portage. He assured them that it would not be as difficult as the Amoskeag Falls.

Samuel had insisted that the women try to sleep some; he had felt refreshed and was confident that he could handle the canoe alone on those waters. Neither of the women took offense and did their best to get comfortable. Their garments still felt warm from the fire; it was the little things that Goody Neff was most grateful for.

The night passed without incident. Samuel guided the canoe down the center of the river, letting the current take it slowly and steadily. The subtle sound the water made as it lapped the side of the canoe was as distinct to him as a signal from his master; both would alert him of something. He was also listening to the sound of the forest, an occasional cry of an owl or the flutter of waterfowl on its shore, and that was all he had heard.

The sun started to rise, and it was directly in front of them; it was a sign that the river had gracefully shifted again, and east was straight on. Mary was stirring in the center. She carefully stretched her cramped body and sat up. She was happy that she had slept through the remainder of the night.

"Samuel," she said. "I will take over for ye."

He did not need to be asked more than once. Mary moved to the back, and Samuel balanced the craft. He passed her without issue and took her spot under the bear blanket. Mary was feeling refreshed and picked up the paddle. The waterway was very conducive to her ability to keep it straight. She had almost forgotten that she could not swim but was quickly reminded when a large snapping turtle created a small wake next to her paddle. The creature, despite the large shell, seemed to do just fine in the river.

Before they left the Lovewell cabin, John had given them the ways of the river. Along with the characteristics of the current, he mentioned that Pawtucket could be reached in a full day if they were steady with their progress. After that, Haverhill could be reached within a half day. He stressed watching for landmarks along the river.

The ruins of the Manning Garrison, he told them, would be on a small island he called Wicasuuck. It had been an early settlement of a fellow who was called Jonathon Tying. The garrison was abandoned after numerous raids over the years and stood as a landmark. The falls at Pawtucket would be a short distance down the river. The trail for portage would be on the south side; it had been clearly marked for many years.

Mary had listened carefully to his advice; the smallest of details had not gone unnoticed by her. She did not want to be a burden to Hannah; her explanation of the event had triggered something in her, and it had boosted her self-confidence, something she felt was required of her.

Samuel had fallen asleep, and Hannah had not stirred. Dawn had broken, and to her amazement, Mary was in control, something she thought would never cross her mind.

TWENTY-THREE

Hannah felt the sun on her face; it was warm, and even with her eyes closed, she could tell it was very bright. She tried to keep her eyes shielded by pulling the deerskin hide over her face; one more moment of sleep was all she desired. She had opened her eyes and saw Samuel curled under the fur where Mary had been a few hours earlier. Confused, she wondered who was guiding the craft. She quickly sat up. Goody Mary was kneeling in the front and was gently guiding the paddle into the river; the canoe was on a slow and steady course. Hannah was relieved and very pleased.

"So ye decided to wake," Mary said. "Tis the day has started, and I fear we are very close to the Pawtucket."

Hannah was fully awake and wondered how the night had passed without her waking. She had had a good rest, one that she needed badly. It soon became obvious that Mary and Samuel had switched positions during her slumber. Mary was at the stern with a renewed burst of confidence.

"Morning, Goody Neff," Hannah said. "How ye know we be close to the falls?"

Mary explained to her that about an hour earlier, "when the sun was there," as she pointed with her left hand to the location they had passed above Hannah's head, "it was at that time we floated by an island with an abandoned house on it."

Goodwife Duston looked up and agreed that the sun was higher in the sky, and shook her head with approval. If that had been Wicasuuck Island, then they were close to the falls. She was confident that they would not make the same mistake as they had the day before; staying alert would be the easiest way to stay safe and dry.

"Shall we wake Master Samuel?" Hannah asked.

"No, maybe after one more hour," Mary replied. "The lad was exhausted; we will need his strength to carry the canoe around the falls."

Hannah agreed with her friend and wondered where she had found her new foresight. Her entire manner had changed; she was sitting up straight with a keen eye on the river. Mary was displaying control over their day, which delighted Hannah.

Hannah's stomach had made a noise; she was feeling a bit hungry, but the sack of supplies was acting as a pillow for the young lad. Hannah would not wake Samuel until they were closer to the falls. Her hunger pains would have to wait, she thought. She picked up the paddle and matched Mary's stroke on the opposite side of the canoe. The vessel glided through the placid water with ease.

Everything about the morning seemed more blissful to both of them. It was like they had awakened from the nightmare that held them in a dark land for so long. The ordeal had to be coming to an end; it was only a matter of time before their future would be determined.

The women silently paddled, both in deep thoughts, and not a word was spoken. They had many questions in their minds. What would they find on their arrival, what of their families, were they too captured, or did they meet the same fate as baby, Martha? They both had witnessed such horrific acts of violence, and their last memory of Haverhill was watching the black smoke rise over the horizon. Whose home would be left standing, would there be anything left, or would all be destroyed?

It had been clear to them that they knew each had taken matters into their own hands, and with that, their freedom was achieved, but at what cost? The events that transpired over the last fortnight were what nightmares were made of; both were convinced it was the work of The Devil himself. The Reverend Cotton Mather's sermon months before only reinforced their beliefs. The forest was the domain of Satan, and the savages that roamed it were doing the work of The Devil.

"Goody Mary, ye be fine?" Hannah asked.

Mary turned and just nodded in her direction, never speaking. Their bond had grown even closer; a nod, a glance, or the slightest of facial expressions was all that was needed for them to communicate. Hannah returned the nod and pushed those thoughts out of her mind; they would know the answers soon enough. She put her back into her strokes and concentrated on the river's current. Pawtucket and the falls would be nearing soon.

That morning had been a pleasant float on the Merrimac; between the falls, the water calm and the current very forgiving. Master Lovewell's description had been most accurate. Knowing what was to be expected was a liberation of sorts, but they were still wary, and surprises would not be welcomed. Mary remained silent and kept steady her strokes; the blisters on her hands were not painful enough to prevent her from her duty.

Hannah watched the shoreline with a keen eye; there would always be a threat of Indians. She had a false notion that the ordeal was completely over. The savages could have arrived at their fishing area up ahead at any time. That was something they continued to remain observant of. Master Lovewell told them the waters were too high at present for their reappearance; she prayed that he was correct.

The entire water was in front of her to admire, and the sun felt warmer and brighter; it had to be April, Hannah figured. They had been away for so many days; the bitterness of winter was now passed. She watched the shoreline as they drifted by; it proved to be a settling meditation for her. The view was something she had not seen, having never been on a boat in the middle of the river.

Along the banks, the trees had grown to the water's edge; they were a mixture of hemlock, oak, and saplings that she did not recognize. The cat-o'-nine tails grew thickly where the trees were not. It was a sanctuary for the waterfowl. She watched a Great egret that had just plunged its head into the water, resurfacing with a fish in its mouth. Hannah wondered if it was an alewife, or as her husband called it, a shad.

A hawk swooped down, looking for something to eat. It had been a gentle motion, free of strain or effort; envy came to her mind. Hannah often felt she wanted to fly away herself. The burden she often felt being an Emerson, the family name that, most days, she regretted. The family name, after all the past years, was still a subject of gossip. The witchery accusations and the execution of her sister still lingered in the townspeople's minds. What now would she have to face: her family perished, her home destroyed, and she with a sack of bloody scalps; it surely would be an uphill battle for her.

"Goody Neff," Samuel stirred. "Ye must be hungry?"

He sat up and opened the sack that had served as his pillow. The Nokechick was running out; he hoped it would be enough to see them to their destination. Hannah had given some of it, the night before, to Master Lovewell as they were leaving his home. His hospitality had saved their lives, and she wanted to share what little they had to express her gratitude.

"Master Samuel, how did thee sleep?" Mary asked. "We are near the Pawtucket, I sense."

Mary took the pounded cornmeal cake from him; he was right, she was starving. He turned and leaned across the canoe and gave Hannah a couple of the dried cakes. The three quietly sat there to enjoy the food as the river's current did its work, guiding the canoe downstream.

Hannah and Mary explained to Samuel, who was ready to do his part, about where they were in relation to the falls. Samuel agreed, having only heard about Pawtucket from his master. The lengthy falls and rapids would be approaching soon. Unlike the Amoskeag, the Pawtucket was a series of rapids, not one giant waterfall. The current was strong and dangerous; surely the bark canoe would not stand the river's fury, so portage was necessary.

Samuel's Master, Bampico, had told the young English boy many things about his life and his ancestors. Bampico's people had once been a part of the Penacook; the tribe would come every spring to fish at those falls. The river was an abundant source of food for his people. Each spring, the shores of the river were an encampment, and fishing during the springtime was plentiful. The Merrimac was a vital resource for all who lived near its shores.

Bampico told the young English lad that years previous to the King Philip's War, the Reverend John Eliot established a praying town called Wamesit. The small village was not far from Pawtucket, just downstream a bit. Eliot had mastered the Algonquin language just as Samuel had. The Puritan Reverend was determined to convert the native people to Christianity; his efforts were somewhat successful. He was from England and had been raised by the Reverend John Knox, who was an ardent Puritan, maybe the worst kind. Eliot preached in their language; many of the Penacook did embrace the teaching that the King James version of The Bible offered.

Bampico had explained that during the war, the English had grown distrustful of all Indians and raided the village of Wamesit and the other praying towns. The colonists set the settlements on fire and tried to capture his people; fortunately, many retreated into the forest and headed north to the summer home of Passaconaway on the Merrimac. More English arrived, the tensions grew worse, which is why his master headed further north from the crotch of the rivers to Canada; the French were more trusting of his people.

Young Samuel was curious about his master's life and the ways of his kind. The stories were intriguing to him, and there were many. The praying town was destroyed, and the captive Indians were held prisoners on Deer Island in the harbor, near Boston. Men, women, and their children were all jailed in deplorable conditions. Those who lived were sold into slavery in the South; only a few who were freed returned to the river, to a burnt-out village. It was a tragic tale; Samuel still could not sort out the reasoning for all the conflict between the French and the English.

"Master Samuel," Hannah said. "What are your thoughts? You are many worlds away."

"Do not worry, our actions were part of God's plan," Mary interjected, figuring he was lamenting the incident. "I am sure of ye."

"My thoughts are filled with stories, and memories of the past are all," he answered them.

He could not sort out decades of trouble; Bampico's word would haunt him. Samuel knew he had to focus on the task that lay ahead. He motioned to Goody Neff to switch places with him. His rest had invigorated him. Paddling would clear his mind. They had finished their brief pause, and he picked up the paddle and started. Hannah watched and mimicked his stride, and the canoe lurched forward.

The sun was nearing the highest point in the sky, it was almost midday, and there were still many hours of daylight left. The sun was warm, and the current favorable; the falls would be in sight soon. They paddled with great focus; home to Haverhill for the women was consuming their thoughts.

The noise from the rushing water over the falls was like a distinct drone in their ears. With every stroke, they got closer, and the falls got louder. The sound was not as furious as the Amoskeag had been; it sounded less intimidating to them, not as angry.

"There," Samuel shouted. "That looks like a clearing."

Hannah turned her paddle sideways, and the canoe veered to the left, in the direction of what appeared to be a spot to land the canoe. Samuel had a good sense about these things, and he was absolutely correct. It was a site to portage the craft.

Samuel jumped out and helped Mary over the gunwale. Hannah climbed to the front and stepped on shore. Each of them took a moment to scour the area for signs of Indians; there had been none. The season was not quite right for fishing. There was a well-worn path that looked to be the way around the falls.

It had only taken a few minutes for Samuel to empty the contents of the canoe into the deer hide sacks, placing the linen cloth stained in blood on top of their supplies. Mary was handed the sack, and she set off on the trail, which was on the north side of the river; it would lead down the embankment away from the rapids and numerous falls.

In comparison to the Amoskeag, this egress was much easier for Hannah and Samuel to carry the canoe. Mary led the charge, and in a short time, the point of reentry to the river revealed itself. Young Samuel waded into the river carrying the front of the canoe; Hannah followed. The supplies were handed off and placed back in the center. Hannah climbed over the edge into the front. Mary resumed the center, and Samuel shoved off the vessel into the current and jumped in with ease.

Looking back to the mighty falls, the noise was deafening; they were much bigger, wider, and longer than either of them had imagined. It would have been a deadly consequence had they not been aware. Once again, Master Lovewell had been a vital resource for this part of their journey.

The trio was once again wet; their leggings, undergarments, and shoes were soaked. Hannah's stolen moccasins that had been dried for nearly a day dripped with water. She did not mind; home was in sight in her mind. There would be time to dry out once they reached Haverhill.

The speed at which they paddled had a sense of determination. The falls were a landmark. Soon, the river would take a turn to the east, the current would increase before long, and Bradley Cove would come into view. The cove would be less than three miles from Haverhill, where they could land the canoe and walk the rest of the way. They could make it before nightfall if they were vigilant.

A mixture of emotions ran through each of their heads: the excitement of freedom, the revelation of what had happened to them, and the knowledge of the outcome for their families. All Hannah had known was what a drunken Bampico told her: that they were all dead. She feared that that was not the truth, and his words were just another act of The Devil.

Samuel continued to watch the shoreline for any signs of life, of the white man or of the Indian. He was aware that they were close. Off on a distant hill, what looked like an old farmhouse, stood neglected and empty. No doubt a remnant of an Indian raid a few years before.

The river turned to the east, and another waterway joined the Merrimac. The area appeared to be very similar to that of the one they left a week ago, where the Contoocook joined the Merrimac; the scene of such carnage and violence.

As they passed the island, it was an eerie feeling at best. That area was the remains of a burned-out praying village of Penacook Indians, twenty years before. What had started as a gesture of goodwill by the English turned so dismal for its inhabitants. The Bible itself had brought down fire and brimstone onto the inhabitants. The fort that was constructed by them was overgrown; the few visible timbers were blackened and scarred from fire. Maybe it was set ablaze to purify the community, while also destroying it.

Samuel gazed in the direction of the empty shell of the village. After nearly two years in captivity, he had some empathy for his captors. He wanted to tell Hannah and Mary the story of the praying villages, the interment on Deer Isle, and the sale of them as slaves, but he did not. Their ordeal for the past few weeks was equally devastating to them.

High above, the sound of seagulls drifted down the river. It was a familiar sound and one that had reassured them that the ocean was near, as well as the end of their journey. The air smelled fresh; a lingering scent the river created was distinct to the area. Bradley Cove was around the bend. Daniel Bradley and his family had settled the area years before. Hannah had been casually associated with his wife during the lengthy sermons; she knew them to be a fine Christian family.

"There, I can see the barn," Hannah told the others. "We made it."

They began to paddle to the sandy spot on the shoreline, where there was a wooden skiff beached as well. It had no doubt belonged to the Bradley family; they had fished the river daily when the weather permitted. Hannah wondered why there was no sign of the family; clearly, they would have seen their approach to the cove.

Samuel was the first out of the canoe, pulling as far on land as he could. Mary scrambled once again over the supplies and onto the sandy beach with the help of Samuel. Hannah could not wait; she jumped into the river, wading hurriedly to the others. The three stood on dry land and took a collective moment to reflect.

"I think we should pray," Mary suggested.

"Ye always knew the right thing to do, Goody Neff," Hannah agreed.

The three of them stood in silence, their heads bowed, with their hands clasped. Mary, the most devout of them, had known the scriptures cover to cover; she chose a verse from the Book of Psalms. Quietly, she recited the words she had read many times during the dark days of the problems with witchery.

"I called to the Lord, who is worthy of praise, and asked Him to deliver me from my enemies. O my God, protect me from those who rise against me. Deliver me from evildoers and save me from bloodthirsty men."

Her prayer rang true to the ordeal they suffered through. It was the right time to show gratitude; they had survived. Hannah thought perhaps God did have a hand in her plan, but it had been her rage, her seeking retribution for the death of baby Martha.

"Amen," they all said in unison.

Samuel went to the canoe to gather their things; they knew Haverhill and the Duston home were only three miles away. He would carry the sack; it was his duty to see the conclusion of this journey with the two women responsible for his freedom.

Hannah and Mary ran up to where the Bradley homestead was. They had hoped perhaps their horse and cart could take them the rest of the way. There had been a distinct smell of burnt timbers in the air as they approached the footpath up the embankment. The tall trees that had surrounded the area prevented them from seeing more than a part of the roof of the barn that was visible from the river. The rest of the homestead was out of view.

"Ye smell that?" Mary asked Hannah.

"Yes, Goody Neff, it's the smell of death," she reluctantly answered. "I fear the worst."

They reached the top of the knoll; the Bradley home had been burned to the ground. The smell was that of the remains of their log house; nothing was left but a cellar hole and timbers toppled into it, a blackened heap that once held life.

"Oh, dear God!" Mary gasped. "This was the work of the savages."

Hannah was in shock. Was this what was to be when she made it to her own home? There was nothing left of the homestead, once a large house. "What had happened to the family Bradley," she thought to herself.

"The barn, perhaps they sought shelter in the barn," Hannah said, rushing in that direction.

Samuel had made it up the path and saw the devastation. He dropped the sack and scurried up towards the barn to catch up with the other two. The family garden, which during the summer months was bountiful with vegetables and herbs, lay like a wasteland from the previous season, untouched, not harrowed. That was not a good sign.

The barn door was open, and it was empty, void of life like the house and the garden. There was nothing left; tools and livestock all gone. The three looked to each other; disappointment and fear can look the same on the faces of the weary. They were all tired, malnourished, and fearful.

"We need to make haste," Samuel told them. "The day is long; soon the sun will leave us."

He walked back down, gathered the sack, and motioned for them to follow. The road ahead, he figured, would lead them to the village; it was in the correct direction, northwest. Mary wiped the tears from her eyes and turned to Hannah, who had a stoic expression, with a sense of anger. They said nothing.

The road led them up the hill from the river to a clearing, which marked the border of the Bradley land. Visible from the road, they saw four crudely constructed wooden crosses planted into the earth. They walked across the field to a mound of soil that was obviously a grave; the four crosses stood as a reminder of their own morality.

TWENTY-FOUR

The level of anticipation that Hannah was feeling was overwhelming to her. She could feel the blood rushing within her body, her heart was pumping faster, and a wave of warmth overcame her, causing her to be flushed. This feeling was similar to how she felt the very first morning, standing there in the snow by the apple tree; was it rage or sadness?

Her thoughts were not of the night on the island, but of the common grave they had just passed. The four wooden crosses had burnt an image in her memory that she could not shake. It had reminded her of the image she thought of, which was the crucifixion of Jesus on the Golgotha. Goodwife Duston was tired; the physical toll on her body had caught up with her, and her mind was causing her turmoil. She had stumbled on the rutted road as they made their way to Haverhill, or what was left of it.

The road was nothing more than a path from the Bradley homestead to Haverhill. It was rough, filled with stumps, rocks, and washes from the April rains. It had slowed their journey tremendously. The sun was falling behind the trees; soon, it would be twilight, and darkness would not be favorable for the remainder of their trek.

After nearly an hour, Hannah insisted on taking the sack of supplies from Samuel; they were getting close, and she knew the young man needed to have a rest. She was pleased that he had run back to the canoe to retrieve the Indian rifle, something she wanted to have to support her story. The hatchet that was in the bottom of the sack, the dried blood, and the long dark hair of her victims stuck to it.

"Thank you, Master Samuel," Hannah said, taking the sack and placing it on the ground.

The three paused for a moment and caught their breath. Mary was also feeling a level of fatigue she had not felt before; she looked down the long road and searched for any sign of civilization. Samuel took the rifle from Hannah, who had opened the sack and was searching for the piece of cloth she had woven, the same linen that was wrapped around the third item of evidence. The ten scalps had begun to smell; the odor was foul and reminded her of her master when he stood too close to her on the trail. The smell of savagery and death was about the same.

"I know ye are tired," Samuel said. "We can be delivered; I am sure of that."

They agreed and started once again, watching their footing; falling was not an option. The road, which was less than a few miles, seemed to them the hardest point of the past fortnight: exhausted, mentally drained, and hungry once again. The supply of food had run dry after the falls.

The road ahead took a sharp bend to the right and started to go downhill. The decline was favorable, and their speed increased. They came upon a junction, and the road was familiar to Hannah; she knew it to be the way to Andover. It was only a short distance to Little River and her home.

Up ahead, they could see a cart being pulled by a horse; there was one man at the reins. Each of them yelled as loud as they could; the driver looked back and pulled the reins to stop the horse. They ran as best they could to the empty cart. The driver was clearly startled by their appearance. If death stunk like rotting flesh, then surely it had smelled like them. Hollowed faces, dark eyes, stained clothing, and filthy.

"Good day," Hannah yelled. "Might we trouble you for passage?"

The driver picked up the musket that was resting next to him and aimed it at the young Englishman. Samuel was still dressed in his Indian garments, the leggings stained with blood, his long hair soiled; they had forgotten what a sight he was.

"No, good sir!" Mary screamed. "He is English; we have been held captive for weeks."

The Puritan farmer jumped down off the cart and gave the weary trio a hard look. He had been on alert for months, since the morning in March when the outskirts of Haverhill had been attacked. He was not going to take any chances. After a moment of studying them, he felt slightly more comfortable.

"Ye be Goody Neff?" He looked directly at Mary.

She nodded and was happy she was recognized and not forgotten. Mary introduced Hannah to the farmer, along with Samuel. He motioned for them to climb onto the cart. Each of them found enough energy to climb into the cart with ease.

The road was much improved, and the horse pulled the cart along effortlessly. The ride was a Godsend, albeit with the ruts and bumps. They relaxed, knowing that in no time the town would appear.

He introduced himself as Josiah Williams. He was living in Bradford and was on his way to Haverhill to pick up supplies for his farm. He had recognized Goody Neff from his dealings with her oldest son before he died in 1691. He knew her daughter, Mary, the second oldest of her children, and would bring Goody Mary to her before arriving at the Duston homestead.

They traveled in the back of the cart for close to an hour before reaching the Neff house. Samuel jumped off the cart and helped Goody Mary down. Mary had insisted that he come into the house. Her daughter was a God fearing and generous woman; she would do what she could for both of them. Hannah climbed down onto the ground and said her goodbyes and agreed that in a few days, they would all meet. She was not a demonstrative woman; Puritan women reserved that for their family. Mary was family to her, and young Samuel was the same age as one of her sons. The urge to embrace them both had overcome her, and the hug was received with good wishes.

Hannah climbed up to sit next to Master Williams, and they proceeded to her home. Her emotions were still getting the best of her, and the not-knowing continued to cause her much trepidation. They did not speak; she could not share her story, specifically with a stranger. His kind-heartedness and generosity would not be soured with the tale she had to tell.

"Master William, our farm is that way. Along Little River," she said, pointing to the left.

"I beg your pardon, but that was destroyed during the raid," he told her. "The Marsh Garrison will be more suitable for you on this night."

There was Hannah's thought, the beginning of the end of what life she had known for nearly forty years. Her home was reduced to a pile of burned timbers. After seeing the Bradford home, she was preparing herself for the worst.

"Let me go in and tell them in the garrison that you are here," Williams gently told her.

Hannah's arrival would be compared to a person rising from the dead; she was aware of that. It had been weeks without any knowledge of her whereabouts. She also had no idea what she would find inside the garrison.

It was now dusk; the sun was still in view at the top of Pecker Hill where the Garrison sat. Hannah's last memory of her husband was when he galloped up the hill in this direction, trying to save the children. Had he been fruitful? Master William was inside the house; she emptied the cart of the rifle and the sack. She waited for Master William's return.

The door flung open, and a burly man with a full beard appeared with a musket in hand. He stood there staring at what he believed to be a specter, an apparition that could not be believed. Hannah knew him to be her neighbor, Onesiphorus Marsh, the owner of the garrison.

"Master Marsh, it is I, your neighbor Hannah Duston," she told him. "Wife of Thomas."

"I know ye," he said. "We all feared you and the others to be dead."

"Master Duston, what ye make of him?" She asked, "and the children..."

She had not finished asking the question when she noticed him. Her husband, Thomas, was standing in the doorway. Hannah was so overwhelmed by the sight of him; she fell to her knees. Her exhaustion had caught up to her, and all the emotions drained whatever energy was left in her body; it suddenly was empty.

"Hannah," Thomas rushed to her side and knelt next to her. "Praise be to God; you have been delivered back to me."

Tears filled his eyes; it had blurred both his vision and his thoughts. The last time he saw her, she was half-dressed, and Indians were approaching; it had been a devastating morning.

"Thomas," she whispered. "What be of the children?"

Thomas was crying; the tears were rolling down his cheeks, and he could taste the salt on his lips. Hannah began to cry as he cradled her head in his lap. He was still in shock that she had returned; he was forever in debt to his faith.

"They are here; they are all fine." Sobbing, he tried to say the words.

Master Marsh had gone back inside to alert the Duston children of their Mother's arrival. All of them have been living on the second floor of the garrison while Thomas was building their new home out close by. The children were preparing the evening meal when the news came. They dropped what they were doing and raced downstairs to their mother.

Thomas helped Hannah to her feet; the emotional side of his stoic demeanor had gotten the best of him. He did not care, for his wife had been delivered back to him. It was God's will; he was convinced of it.

"Mother, Mother," the children all rushed out to greet her. They, too, were overcome with emotions, the youngest grabbing her and hugging her legs. It was all too much for them all, tears in everyone's eyes; the family reunited after weeks of uncertainty.

Her oldest was nearly nineteen, named for her mother; she was the most emotional. Her tears of joy were uncontrollable, as her younger sister Elizabeth had been. They stood next to Hannah and held her so tight that they feared that if they let go, she would disappear again. All of her children were present, all eight of them; it truly was a miracle.

"Elizabeth, take your sister inside and get a bath ready for your mother," Thomas told the two oldest children. "Nathaniel, help your brother Thomas to fetch enough water for the basin."

Thomas knew that his wife needed food, a bath, and sleep. Her body had been ravaged and needed care. He instructed the others to go back inside and tend to their supper. He would be in with their mother right away. Master Marsh took the sack and the Indian rifle into the garrison and thanked Master William for his help that day. The cart continued back to town, descending the hill.

Thomas put one of Hannah's arms around his shoulder and assisted her into the garrison and up the steep staircase. The girls had hung the cast-iron kettle over the fire in the hearth. Clean warm water would set her right.

The boys put the washing basin in the bedroom where their father slept. The garrison was a blessing for the Dustons; it was not their home, but it certainly felt like it now with Hannah there.

The supper was nearly ready; freshly made Johnny cake and rabbit stew would satisfy the hungry clan. The girls helped their mother out of the soiled, wet, and bloody clothes she had worn for many days. They respected their mother not to ask what had happened; they were just happy to have her back. She was a modest woman, even around her children; they had given her a blanket to wrap up in as they waited for the water to heat.

The bath water was tepid at best; it would warm the cold from her body and help wash away the memories of her ordeal. Hannah thought it was heavenly; she had been wet and cold for days. The girls helped her with her bath, the lye soap was used to scrub her face, and her hands that for so long had been stained with blood. It was a difficult endeavor, but the result was acceptable.

Clean clothes were laid out, but the night shift and the undergarments were not hers. She had figured all was lost in the attack, her belongings reduced to soot. The girls helped her to dress and climb into bed.

"Hannah, have something to eat," Thomas came into the room.

He was carrying a clay bowl with warm rabbit stew and a Johnny cake. He sat down on the edge of the bed next to her and helped her eat. He could not help but notice the condition of his wife. The warm water might have washed the blood and dirt away, but it did not remove the scars in her eyes. She had lost weight, her eyes sunken in her once robust face, and dark circles around them were uncharacteristic of her appearance. There still was blood under her fingernails, and the blisters on her hands did not go unnoticed.

Master Duston did not ask what had happened or how she made it back to him. He was just in debt to the Lord Almighty that his prayers had been answered. There would be time to get the full story, but he knew sleep was what she needed.

Thomas took the empty bowl, kissed her on the forehead, and blew out the candle. He took a moment to watch her in the darkness, and she drifted off to sleep in seconds. He closed the door; tomorrow would be a day of revelations.

TWENTY-FIVE

The morning sky over the Marsh Garrison was gray, almost opaque, with no hint of revealing the sun. Master Thomas was up before dawn, his chores nearly completed, and stood in the doorway of the fort and looked to the horizon for any break in the overcast. "Tis a dismal day," he thought. It was indubitable that rain would come. Thomas Tusser's very old poem could not have been a more accurate description of the morning; *Sweet April showers do bring May flowers.*

He was glad to have Hannah home; she brought such determination to the household. Her pure presence invigorated everyone she came in contact with, a force of resolve in every situation. She managed everything in the Duston homestead from teaching The Bible to reading poetry to the children. Thomas had missed her and had prayed for her return every day.

The previous day had been as cloudy to him as the present day started. His reaction to seeing his wife had overwhelmed him to the point of disbelief; he was uncertain how she had been delivered back to him. He knew it had to be God's providence. He would be forever in debt to his savior.

"Morning, Thomas," Master Marsh appeared behind him in the open doorway. "Tis a gray day, no planting the fields today."

"Ay. That may be. The seed be best laid by, lest it come to naught and rot in the wet earth," Thomas replied, agreeing with Onesiphorus.

Master Marsh left the Garrison and walked in the direction of the barn. His morning routine, after checking the perimeter of the property, was to care for the livestock. Along with the horses, there were hogs, sheep, and chickens in the attached coop. There was always something to do; everyone played their part.

Life continued in Haverhill despite the daily threat of more savage reprisals. King William's War was winding down, but not entirely over. The French were still aligned with the Indians until the disputes were settled across the ocean; the Massachusetts Bay Colony and its brethren had to remain on alert. The Militia remained active in and around the colony, and the Marsh Garrison always had men stationed there.

Thomas went back into the garrison. He wanted to wake Hannah, but knew her exhaustion had gotten the best of her and she needed to rest. The children had also been up since daybreak; they, as well, had duties to do. There was always a need for a fresh bucket of water or wood for the hearth; each of them, despite their age, contributed to their family.

Nathaniel was next to the fire, stacking an armful of cord wood. He was only eleven, but he could swing an axe like his mother. Hannah, in the early days before the children, would split her own wood for the fire when Thomas was working the fields. He loved the fact that his wife was no-nonsense about most things. She often would lecture him after he disapproved of her working so hard. *"If I don't do it, ye tell me who will."*

The pitcher of cider was on the sideboard; it was left from breakfast. Thomas sat down at the trestle table and motioned for Sarah to bring him the pitcher and a glass. Sarah was almost nine. She took pride in her service to him; her duty was to bring breakfast to the family.

"Father, how be mother this morning?" She asked while pouring the amber liquid.

Thomas had explained that she was still resting; he did not want to disturb her. She was tired and needed to rest to regain her strength. He sat there and was reminiscing about life before the raid in March. The cider was cold and fresh from the last season of apples from his prized orchard.

Hannah had a very difficult time birthing the baby, Martha. It was a troubling day for him; the loss of three other children before, losing another would be devastating to Hannah. Goody Neff was a knowledgeable midwife and extremely helpful during and after the birth. He was pleased that Master William had told him he had found Hannah, Neff, and a strange English boy dressed as a savage on the road to Andover. He just had to be patient to get the full account of events.

"Father! Father," a voice called from the top of the stairs. "Mother is gone."

Thomas jumped up from the table and ran up the stairs to where his older daughter stood at the open door to the bedroom in a panic. Young Hannah was very concerned that her mother was not in the room. She had gone in very quietly to empty the night pot next to her bed. That is when she discovered Hannah was gone, no sign of her mother.

"Are you sure?" Thomas asked. "Did you check the privy?

The Garrison outhouse was around back, far enough away that the smell during warmer months was not perceptible in the house. There was only one door in the Garrison, so Hannah had to have left very early, he thought. The other children came running up the stairs, each of them concerned that they had just got her back; they could not lose her again.

"Thomas, go to the privy, see if she is there," His father told him. "She may have been taken ill."

They looked around the room, and there was no sign of her moccasins or the borrowed cloak that was on the hook. Thomas was convinced she had left on her own free will, dressed for a cold morning. He had hoped that the burden of what had happened would not cause poor judgment, and it would not be so strange that her mind would play tricks on her.

They searched the rest of the upstairs of the garrison, no sign of her. Thomas rushed down the stairs and looked about the center room for any signs of her departure. The ceramic carafe of cider sat in the center of the wooden table. It triggered something inside of him, a revelation of sorts; he instantly knew where to find her.

"You all stay here. If she returns, fire one shot from the musket." Thomas told them.

He grabbed his favorite rifle and jacket and rushed out of the dwelling. He ran into the barn and found his horse enjoying some hay that Master Marsh had fed him earlier. In a matter of seconds, he was galloping down the hill in the direction of what was left of the Duston homestead. He passed it and kept going. He was determined to find Hannah; the route he was going was the same way he had last seen her that morning of the raid in March.

Riding past their house, the remains were that of a mere cellar hole. Burnt timbers and a stone fireplace left standing, everything lost when it was set ablaze. All they had now were donations from the neighbors, and even the clothes Hannah wore were there because the children could not wear them.

Thomas used the heel of his boots to speed the horse along; he galloped by the river's edge, the field all turned and ready for planting. He was headed for the apple orchard, that is where he would find Hannah. He loved that orchard; it was one of the first fields he tilled and tended. He had mastered the art of planting saplings, so young and delicate. He nourished them like children; the bounty of his apples now fed his own offspring. It was a full circle for him.

He slowed his stallion to a cantor; he did not want to frighten Hannah if she was, in fact, there. Ahead, just off the trail, he spotted her; she was kneeling on the ground next to an apple tree. He dismounted and walked quietly to her. The fresh grass softened his steps; he made no noise.

Hannah was next to a fresh mound of soil, which was the final resting place of Baby Martha. She was on her knees, and tears had stained her face. She did not mind the dampness of the cold ground; she was in meditation, far away in her mind, reliving the horrid event.

"Hannah, my dearest wife, I am here," Thomas whispered to her.

He knelt behind her and embraced her with both arms. Her body was cold and rigid, almost like a statue. He needed to make her understand that he would do anything for her; his devotion had been tested many times of late. He would keep hold of her as long as it took.

Her body started to shake, and she began to cry again, fresh tears streamed down her cheeks. He held her tighter, and his own eyes filled with the salty liquid; it had been the second time he displayed his own vulnerabilities.

The mother and father of a baby taken too young knelt next to the grave, trying to sort out the events. It was a harsh world they lived in and a harsher reality of the actions that needed to happen to prevent another incident.

"Thomas, the anger in me is greater than my love," she told him. "I have much to tell ye, I fear my soul was lost with Martha."

"Hannah," he whispered to her. "Dear wife, there is much to be discussed betwixt us, yet by God's grace, we shall endure this trial together."

He held her even tighter, and her body became less rigid, her head relaxed, as she rested it on his shoulder. They sat in silence for enough time to show respect to their baby. When the tears ran out, she felt her heart breaking, becoming less filled with pain. It was a glimmer of hope for her that her resolve was returning.

"Shall we go back?" She looked to Thomas.

"We shall walk, and use the solitude to reacquaint each other with the events that led to this day." He needed to know the entire story.

Hannah nodded. It was time to tell her husband everything. He needed to know what was in the deerskin sack; the contents would be her evidence for those in disbelief.

Thomas stood up and extended his hand to her. She took it and relished in the fact that he would see her through this time of disclosure; only after that could they look to the future.

They each took one last notice of baby Martha's grave, the fresh mound of soil marked only with a handmade wooden cross. Hannah knew surely there were many unmarked graves in the village, each with a tale as tragic as hers.

Thomas took her hand, and they walked slowly in the direction of the garrison. There would be plenty of time for her story to unfold. The rain had started; it was gentle, and neither took notice of it.

TWENTY-SIX

It had been almost a week since Hannah and the others returned. The reunions should have been a joyous time. The women were back in their homes, sharing the story of their ordeal and the escape that followed. It had been an unpleasant time for both of them; for Goody Neff to tell her children that she and Goodwife Duston had taken matters into their own hands was the hardest. As a healer and a midwife, Mary regretted that they killed the sleeping Indian children; it was the darkest part of the story she told. Those who heard her story felt that their actions were justifiable, as The Bible said, *"an eye for an eye."*

Haverhill as a community did not fare well; there had been countless homes burnt to the ground during the early morning attack. Most of the homes, like the Duston farmhouse, were located on the outskirts of town, the area considered to be the frontier. The Indians ransacked them, stealing what they could in a matter of minutes, before the torches were thrown against a wall. It was still unclear to the village why some were captured, and others killed.

Twenty-seven members of the community were slain, left for dead in the snow banks, or burned in their homes. Men, women, and children were not spared; the savage attack was unprovoked and had caught them off guard, virtually defenseless. A mistake that would not be repeated. The assault was a reminder of the hard life they had chosen and reinforced their own mortality. They took solace in the fact that those who lived could continue to carry on the work of the Lord in the world.

The news of their return traveled fast throughout the community; it reminded them of the time when the first charges of witchery were announced. The Puritans' nature and even their doctrine were rooted in forms of gossip; unlike the trouble in Salem Village, this story of Hannah had hard evidence. They embraced the story, wondering how much of it was the truth and how much of it was distorted. Goody Neff was known to be a God-fearing woman who attended sermons regularly. Goodwife Duston attended not as regularly; the fact that she was an Emerson had many wondering if her violent behavior was a family trait. Everyone knew of the trouble with her father and the demise of her sister, Elizabeth. The general feeling was that any shred of good news was a welcome relief, something they could be thankful for.

It had been a time for reflection for all parties; many of the sermons that Reverend Benjamin Rolfe preached included empathy for those who survived and for the less blessed. His congregation in Haverhill met on the Sabbath at the meeting house; the attendance since the raid had increased weekly. That pleased him; he welcomed the brethren and wanted to keep the momentum of his words to spread throughout the entire colony. The

Indian raid on March 15th was just over a month before when he spoke to his brethren to confirm the deliverance of Goodwife Duston and Goody Neff.

"Who be at the door?" Hannah asked.

"Tis a courier, from the meeting house," Thomas told her, holding a folded piece of paper.

He sat down at the table. He and Hannah were having some cider and a bit of cheese when the knock at the door came. The children were all out and about doing their chores under the watchful eye of two militia men who had been stationed at the garrison.

Hannah and Thomas were doing their best to resume their life; it was important to them both to put the past behind them and move forward. Living at the Marsh Garrison was only a temporary solution to being homeless. All the Dustons were contributing to the new house that Thomas was building less than a mile from the remains of the old one. He had hoped that by the end of the warm months, he could move his family into the new house, as the garrison was a constant reminder of that morning and their mortality.

"Ye know whom sent it?" Hannah asked.

Her husband broke the wax and unfolded the parchment. He sat silently reading the message before laying it on the table in front of Hannah. The news of Hannah had, in fact, reached Boston. The letter was from Reverend Rolfe, their local minister, who was requesting the Dustons to call on him the next day. It had been a request from Reverend Cotton Mather, of Boston, for Rolfe to first interview Hannah and to make a written statement.

"Tis good news?" Hannah said. "The good Reverend can hear my story; it will help with the bounty."

Thomas was still worried whenever she spoke about her ordeal; it was a justified consequence, and the evidence Hannah returned with was a curiosity for everyone. The Indian rifle, hatchet, and the dried scalps were tightly tucked away from prying eyes, especially the children. He knew that the bounty was not the only driving force for her actions; what the savages did to her, her family, and the community outweighed any monetary gain.

"Hannah, we shall go on the morrow to the parsonage of the Reverend, and there bring forth the evidence," he told her. "Tis a good sign from the master."

She picked up the last bit of cheese from the wooden trencher and washed it down with cider. Hannah was worried that the prominent Reverend Cotton Mather would request a written account of her story. She could never forget the sermon that he had preached the day of her sister's execution; it was not forthcoming to her sister or to her charges. Elizabeth went to the gallows believing that Mather had written his words to her confession and coerced her to sign it; Hannah knew that to be true. Her sister told her that the day she visited her in the Boston Gaol.

Hannah got up and went over to the hearth; the fire was only embers, and the heat it emitted was perfect for simmering her stew. She poured what remained of the cider into the cauldron and used a wooden spoon to stir it. It was cooking very slowly. Using the same spoon, she pushed on the trammel to swing the pot away from the heat. Burning the evening meal was something she would not do.

"Shall we go?" Thomas asked, standing there with her woolen cloak.

They were off to see the progress of the new home that Thomas was building. He had been very busy the past few weeks; his kiln was fired up daily, baking new bricks for the construction. He was a master at providing for his family. He had wasted no time in securing a spot for the house. It was not a mile from the old one; this fine home was two and a half stories, built of brick, and was located in a more secure location.

Hannah was pleased with the new house and was very anxious to be in it. The Marsh Garrison was perfectly fine, but it just wasn't her home. She took his hand and smiled. It was time to go back and begin her teaching again; the younger children were ready to learn more. Hannah believed education was the remedy for most things.

They strolled past the ruins of the old house. Hannah turned her head to prevent viewing it; she knew it to be a sad reminder of the past. Her concern now was the future. Thomas was always looking to her for any signs of melancholy, an affliction that was common after such events. She had shown no signs of remorse or repentance.

The next day, they left right after the morning meal for the center of Haverhill; the parsonage was on Water Street, near the river. The journey was almost five miles from the garrison. Thomas walked, and Hannah sat astride his horse. Before they started, he had placed the stained linen cloth that encased the scalps, along with the hatchet, into his haversack, and positioned it over his shoulder. The Indian rifle was slid into the leather scabbard that was attached to the saddle. When they left, Master Marsh assured them that the children would be looked after.

"No need to trouble your mind," he told them. "We are prepared for any trouble."

The road to the center of town was not as popular as the others. It was slow going for the first couple of miles; the outskirts of town were still sparsely populated. The center of Haverhill had not been affected by the raid. The homes and residents were still as they had been. The community had grown to over five hundred souls since it was founded by the Reverend John Ward in 1640.

The streets in the center of town were the best to navigate on, lined with maples and the mighty elms; they had stood the test of time and the harsh winters of New England. It had been a drastic comparison to the nearby wilderness where the savages and The Devil took up residence.

The meeting house had been built a few decades earlier and needed repair and enlargement. The weekly meetings on the Sabbath were even more popular since the raid; the room was always cramped and crowded on that day. The wooden structure was next to the burial ground for the town. The Reverend's dwelling was close by, on the same acreage.

Thomas helped Hannah to the ground, and he tied the stallion to the iron fence that surrounded the parsonage. The building was a two-story gambrel-shaped home, with a granite step walkway and six-over-six leaded windows; it had been one of the oldest homes in the town. They had not made it to the front walk when Reverend Rolfe appeared in the front door. He had been sitting patiently watching through the window in the parlor for signs of their arrival.

"Master Duston," Rolfe greeted him first with his hand extended. "Goodwife Duston, welcome."

The Reverend Benjamin Rolfe was fairly new to Haverhill after being appointed when the founder, John Ward, retired in 1693. He was always referred to as the new pastor, as Ward had spent fifty-three years preaching in the same meeting house. Rolfe was dressed all in black, with a stiff white collar and white linen cuffs showing. Hannah could tell that the fabric of his coat was fine wool, probably imported from England. He was dressed more formally than they had expected, which presented a more distinct meeting, one with purpose.

"Pray you enter and keep me company in the inner room," he gestured with his extended arm.

The parlor of the parsonage was modestly decorated and comfortable. It had an air of piety and reserve, perfect for a Puritan pastor. It had housed the most important individual in town, and it reflected this. First, for the founder and then his choice to succeed him, the house was simple, functional, and purposeful. The modest, well-made furniture was arranged for a meeting; the gate-legged table with its leaves open was the centerpiece of the room.

"Take your rest," Rolfe told them. "Make ye the most comfortable."

They sat down and waited for the pastor to begin. The contents on the table were some parchment, a pen, and a pot of ink, nothing else. Thomas knew that he would take down every word they told him; this would be the official record.

Rolfe began by asking the simplest of questions, about their health, the children, and what was lost as a result of the raid. He listened intently, never writing down any of their words; he did not want to miss a detail during the oral explanation. He only nodded and made slight moans. Hannah could not tell if he was approving or condemning her actions as she shared her story.

The raid had taken its toll, and he wanted to confirm the rumors and understand the state of mind that Hannah was in. He spoke only once during the interview, when he offered his sincere condolences for the death of baby Martha and agreed that no mother should witness such a deplorable death of her newborn.

He did notice the intensity twice during the discussion; first when she described the death of her baby, and again when she had taken matters into her own hands: the description of the hatchet landing on the head of the savage, and the amount of blood that was forthcoming. The portrayal of those events was, to the minister, spoken from a person of mixed sadness and revenge. In earlier times, perhaps, these actions could be taken as a form of witchery; he now knew better and would never again make that mistake.

"Thomas, will you show me what you have brought?" The pastor asked.

Thomas stood and took the haversack off his body. He took the items and placed them on the table. He gently unwrapped the linen to expose the ten scalps, which were dried and distorted from their original condition. Rolfe picked up the hatchet and examined it closely, slowly turning it side to side. The dried blood and the black hair of the savages still stuck to it. He was exceedingly curious, and when he looked at the removed flesh, he did not pick it up. He was satisfied at that point with his inspection.

"Master Duston, what of the musket?" He asked. "Would you bring it here?"

Thomas nodded and left the room; the flintlock musket was in the entry hall, leaning in the corner. The pastor wanted to get all his thoughts together before passing judgment. The long-barreled musket was indeed a trade gun, one from Canada. The French supplied them to the Abenaki for being allies and to use against the English settlers.

Hannah sat there trying to keep her composure; the Reverend had really not addressed her directly for most of the interview. A woman, once married, lost most of her rights. This coverture was a common law doctrine in the colony, which said that the husband would cover her legal identity. The husband was the supreme being, from the meeting house to the ballot box; a woman was a necessity for procreation and household chores.

"Ye have a compelling tale, one that needs to be told." Rolfe told them. "There are unfortunate changes to the law."

Thomas and Hannah looked to each other. What could go wrong now was on their faces. Would she be arrested, dragged to jail, or worse, the Boston Gaol? Was it because she was an Emerson that the community had never embraced her after her father's violent tendencies or her sister's execution? Was it not bad enough that her younger brother, Thomas Emerson, was killed along with his wife and children, the very same day of Martha's murder?

"Do tell, Reverend, we are prepared for your thoughts," Thomas told him.

It seemed that the General Court of Massachusetts had rescinded the law on bounty once again. The amount on the scalps of native Indians had gone from 50 pounds to 25 to 0. The last alteration to the decree was in December, just three months before the raid.

Hannah did not say a word; she sat there as stoic as possible, this can't be happening was all she thought as her blood rushed through her veins, a feeling she was all too familiar with. She could feel that her face had become flushed; anger was now being confused with disappointment. Thomas sensed her mood change and reached his right hand out to hold hers.

The pastor could see that they were deflated by the news. He was truly convinced that Hannah's actions, though violent and unprecedented for a woman, were justified. She and Goody Neff, along with the captive Samuel, took the most extreme measures to escape and be delivered back to their homes. The evidence that was presented was proof of the necessity of the savage's elimination.

"Pray, have patience with me whilst I frame a humble Petition unto the Great and General Court in Boston," Rolfe told them. "Tis concerning the payment of the bounty."

The mood for the Dustons turned quickly, a subtle sigh of relief escaped Hannah, and the grip on her hand had lessened. The Reverend took the pen and dipped it into the pot. He began to write; the noise it made as it scratched the surface of the paper reminded Hannah of a barn cat trying to get into the house. The entire writing process took over an hour; Rolfe, a learned man, had perfect penmanship, and the words seemed to flow from his hand. Occasionally he paused as he looked outside the window to gather his thoughts.

"Master Duston, this writing is a petition for the bounty payment," Rolfe told him. "Pray, read it, and it requireth thy signature."

Thomas leaned over his writing; it was addressed to the Right Honorable Lieutenant Governor and the General Assembly of the province. It took him some time to read, even though he was well-versed in the written language; he wanted to be sure it was correct, no inflections or introversions on his part.

He was satisfied with the document and looked to Hannah to assure her that it was correct. It was more an appeal to the court than a confession. The Reverend Rolfe had done a fine job straddling the fence; he cast no judgment in either direction. The Dustons had lost everything, and this could help ease their suffering. Thomas used the quill to sign it; as important as this was, Hannah's name was not even on it, only being referred to as his goodwife.

Rolfe carefully began to sprinkle pounce onto the freshly written document; this would dry the ink faster and prevent any smudging of his written words. Hannah watched with intensity, knowing that the fate of any reward rested on that parchment.

Thomas stood and gathered the evidence while the ink dried on the paper. Hannah stood up and helped place the items back in the haversack. Hannah picked up the rifle, which she had carried long enough and was well acquainted with. The Petition was rolled and tied with a black ribbon. The Reverend handed it to Thomas and patted his shoulder, a subtle affirmation of success. The next step he knew was to present it to the Boston Assembly.

The three stood in the entry hall of the parsonage, and at the request of the Reverend, a short prayer was said before their goodbyes and well wishes. When the prayer ended, Hannah raised her head, her eyes met the pastor's, and she only slightly smiled; she would only show her gratefulness for his help. Happiness for her was only a memory. Thomas shook his hand, and they walked down the walkway to the horse.

The Reverend Rolfe stood for a moment before going inside. He watched as intently as he listened to them. That meeting had been a fruitful one; not only had he gotten enough details for further sermons, but he was now able to write a full report to share with Cotton Mather, the one man he had admired so much.

TWENTY-SEVEN

The time passed slowly for Hannah since her return from captivity; she was determined to put it all behind her. "The past is the past," she thought. Living at the Marsh Garrison had grown weary in her mind. She had longed for her own home and more privacy. She had been reacquainting herself with Thomas, which had also taken some time. The intimacies they shared were less frequent and often in a rushed manner, something she took no pleasure in, though she was happy for Thomas that he was satisfied. After all, she knew it was her duty. Her happiness would be restored when she was in her own home surrounded by her family.

April passed without incident; the rains had stopped in May, and summer had approached quickly. Thomas and the boys finished clearing another field, and the planted corn was now emerging from the fertile soil. Soon, the garden would once again be abundant, and they could stock the root cellar of the new house with its rewards.

There had been no word from Boston in the weeks that followed their meeting with Reverend Rolfe. The bounty on the scalps would be a bonus to the household;

funds were running low, and Thomas feared that the house might not be completed before the snows would come. A positive message from the court would change everything.

Goody Neff was taken ill in May, and without a doubt it was from the time in the wilderness that caused harm to her body. Her advanced age of nearly fifty-two years and her physical condition played a role in what everyone thought to be consumption.

Widow Neff lived in the family home with her oldest daughter and her husband, who took great care of the elder. She had lost a tremendous amount of weight during her confinement with the Indians and continued to do so once she returned. Mary instructed her caregivers herself for her own care, starting with her bed, which was brought outside under an arbor so she could rest in the fresh air. There were candies made of Horehound that she would use during the day, and at night she took it as a syrup made from the same mighty herb. It had taken some weeks, but the color in her cheeks was restored, and a full recovery occurred.

Samuel Leonardson had stayed at the Neff home until his father traveled from Connecticut to gather him. Samuel had adjusted to life in Haverhill for a few weeks, helping around the farm as best he could. The time with the Indians had taken his youth away; as a boy of nearly fifteen, he was hardened, suspicious, and uncertain with the prospect of a bounty for his actions. He also had a desire to put it behind him; the attacks had not stopped in the colony, and he was in constant fear that the Abenaki would take retribution against him for betraying their trust. Samuel wanted nothing more than to gain as much distance from Massachusetts as possible and to start again.

His father arrived and brought the news that his beloved mother had passed. After his abduction, she was never the same woman; melancholy and sadness filled her. She literally died of a broken heart; it was shocking news to Samuel. His father's love was not enough to console him. Master Leonardson thought it was best to quietly leave Haverhill and return to an undisclosed town to start again. It was a gross reality that he had lost eighteen months of his boyhood, and along with his mother, he, too, was a changed person: the fewer people who knew of his whereabouts, the better. He was still a young man and had his life ahead of him.

The people of the colony were all too inquisitive when it came to the delivery of the three; mostly, they wanted to meet Hannah and hear her tale firsthand. After Samuel's departure and during Mary's convalescence, Goodwife Duston received the larger share of notoriety. She had not often attended the sermons on the Sabbath; when she did, she had become more open to the guidance of the Lord as preached by Rolfe.

The support she and her family received from the townspeople was, at times, overwhelming. There were letters of good thoughts and appreciation dropped at the garrison. Sometimes, a basket of fruit or a sack of cornmeal would accompany the written message. Hannah had been more than thankful when someone dropped a piece of broadcloth, or some used clothing, for her or the children. The Dustons lost almost everything in that early morning fire, including her books that gave her solace when she read them.

The social acceptance that was bestowed on her from the community had almost cleared her thoughts of what she felt like for being an Emerson; that would never go away. Her unmarried name carried a weight of dread; it was associated with violence, witchcraft, and execution. A combination of the worst traits a family should bear witness to.

Michael Emerson and her own mother, Hannah Sr, did not come around much after Elizabeth's conviction; they barely visited, and when they did, it only brought up feelings of remorse and regret. No one ever spoke about what had happened, least of all her parents. The birth and death of those twin babies was a secret that was sewn into the sack with their tiny bodies many years before. The estrangement between Hannah and her parents was as wide as the Merrimac River and as deep as the ocean.

After Hannah escaped and returned to Haverhill, her parents did not come around at all. Their neighbors also did not bring up the past, it was a dark time for the Emerson family. But, a question would always arise; why one sister had been denigrated as a child murderer and the other celebrated for being one; this quandary had weighed on the Emersons' minds every day.

The Reverend Rolfe associated the new attitude with changing times after the last person accused of witchery died in prison in 1693, the same year as Elizabeth's hanging on Boston Common. In all, twenty members of the colony met their death by some form of execution, most commonly hanged on Gallows Hill in Salem Village. The few that were imprisoned, like baby Martha's namesake and Hannah's cousin, Martha Emerson

Toothaker, died of sickness in the Gaol, because she did not have the funds to pay the fine to the courts. The irony was that her charges had all been dropped against her. It truly had been a miscarriage of justice, a stain on the experiment that was once called *the city on the hill.* Governor Winthrop had been correct; the eyes were on all of them, a stink eye at best.

One judge who was involved had sought public clemency for the mishandling of the trials and for his personal blindness to such nonsense as witchery. Earlier that year, after the Abenaki raid, Judge Samuel Sewall publicly repented his role in the wrongful executions, seeking forgiveness for his guilt in a public forum in Boston.

Reverend Cotton Mather had not been a judge but had been heavily involved during all the proceedings; he had clutched the opportunity from each person charged to interrogate them to add testimony against them. With each charge over the months, their dialogue only added to his arsenal for his fire and brimstone sermons. He had yet shown any remorse for his involvement; he did, however, profit from the sale of his sermons that were published.

Goodwife Hannah had plenty of time to think about all that had happened; her days were full of mending clothes to fit her or the children. Creating a home full of love and continuing to educate them on The Bible, the one book that was damaged, but still readable. She was patient when she needed to be; the appeal to the assembly needed to be brought to Boston and presented in person by Thomas, her presence was not needed. They were waiting on word from Reverend Rolfe on their next steps; she was convinced a message would come any day.

Her foresight had been correct, and the following day a courier arrived with a letter addressed to Thomas. She had recognized the seal to be that of Reverend Rolfe's. Once again, as Thomas's wife, she dared not read it before he arrived, never forgetting the role she was meant to occupy.

Her husband arrived from a day at the new house. The construction had shown progress daily. He was exhausted but happy with the fruits of his labor. Hannah greeted him with a tankard of ale, and he sat down at the trestle table. The letter was there waiting for him, the seal ready to be cracked. It was, indeed, instructions for the next step of the petition. Rolfe had included specific details for their presence in the city; they needed to be there the following day.

"It is his pleasure that we be found in Boston on the eighth day of June,' Thomas told her. "Should we set forth on the morrow at first light of the day, we surely would arrive."

The letter stated that they should make their way to Hull House, home of Judge Samuel Sewall. The revered judge would answer any concerns about the procedure before presenting the petition to the courts. Thomas felt strongly that this was a good sign; Sewall was to be a good and fair man, one who appeared to be of wisdom and piety.

Hannah did not need to be told twice; she was ready to go. With the help of the older girls, they could hastily prepare provisions for the journey that night, and the boys could tend to the horse. The sooner this chapter in their life was over, the sooner they could move past it. The children would be fine. Thomas Jr enjoyed playing the figure of authority, and Master Marsh would keep a watchful eye on them.

Thomas agreed with everything she said; it was Hannah's petition, and he was aware of that fact. Her signature, he felt, was exchangeable with his; it was the courts that thought differently. Attitudes and times were changing, but not fast enough for him and his wife.

Hull House was the home of the esteemed Judge Samuel Sewall. It was his wife's family estate located in the city of Boston near Summer Street, not a stone's throw from the Commons. They had not been back to Boston for four years, almost to the date of Elizabeth's hanging. Thomas knew that he had to stay clear of the tree where she was hung; there could be no distractions for either of them. It had taken Hannah many weeks to put that behind her. Stirring that up now would only set her back.

Daybreak came sooner in June, the days were longer and much warmer, both were advantages for the day ahead. With favorable anticipation running through his mind, Thomas barely slept.

Hannah had slept; she felt it was God's will that aided and guided her back to her family. She knew in her soul that this outcome would be a good one.

Thomas had decided it would be faster if they rode together on the stallion; he was a fit horse, and it would save time. They could make the forty-mile journey to the center of the city the following day, with enough time to rest before arriving at Hull House. Hannah mounted the horse first, sitting behind the saddle. A blanket was folded and attached behind the saddle to soften the experience for her. Their saddlebags were full of the evidence they needed to present and the prepared food, and they were off.

The ride was taking longer than he thought; they rode, walked, and rested throughout the day and found a spot to rest on the blanket for the night just outside the city. It was sunup when they crossed the mile expanse of the narrow peninsula called the Boston Neck. They passed the new scaffolding, which was now used for executions of mothers convicted of infanticide to heretics; changing times were slow, and some attitudes had yet to change. Public executions were still a crowd pleaser and a boost to business for the purveyors of food.

Boston had grown in the last four years, Hannah thought. The streets were mostly cobbled, and the homes that lined the main squares noble, creating a presence of a real city. It was said that Boston was the largest city in the colonies. Thomas had read that there were more than six thousand people during the last census; he was in awe at what he saw. The good Reverend from Haverhill had only given an address for Hull House; directions were not included in the letter.

"What business have you with Judge Sewall?" A fishmonger asked Thomas when he inquired for directions.

Thomas was taken aback by the direct question; it seemed that civility in a large city was something that was lacking, and he did not answer.

"Where ye from?" A fruit vendor asked Hannah as she bought an apple.

"Haverhill, in the north," Hannah answered.

"Aye me heard of the place, the Indian killer comes from those parts," she replied.

Hannah had followed suit with Thomas and was surprised by the woman's comment. She took the apple and asked for directions to Washington Street. She gave Hannah directions; it was the main throughway in the city, and it could not be missed. The last bit of their trip was meandering around the crowds of people that were just waking up, most of them vendors, all hocking at them as they passed by.

They found the house on the corner of Washington and Summer streets. It was a fine house, Thomas thought, three stories tall with a gated front yard, what appeared to be an orchard in the back and quarters for servants. A grand house, it was one stately in the midst of many. They dismounted. Hannah was relieved; she had never ridden that long before, and her arse felt it.

Thomas pulled the metal chain and heard a distant clang of a bell. After a moment, a finely dressed servant came to the gate and inquired what their business was. Thomas showed him the letter from Reverend Rolfe; the judge had requested their presence.

"Hannah Duston, the Indian slayer?" It was all the man servant said.

He graciously opened the gate, and he took the reins of their horse. He assured them he would brush, water, and feed the animal. He motioned for them to proceed up the walk to the front door. The Dustons were taken aback by the reactions they encountered that morning, from rudeness to gentile hospitality. Boston was truly an eye-opener that June morning.

Judge Sewall was standing in the front door of his manse; he was a fine-looking man of forty-five. He had long grey hair and was fair-complexioned. They could tell he was a fine man, a gentleman, dressed in the finest of breeches and waist coat. His wife was also named Hannah. She was standing behind in the foyer, a pleasant-looking woman, younger than the judge and dressed equally pristine in a summer day dress.

"Pray come in, Master and Goodwife Duston," he welcomed them. "Ye have made good haste on your journey."

"We give thanks, Judge Sewall, for you receiving us," Thomas replied.

The house was grand, the floors hardwood with carpets, rich in color and design, older than most dwellings. The polished furniture was all carved mahogany, ornate and perfectly appointed, imported from England. Numerous paintings adorned the walls. There were portraits and only one landscape. The chandelier in the foyer was something neither of the Dustons had seen before; the candles glowed, creating prisms of light through the crystals. Directly in front of them, a grand staircase curved to the left, creating an illusion that it floated to the second story. The butler offered to take their cloaks; he was an Englishman.

"We have refreshments," the judge's wife said.

They were escorted into the parlor, another fine room that was richly decorated and most comfortable. There was a tea service set on a small table next to a fancy sideboard filled with crystal glassware and silver items. The tea set was complete with bone china tea cups, the finest she had ever seen. Hannah was fearful of using such finery.

The judge was well versed in all that transpired during Hannah's time with the Abenaki; the purpose that day was for the judge himself to assess the petitioner and grant his approval or dismiss the claim. Since Hannah was a married woman, Thomas was there to represent her for a judgment to be acknowledged; it was the law for married women.

"Ye brought the evidence?" He asked. "I saw the musket in the sleeve on the horse."

Thomas had borrowed a proper leather satchel from Master Marsh; the scalps and hatchet were produced. The blood-stained cloth was a crude reminder of the troubles that had continuously plagued the colony. The Judge had already, at his wife's request, placed a clean white cloth on the table to protect it from such reminders. Mistress Sewall did not want such items in her home, much less touching her fine linen.

Sewall had only asked Hannah a few questions; the rest were directed directly to Thomas. The judge did not take any notes or present his character to appear to be in favor of or against the petition. One question that he asked was in reference to what they had lost during the raid.

"Master Duston," he started. "After such loss and tragic events, I pray, tell me how your family looks toward God's promise? How do ye find your way forward?"

Thomas was very stirring and thoroughly emotionless as he described the loss of their home and the murder of their newborn baby, Martha. The events were tragic, he agreed with the Judge, and he had hoped the reward would assure the completion of the house he was building, a garrison to protect his family in the future. He was confident that through prayer, God would deliver providence as he had delivered Hannah.

After the debatable hullabaloo in Salem, Hannah had sought forgiveness for her own tragic actions, and Sewall needed perspective from another. He needed to get his judgment correct; he was acutely aware of the notoriety that Hannah's actions had created in the colony.

Hannah, the judge's wife, motioned to the servant to pour more tea; it had allowed her to turn her head and dry her own tears. Thomas's story had touched a chord within her, having lost a newborn a few years before.

Judge Sewall sipped his tea, a man of not so many words. After a few moments, he nodded and granted his approval for the bounty claim. He explained that the final word would come from the General Court. Thomas was humbled and very appreciative. He gathered the items and placed them back in the satchel; he knew the next step. They would now go to the court clerk and submit the document that Reverend Rolfe had composed a few weeks before.

They gave thanks for the hospitality, and the Judge in turn wished them good fortune, for the providence of Hannah's deliverance was all the proof he had needed.

They walked to the gate, and the man servant was there with their horse; the stallion looked to be in good form. They said their good wishes and thanked him for his kindness. He opened the gate, and a crowd rushed from the street to the Dustons as they walked the horse onto Washington Street.

"Are you Hannah Duston?" A woman yelled.

"Aye, I have seen tis early this morning when asking for directions to the judge's house," the fishmonger yelled to the crowd.

"You be a fine example for all of us," another yelled. "Those savages shall reap what they sow."

The Dustons did not know what to make of it. Thomas grabbed Hannah's hand, securely holding it tight as they made their way through the crowd that was forming. He was puzzled at best. There they were in the largest city in the colonies, and his wife was recognized. Was this favorable, or something they should fear?

It was only a matter of seconds, before someone clapped their hands together; it was loud and a commanding sound. Like a ripple on the water, the rest of the onlookers began to clap, shouting well wishes to the Indian killer.

Thomas and Hannah walked slowly through the crowd without stopping, guiding the horse to follow. Some reached out and touched the arm of his wife; it was a gesture of approval, nothing more.

They headed in the direction of the General Court, which was just a short distance away on State Street. The crowd did not follow, and they were grateful.

On Washington Street, they encountered an Indian family walking directly towards them. It was not an unusual sight to find a few of the praying Indians in the city, converts to the Christian way of life; they kept in their place alongside the Africans.

Hannah watched them as they got closer; they were partly dressed in garments they had made, similar to her Abenaki captors. She took a deep breath and was prepared to stand her ground. Thomas sensed her uncomfortable stance and squeezed her hand firmer. The young Indian was a squaw who looked to be about ten years of age. The child stared at Hannah, never breaking eye contact, as she walked. It had been a haunting stare, her black eyes lifeless and penetrating. The hair on Hannah's neck stood.

The Indians appeared not to know who she was and passed without incident, a relief welcomed by them both.

TWENTY-EIGHT

They were both grateful that their master bestowed on them a fine day in Boston that so far was prosperous; the blue sky assured them that rain was not arriving anytime soon. The city had been hard enough for them to make their way through; the prospect of rain would only cause more confusion and discomfort. State Street was easy to find. The Provence House, as it was known, was bustling with activity. The building was the official seat of the Governor and his council; it seemed all of the city had business within the structure.

Thomas tied his horse to the ornate hitching post in front of the building and retrieved the musket from the saddle. He looked at Hannah, his eyes expressed self-confidence and distress, a deadly mix when so much was on the line.

Hannah grabbed his hand and turned to the entry gate. Two court guards were questioning every one of what their business with the assembly. The petition was produced, and one of the guards read it while the other looked inside his satchel. They saw the bloody linen and were instantly overcome by the putrid smell of the dried scalps. He closed the leather flap as quickly as he had opened it.

"Let thee in!" A shout from someone on the street. "That's Hannah Duston, the Indian killer."

Thomas looked and saw the fishmonger from earlier. He must have followed them from the Judge's house. The crowd stopped and took notice; they began to shout good wishes to Hannah. The soldiers had heard of the raid in Haverhill, but it was the first time they laid eyes on the Indian killer herself. They opened the gate and instructed them to go to the second floor to the office of the Deputy Clerk of the General Court.

The office was identified with a brass name plate on the door, which was ajar, and the Dustons quietly walked in. The entire room was filled with other men, all trying to capture the attention of the clerk behind the rail. He was responsible for reading all the documents and weighing their importance. The queue amazingly parted when the presence of Goodwife Duston entered the room; she was the only woman there.

The Deputy Clerk looked up from his reading, his concentration broken, and stood looking at the petitioners from Haverhill. He had recognized her by reputation only, and the fact that the Judge had sent word earlier in the day that she had arrived in Boston. It would seem Sewall had already made his judgment.

The clerk motioned for them to approach the rail and asked to see the petition. He stood at the barrier reading, and being convinced of its merit, he nodded to the soldier guarding the chamber door. He did not even look at the evidence, which would be the role of the General Court and the Governor if he so chose.

"Do ye have the filing fee?" Was all the clerk spoke.

Thomas took the pouch from his waist and paid the money to the clerk, two schillings it would cost. A mere pittance as an investment for the approval of the reward. The soldier approached them and escorted them into the court chamber. He instructed them to wait and took the petition to the desk near the council seating, close by the Governor.

Governor William Stoughton presided over the court and was normally present for all proceedings, especially those concerning the public treasury. His reputation had preceded him. As Governor, he had presided over the Salem Witch trials. He was the chief judge and appointed himself as prosecutor, a deadly alliance for many. His approval of spectral evidence was considered unlawful by many; his most ardent opposition to such nonsense was the Reverend Cotton Mather. Stoughton's judgments were unmerciful and had deadly consequences.

Hannah knew who Stoughton was; he alone could have released both Master Toothaker and his daughter, Martha Emerson Toothaker, before they both perished in the Boston Gaol. It seemed wherever Hannah turned, the tragedy of her family's past would be staring at her as the young Indian squaw had done earlier in the day. Perhaps Stoughton would not make the connection between her and her dysfunctional family. She wanted nothing more than to be at her spinning wheel, spinning the flax into something useful.

The court was finishing up the case at hand. Thomas watched the secretary as he approached the center judge with his document. The committee all looked in his direction and turned back. The hush over the room was evident that the Dustons would be heard next, taking priority over the others that had been waiting.

Thomas was escorted to the center of the assembly hall, where he then handed the evidence to the secretary, who in turn brought the items to the committee. The Governor was on a rise, sitting at a large oak podium behind the committee, and seemed to be ambivalent about the case; perhaps he remembered the troubles in Salem and the fate of Hannah's relatives. Thomas refused to think about that and only wanted his voice heard.

After explaining his petition and the endorsement from Judge Sewall, he spoke clearly and concisely. Hannah listened and thought perhaps he had lost his calling. She was happy that they did not have to wait to present their argument. The committee took one last look at the scalps and the hatchet. It was clear to them that the musket was French in origin and given to the savages to use against the English.

The committee secretary brought back the items, and he shook Thomas's hand. He explained that they would pass the judgment within a week, and a courier would be sent to the Reverend with further instructions. He thanked him again for his well-delivered argument and his condolences for their loss. Hannah did receive a nod from the committee when it was all said and done. She took that as the best they could do and headed to the other chamber, Thomas at her heels.

When they entered the hallway, it was filled with well-dressed men, all standing against the walls waiting for the Dustons to emerge from the Governor's Chamber. Each of them hoped to get a glimpse of Hannah. As they walked to the top of the stairs, they stopped, looking down. They saw that the entire first floor of the court entry was also filled with onlookers. Hannah Duston had become a hero, a defender of her family, and the most admired woman in the colony.

It was all too overwhelming for Hannah; she needed to move past the crowd as soon as possible. She herself was haunted by her own demons over her actions, which gave her great pause daily. They started to descend the large staircase when, once again, a single clap of hands could be heard, then the entire entry filled with clapping. The emotion that she felt was a mixture of happiness and embarrassment, and she quickly exited to the street.

The visit to the General Court was now over, and the next and final visit was to the Reverend Cotton Mather's home, where they had been invited at the request of Mather. It was to be a luncheon meeting. Hannah had dreaded meeting Mather the most; she was fearful of losing her self-control when confronted by the fire-and-brimstone preacher.

The Second Church of Boston was the domain of the thirty-five-year-old Reverend and author. Mather was the son of another prominent preacher, Increase Mather, who had been the President of Harvard, something the younger aspired to. The church had been on North Square, close to his home on Hanover Street; it was but a brief walk. The crowds were still present and followed the Dustons as they made their way to the north end of the city.

It, too, was a formidable home, made of brick with large windows and a center chimney, no doubt a fireplace in every room. It did not have the gardens that the Judge had; it was in its own right stately. The hitching post was directly next to the short walkway; there had been no gate and no manservant to greet them. The Reverend presented a more pious and reserved life; he was considered to be a leader amongst the Puritans, but his followers would not approve of such displays of wealth.

Thomas took the rifle from the hitched horse and walked to the front door. Hannah was behind him, and he grabbed the knocker and let it strike just once. He was trying to show solidarity with Hannah; the meeting was only to appease the petition and to set the record straight after the first interview with his fellow clergyman, Reverend Rolfe.

The door opened; it was the Reverend himself; this gave them both a moment of reflection. There had been no manservant, or butler, to greet them; they thought this was strange. He was also younger than Hannah when viewed in close proximity, not as old as either of the Dustons. The only time they had actually seen him was the fateful day of Elizabeth's execution; his sermon had been devastating for her to hear. And the confession that he claimed her sister confessed to him was pure blasphemy on his part; Hannah would not change her opinion. She would do her best to show a reserved emotion and would let Thomas speak on her behalf.

He was dressed in a black clerical gown; this was his way to show his education. He had attended Harvard University at eleven and graduated when he was fifteen, a well-educated man. A master's degree in Divinity was just another accomplishment for Mather. He was adorned with a periwig, something he was known to wear both in public and in private. This was perhaps the biggest disagreement he faced with Judge Sewall, his good friend. Sewall found the periwig a contradiction to the Puritan faith of piety and only represented vanity.

Mather welcomed them into his home and personally took their cloaks and hung them in an armoire in the foyer. The house was a contradiction. It represented an imbalance of practical and elaboration. Hannah remained guarded as he welcomed them into his home.

"Pray. Come and partake of a late repast," Mather told them.

A late lunch had been prepared in the dining room, and it was a welcome treat for them both. The day had grown long, and the tea and biscuits earlier had not satisfied Thomas's hunger. Hannah could go hours without eating; her time in the wilderness had pushed her own boundaries.

They sat down and admired the table and its refinement of pewter chargers and blown glass cups. A young boy entered the room, well dressed in breeches, a waistcoat, and white gloves. His complexion was not African and not native; he was definitely a curiosity to the Dustons. He approached them with a glass decanter filled with wine. Mather nodded, and he poured, filling the glasses and leaving the room.

The Reverend was pleased that the Dustons had taken his invitation. This was his opportunity to gain knowledge of the Abenaki raid and the ordeal that Hannah had suffered. He did mention he was writing a sermon that he would publish after he delivered it in his church nearby.

It was clear to Hannah that he was presenting himself as a kind and thoughtful minister, only wanting to gather the truth so others could learn the true nature of

God's deliverance of her from the savages. God's prudence had brought them together, and he wanted his congregation to be enlightened by his grace.

The meal was served by the same boy: smoked fish, roasted potatoes, and turnips. It was tasty, and the wine went well with it. Thomas could not even remember the last time he had had wine outside of the Sabbath; in the taverns of the north, it was cider or ale. Hannah had never drunken wine before, having never taken communion on the Sabbath. She had been baptized as a child but was never a full participant in her church, freely admitting that she took little interest in the teachings of the Parish. She preferred to educate herself along with her children, letting them come to their own conclusions. It was just another Emerson trait, attending on the Sabbath, just enough to keep the prying eyes happy.

The conversation during the meal was one of passion, each of them feeling strong about their own values on subjects such as the French, The Devil, and the work of the Lord. All three areas of discussion were centered on the deliverance of Hannah from her captors. Mather was indeed a well-educated man and clearly informed on the plight of Hannah and the others.

"Pray tell, are ye familiar with the Book of Judges?" Mather asked.

Hannah had to admit that her Bible study was lacking of late, but Thomas was aware of the story of Jael, who had murdered the general Sisera while he slept. She had driven a tent spike into his temple while he slept. This fulfills a prophecy that the glory of victory came from a woman, her actions as a vessel of God.

The Reverend felt that by comparing Hannah to Jael, the incident was not one of revenge but one of a heroics, a Godly woman who had delivered her people from the enemy. The Abenaki had been their enemy, and Hannah's actions were justified; he felt strongly about this. Both of the Dustons took a slight sigh of relief; there was an approval from an authority that in the past had been an adversary.

They finished their lunch and moved into the parlor, which he referred to as the front room. Again, it was most comfortable without being intimidating. Hannah's opinion of Mather had changed slightly, though she thought she would never forgive him for the disservice he had shown to her sister.

Mather asked to see the evidence that Thomas had brought. The scalps and the hatchet had been handled by many people that day; he was in fear of the condition and thought to himself he would not present them any longer. They needed to be tucked away for safekeeping for the future; they could not afford to lose them.

Hannah looked out the window, and the sun was casting a long shadow; the sun was beginning to set. Mather sensed the same and thought it was time they made their way back on the road north. Thomas also did not want to find his way out of Boston in the dark.

The Reverend stood and thanked them both for their time and the trustworthiness to him. It was not an easy task to keep reliving the raid. He reached out to Hannah and shook her hand first. It was totally uncharacteristic of him; it gave thought to both the Dustons that perhaps the times were changing.

He offered up the suggestion of a prayer, one of guidance and resolution for them both and their family. His motivation for the meeting was to hear first-hand the account and perhaps to seek some forgiveness for Elizabeth's confession. Mather knew the embellishment of her words did not fare her fate very well. This was something he would never admit to anyone, let alone her sister.

They said their goodbyes and were pleased to see his boy watering the horse; it had been a wonderful gesture to end their day in Boston. They feared a long night was ahead for them. It was now in the hands of God and the courts. Neither could wait to be in their bed.

TWENTY-NINE

The summer heat had been very beneficial to both the garden and the construction of the house. The heat caused the strawberries to grow plump and sweet, and it aided the brick laying, helping to dry the limestone mortar faster. Thomas had mastered the art of burning shells and limestone to create the mixture to hold his bricks in place. The house had taken shape, and soon the family could leave the garrison and finally be in their own home.

Hannah was out in front of the garrison with the girls. That morning, they had picked a bountiful amount of strawberries from the bed, and they needed to dry them in the hot sun. The heat from the sun would remove the moisture, so they would not mold. The berries would be tasty later when they would be added to cornmeal in the cooler months.

They had moved the trestle benches out of the main room and placed them in the direct sunlight, neatly arranging the quartered berries in tight rows. They hoped that would speed the drying process. Hannah's task was to cut the berries into four pieces, and the girls placed them on the bench. She looked down at her stained hands, and the juice of the strawberries ran bright red through her fingertips and under her nails. It was a visual reminder of the incident on the island, and she would not allow herself to go there in her mind.

"Mother, there is a horse and rider a-comin' up the way," Elizabeth, Hannah's second-oldest daughter, shouted.

Hannah and the other girls stopped to look down the dirt road in the direction of the village. The rider was nearly in a gallop as he approached the garrison. Dressed in black, wearing a wide-brimmed hat, Hannah recognized him as the Reverend Rolf. He was waving with his left hand, seemingly elated to see the Dustons at their place of residence.

"Goodwife Duston," Rolfe shouted. "I have news, I hope to be favorable."

The Reverend pulled the rein tightly, and the horse abruptly halted. He dismounted with ease and showed reserved excitement as any man of God could. He did not wait to be greeted and proceeded to retrieve an item from his leather bag attached to the side of the horse. It was wrapped in broadcloth and tied together with a cotton string.

"Elizabeth, fetch me a bucket of water," Hannah whispered to her.

"Is Master Duston close by?" Rolfe asked. "I think he would be pleased that his efforts have come to fruition."

Hannah motioned for Sarah, who was almost ten, to run to the new house and gather her father. He needed to be here; the Reverend was clear about that. Elizabeth brought back the wooden bucket, and Hannah tried furiously to wash her hands. The stain of the berries was much harder to remove than that of the blood of the Indians. Her daughter handed her some freshly made soap and a rag, both of which helped.

Hannah walked to the garrison door and welcomed Rolf inside. He was carrying the parcel along with his leather satchel. The girls remained outdoors, finishing the task at hand. They would wait for their father before entering; he would instruct them when it was appropriate to do so.

"Goodwife Duston," Rolfe said. "Accept thy apologies for my hasty arrival, but these items just arrived from Boston this morning,"

Hannah pulled a stool around from the hearth and sat down at the table. The Reverend placed the parcel and his bag on the table and found a small bench next to the table. He sat across from her and smiled. She knew it had to be good news; his demeanor was a bit infectious, something she had longed to feel again.

"Let me begin with this," he told her.

He reached into his leather bag and produced a copy of The Pilgrim's Progress. The novel that had been written by John Bunyan, it was one of Hannah's favorites; her copy had been destroyed in the fire. Rolfe handed it to her, and she grabbed it with both hands and pressed it to her chest, like a mother with a newborn. It made her happy; it was such a kind act.

"Oh, Pastor Rolfe," Hannah spoke with such serenity, "You have pleased me once again."

Rolfe knew that the entire community had come out to show support with gifts and good wishes. He also had noticed that Hannah, of late, seemed to be attending his sermons more frequently, and that had pleased him. The novel was an allegory, one that resonated with Hannah and her story of salvation. He was also convinced, like in the book, that she was seeking a spiritual outcome from her journey into the wilderness.

Thomas suddenly appeared in the opened doorway; he had raced back to the garrison, and he was hot and out of breath. His face soiled from the dust of the kiln, as he had been firing the last of the bricks for the nearly completed house. Thomas, like Hannah, could not contain his eagerness to meet the Reverend.

"Welcome, Master Rolfe," Thomas extended his hand. "It is a blessing to have thee beneath our roof: pray, what business brings thee to our door this day?"

Rolfe assured them he came only with good intentions and well wishes. Hannah held up the copy of the novel he gave her, which pleased Thomas, for his wife had been without books for reading for some time. He also produced a letter with the mark of the General Court in Boston, the wax seal thick and solid, fixed to the folded parchment.

Thomas sat down next to Hannah, and the Reverend slid the letter in his direction. The curiosity of its contents was causing them both mixed emotions. If it were favorable, then the funds would be used to finish the house, something they both longed for. If it was not in their favor, then perhaps a charge against Hannah, or a fine could be imposed. That would be detrimental to the entire family.

"I fear the outcome of this document," Thomas told him.

"Firstly, Goodman Duston," he began. "I have brought a token for thee and thy dame, come all the way from the Maryland Province."

He stood up and retrieved the parcel from the other end of the table. He placed it in front of Hannah next to the letter. Thomas reached for a knife from the sideboard and cut the string that was around the parcel. Hannah started to unwrap it. A letter was in the wrapping, which Thomas read. It appeared that Hannah's story had spread all the way south, to the Governor of Maryland. Francis Nicholson was moved by her story and her plight and sent a generous token of favor to her.

Hannah slowly unwrapped the item; she was curious about what it was, as the other two were. A beautiful pewter tankard was revealed, perfectly cast and polished. Truly, it would be a prized procession of the family and a positive reminder of her ordeal.

"Now thee must open the parchment," Rolfe told Thomas.

The sound the wax seal makes as it is cracked is very distinct, one the Dustons were not familiar with until recently. There had been other gifts and letters from the colony, but those on that day had to be the most important and impressive.

The letter seemed lengthy, and Thomas read it silently before he explained it to them. It had taken a few minutes for him to comprehend it; he read it twice to be clear.

The court had awarded a bounty on the ten scalps produced at the petition; it was unfortunate that the bounty had been repealed, but due to the extreme situation of the events, they all agreed to award the parties an amount. Goodwife Hannah Duston's husband would be awarded a total of 25 pounds for Hannah's efforts, and the sum of 12 pounds, 10 shillings each to Mary Neff, and to the guardian of Samuel Leonardson for his role in the incident. It was a favorable ruling, but not as much as they hoped.

"Thee must collect in person in Boston," Thomas continued.

Each of the petitioners must collect in person the bounty from The Town House, which was the seat of the Massachusetts General Court. It would be paid from the general treasury in paper currency, known as Bills of Credit. It also stated that Mary and Samuel had been notified by a letter and would have to journey to Boston as well.

Hannah could tell that her husband was holding back his true feelings regarding the court's decision. She reached over and grabbed his left hand, in a gesture of solidarity and support. She knew that 25 pounds was more than enough money to finish the house and maybe even buy more land; expanding the farm was always something Thomas wanted to do.

"Methinks a draught of some small cheer is needed to mark the great providence the Lord hath bestowed upon us," Thomas announced, hiding his true feelings.

They agreed. Hannah stood and went to gather the beakers, and Thomas went outside to the cellar for a crock of ale. It was stored in the damp and dark to keep it cooler and prevent it from turning. The root cellar was an essential part of their lives, storing food and refreshment.

The three sat and drank the amber liquid; it was refreshing on such a hot day. The conversation had ceased, and they sat in silence, each in deep thought. Hannah looked at her stained hands as she drank, the color vibrant and horrifying; would her mind ever let her forget what had happened? Thomas was bitter that the reward wasn't more; the courts should have been more generous, and Reverend Rolf could not wait to return to the parsonage to work on his next sermon. The day's event had proven to be a resource he could not pass up.

The children were all outside waiting to be allowed into the garrison; they, too, were waiting with much anticipation. The ale was finished, and it was time to say good day to the Reverend and thank him for all he had done. The Dustons were truly grateful for his help and guidance. Hannah assured him she would see him on the next Sabbath; his sermons had inspired her to be more open.

Elizabeth had saved a small basket of strawberries, which she gave to the Reverend Rolfe once he had mounted his horse. That gesture of kindness did not go unnoticed by her parents; they each thought, throughout all the adversity the family had gone through, they would be fine.

The children gathered around the table; they were in awe of the pewter tankard on display. Thomas picked up the letter to keep it safe and placed it in his satchel hanging on a hook by the door.

"Methinks I must return to Boston with all haste," Thomas announced to the family. "I shall set forth at first light on the morrow."

The rest of the day passed with little conversation. Thomas returned to the new house to gather a few things and organize the next day's work. He would be gone for a couple of days, to Boston. There was a lot to do; banking was at the top of his mind, and he had no time to feel anything other than progress.

The girls had gathered the berries as they finished drying and moved the bench back into the garrison. The evening meal would need to be started as well, and they needed to fill their father's saddlebag with some food for his journey south.

Hannah tried again to remove the stain from her hands. It was a silly thought, but she could finally wash her hands of what had happened that night on the island. She knew all too well that, scrub as she did, her hands remained stained. It would take time for the stain and the memory to fade.

THIRTY

It had always amazed Hannah the concept of time, how fast life would pass when things were of good nature, and how long it would take when things were awry. The summer had flown past like a breeze from the south, and autumn came and went in a flash. The harvest had been bountiful from the new fields that were planted with radishes and turnips; they loved the cold soil.

It was the prior June when Thomas had returned from Boston with the bounty in hand and a fresh outlook for the years ahead. The money had gone a long way; it was first used to finish the new house, which had been a blessing for the entire Duston family, who had grown tired of living at the garrison. With what was left, he was able to expand the farm with a small parcel of land, which, once cleared and tilled, was perfect for late planting of root vegetables. It all seemed to be going to plan; Thomas was happy, and the children were back into a routine of chores and learning.

It was the beginning of the new year, and Hannah herself woke that morning not in the best of health. She had taken ill the morning before, and the sickness returned the next day. She was now in her fortieth year, and she was hesitating to push herself. The girls insisted she remain in bed; they would see to the fires, the meals, and the upkeep of the house. Hannah could not argue with her daughters, who were as strong as she and as self-reliant.

Hannah was in her new feather bed; the room upstairs was kept warm from the large center chimney in the house. It was late afternoon, and the sky was gray, with a foreboding appearance. There was a snowstorm on the horizon; all signs led to that assumption. She felt safe and secure, wrapped in a quilt she had made in the warmer months.

The light of the day was fading; she was thankful for the new Betty Lamp that was purchased. The small iron dish was filled with fish oil, and the light was more than enough to read by when placed near her bed. She had been rereading the book that Reverend Rolf had given her; she took her time with it. The Pilgrim's Progress was having a profound effect on her.

She was about halfway through the novel and wanted to relate the main character to her own life, her own struggles. The book is centered on Christian, and the first part is narrated as a dream. He was from the City of Destruction, trying to make his way to the Celestial City. He was weighed down by sin and slipped into hell, where he had to cross through the Slough of Despond, a mire of boggy, swamp-like terrain where temptation was close by.

Hannah would read some of the novel and take a pause; she was trying to sort out what she had experienced compared to that of what Christian was experiencing. He had left his family, too, in the City of Destruction and journeyed into the wasteland, hoping for a place of deliverance that would be revealed to him. His obstacles, at times, were insurmountable, but he pushed forward.

She thought she was reading her own story; she, too, had left the morning of the raid, her city in flames, the fate of her family unknown; destruction was all she knew that morning. Baby Martha and the apple tree were her Slough of Despond, but she pushed forward.

Hannah sat up in bed and pulled the quilt tighter to her body. The wind had picked up, and she could see snow begin to fall in the fading light of the day. She hoped the lamp would stay lit; she wasn't tired and wanted to continue to read about Christian's search for his enlightenment. She picked up the book and began again.

As she read his story, Christian was walking through a field with no end in sight, it was one foot after the other. A trance-like state that kept him moving in the direction of salvation. He met an evangelist along the path, and he directed him to the Wicked Gate for deliverance, but he could not see it and sank into the mire. Help came along and pulled him out. Help was there to guide him.

Hannah put the book down and had a memory resurface that she thought was lost to her. It was that night on the trail when everyone was asleep, the fire only a pile of burning embers. She had heard a voice; it had called to her from the dark forest. She was able to not wake Goody Neff, who was sleeping next to her, and walked into the darkness. The ground was snow-covered and near the river, where she thought the voice had originated.

It was all coming back to her, the unseen visitor, the voice of Tsienneto. He had been watching her and explained he was a very old advisor of weary travelers in need. He predicted that the way would appear to her. The voice had been right, the plan worked, and her deliverance was inevitable. How did she not remember the details of that encounter? The novel had caused her to recall Tsienneto and his words.

Was the old Indian advisor an Evangelist, was the forest her Slough of Despair, and was the river the Wicked Gate that she had to go through to reach the Celestial City? Was Samuel the same as the character "Help" in her own story? Hannah felt a surge of energy within her body, as if the sun was warming her face in an early morning spring, as she sat next to the river. It was an enlightenment she felt, something she feared that, being an Emerson, she would never feel.

Elizabeth had come to mind; it had been well over five years since she first went to Boston with Thomas, the visit to the prison, and what followed on the Common had been neatly tucked in a dark place in her mind. Now she was not fearful of her memories but could embrace them. Elizabeth's unfortunate demise started long ago; it was with her father when he crossed the ocean. Evil appeared on the shores of Massachusetts, and it had crossed paths with all of the Emerson family. That thought had saddened her; she missed her sister and hoped she was delivered to the Celestial City atop Mount Zion, and at the same time hoped her father would sink into the mire.

She took no pleasure in that thought and would seek counsel from the Reverend Rolf after his sermon on the Sabbath. Hannah was becoming more devoted and absorbed as much from his words as she did from the book she was reading.

The light of the lamp would be out soon, the oil all but burned away. Thomas would be coming to bed soon, and she wanted to be fast asleep before he arrived. The sickness from the morning was all but gone, but she knew it would return again and again. Thomas would have to wait until morning before Hannah would break the news to him.

She blew out the lamp, the room faded into darkness, but the glow of her inner light warmed her belly and her soul.

THIRTY-ONE

Hannah could hear the footsteps coming up the stairs; she knew it to be Thomas. She could recognize his gate anywhere. After forty-seven years of marriage, there wasn't much she didn't know about him. She was still in her bedroom reading The Bible that had been damaged that fateful morning twenty-seven years prior; it brought her solace. There was a soft knock at the door. Thomas was always respectful of his wife; her alone time was like the comfort of her favorite quilt. The door was ajar, and it creaked as he opened it; he paused hoping she was ready for the day.

"Goodwife, art thou prepared to journey to the meeting house?" He asked her. "Tis a solemn day for you."

Hannah only smiled and placed The Bible on the table next to her chair. Her thoughts were mixed, and she recalled another day when her mother asked her the same question. She was married at nineteen, a young woman and one who, in retrospect, needed to distance herself from the toxic household of the Emersons. She was forever grateful to Thomas for taking her away and legitimizing her first child. Hannah Jr was born just over eight months later, something she never regretted.

"What wast thou reading?" He asked.

"Tis the Book of Psalms," She answered. "My times are in hand, be the passage."

It had been an appropriate verse to mark that special Sunday in 1724. Hannah was sixty-seven and had lived these last years in the house that Thomas built, and not a happier time for her was had. Baby Lydia had grown into a bright and intelligent woman of twenty-five; she had been the light in Hannah's eyes. It had been twenty-seven years since baby Martha made her way to the Celestial City, a morning she would not forget.

Thomas and Hannah had raised their children without remorse or judgment of the past. If the family was to flourish, then the sins of long ago had to be recognized and dealt with; mortality was always around the corner. Times were still precarious for the colony. King William's war ended in 1697, but as fate would have it, another conflict began.

Queen Anne's War had been raging throughout the frontier for over twelve years, ending in 1713. It had taken its toll on Haverhill when, in 1708, the Indians and the French raided the town once more. Over two hundred armed men staged a surprise attack, killing sixteen before the local militia forced them to retreat. The entire colony was once again on guard, causing memories to resurface.

Hannah had taken the last raid to heart, losing a friend and a confidante. The Reverend Benjamin Rolf was killed trying to defend his home that dreaded morning. A French soldier shot him through the front door and murdered his wife and his newborn son. Reverend Rolfe had been a young man when Hannah had first met him;

a patient and empathetic pastor, one that Hannah could relate to. His sermons were thoughtful and inspiring, never judgmental or authoritarian. It was at that time, after his death, that Goodwife Duston retreated to her bedroom on occasion with her Bible; there she reflected and sought spiritual guidance through her readings.

"Mother, I have thy best mantle; this is the one thou should wear to the meeting-house this day," Lydia announced as she stepped into the room.

Hannah could not have been more proud of her children, all ten of them. Lydia was still living at the house and was a God-send helping her with all the duties of a mother. She had the garment draped over her arm, and she had repaired the hem of the woolen cloak. It had been one of Hannah's favorites, a rich, deep green that she had dyed herself, mixing blue indigo and yellow from the yarrow, to create a deep green hue. Looking one's best for the Sabbath was a trait for all church members in Puritan society.

"I thank thee, dear child; what thoughtfulness thou hast shown," her mother replied. "Shall we descend and make ready the wain?"

Thomas took the cloak from Lydia and then took Hannah's hand. He thought her health and spirits, that morning, were great. The smallest of gestures were always the ones that were noticed by his wife. The three went downstairs to the hall, where all life in the household had taken place. The hearth had a small fire emitting heat in the large room. It felt comforting to them on such a special morning. It was May, the showers of April had passed, but it was still a cool morning.

Timothy was gathering the horse from the barn. He was preparing the carriage for the ride to the meeting-house; the journey would take nearly an hour, and arriving late was not in good character for any of them. He would be turning thirty soon, and he was still living on the farm and was extremely helpful to Thomas with the daily duties.

Hannah did not want to be tardy, for she would be presenting herself to the brethren after the sermon. It was to be her acceptance into the church as a full member of the congregation. She had been baptized as a child but never fully embraced the teaching or the requirements of the Puritan faith.

She was tormented with self-doubt of unworthiness and sinful behavior that would prevent her from seeking God's full acceptance. She had always felt that her actions from an early pregnancy as an unmarried girl, and her inability to rescue her sister from wickedness by her father, were judged by the Almighty. She also took to heart her lack of support for her cousin during the madness in Salem. These were out of her control, or were they?

This was a question in her own mind for many years. In fact, during her captivity, she had countless hours to dwell on her lack of action, which plagued her. When she took matters into her own hands on the island, it was a mixture of rage and defiance, for the murder of her child, the destruction of her home, and standing up to the oppression she had felt for some time. She had blamed the church for the feeling of subjection, a fault she had known not to be accurate.

Thomas helped her with her cloak, and Lydia handed the bonnet to her. They were ready to go into town; there would be no looking back for Hannah. The day had come.

Timothy was standing next to the wagon. He helped his mother and sister into the back, where cushions of grain sacks and blankets were placed to ease the discomfort. Thomas sat up front, taking the reins. He gave a gentle snap.

They were quiet; not a word was spoken. It was the Sabbath, and on that day each week, many activities were forbidden. Work and play were frowned upon, as was lively behavior and excessive eating. Prudence and piety went hand in hand on Sundays in the colony. The eyes were still about, just not as hypercritical. The tide had shifted in the community to a more accepting change.

The new pastor in town was the Reverend John Brown. He, like Rolfe, was a Harvard graduate and was a very young man. He arrived in Haverhill after graduating in 1719. He was barely twenty-two, and with an outlook that befitted his generation of thinkers. The fire and brimstone that was of Cotton Mather's day had passed. His platform was one of moral order, and not of emotional distress.

Shortly after he arrived in Haverhill, every member of the Congregation wanted to meet him, for he was so young and had a reputation befitting of an open and patient pastor. He had taken the liberty to call on Hannah at her house, something that was not done since the time of Benjamin Rolf. Hannah missed him dearly, as did the rest of the Duston family.

From the first meeting with Jones, they had a mutual admiration for each other. The age difference did not matter; spiritual growth can happen at any age, he preached. He did not ask about her past, though he was well versed on her ordeal. Hannah Duston was still a name in the colony that was revered and respected. She was thought of as a heroine. Her story was immortalized by Cotton Mather in his preaching and his publications over the years, something neither Jones nor Duston mentioned during their time together.

Hannah grew to enjoy the sermons on the Sabbath and attended more regularly. Jones had a way of speaking that quieted her thoughts and gave her the uneasy confidence that what she had always been taught about the faith might not be entirely true. She had always thought that the taking of a life required moral accountability and that trauma would prevent the salvation of her soul. These were actions she knew well, but still they prevented her from fully being accepted into the church.

Brown had stressed to her that true conversion was an inner peace, a transformation, from that which was initiated by God and validated by society, a scrutiny that would determine if one was a visible saint when their inner grace was confirmed. A Confession of Faith would be a way for Hannah to be fully regenerated in the church. Brown offered her guidance and help with her spiritual journey.

Hannah approved of most everything that Brown preached; his methods had soothed her inner torment, and she trusted his judgment. Their meetings were more frequent over the past months, and in her words, she was ready. It was shortly after the new year had started that her decision was made.

"Sir, I have sat long and often delayed with my thoughts," Hannah told him. "I desire to give word of my faith and enter the covenant, if the church would have me."

That was the beginning of the process for the reconciliation of her life, her actions, and finally the acceptance into the church. Throughout all the meetings with the Reverend, there was little discussion of her captivity and what it took for her return. Brown, like Hannah, was a fan of The Pilgrim's Progress. The book was a relatable source of metaphorical dialogue that they used to create her Confession of Faith. This written record would be presented to the congregation on that Sabbath, after his sermon.

The road into town had been worn over the years. The highway man's plow would occasionally smooth out the ruts that were formed during the mud season. That morning, the ride was relatively smooth and short. Hannah, still deep in thought, was getting nervous. What if her confession was not truly accepted? "Could something like that ever occur?" She silently questioned.

The First Parish meeting house was coming into view. It was a plain structure, no steeple, and the clapboard had weathered over the years. It was Jones' desire to have the building whitewashed again, the appearance fresher, brighter, not unlike his sermons.

Timothy jumped off the wagon and grabbed the bit to direct the horse and carriage to the elm next to the meetinghouse. The grass was green, and there the horse could graze and rest. He helped his sister and mother out of the back, and the four walked to the front door.

Hannah fixed the bow of her bonnet, adjusted her mantle, and lowered her head. Thomas went first, followed by Timothy. The men went first, and the women trailed behind, walking slowly, never making eye contact. They were not allowed to sit together, the men to the right and the women to the left. Older members are seated in front, along with prominent members of the community, as close to the pulpit as possible. Social standing still carried weight among them.

The inside of the meeting house had a distinct smell of dampness, wet wool, and unvarnished wood. There were boxed seats on either side of the aisle, most of them full when they arrived. Hannah's news of her confession of faith had caused a bit of a stir in the community; the attendance was higher than normal, well over 150 souls. Curiosity can be a driving force when it comes to church attendance.

Hannah could feel her heart race; the beating was rapid and pronounced under her cape, and she feared it would explode. Her face was becoming flushed and warm, but she did not look up until she reached the front of the church. Without trying to make eye contact, she slid into the front row. There had been space saved by the reverend for both her and Thomas, each on their respective sides. The children were somewhere in the back on benches that were brought in.

The row was filled with women elders, some she had known, but most she did not. For years, Hannah had distanced herself from the church, so the ones she had known were older and from earlier times. Thomas was across the aisle, amongst the most prominent and oldest of men, too far away to hold his hand, and too obvious to make eye contact.

She could not tell if any of the other children were in attendance; the bonnet only allowed her to see forward. Head coverings for women were mandatory and were expected, by church doctrine, to remain on at all times during services. Normally, she would have worn a cornet beneath her bonnet, but she was distracted and forgot it. The men were allowed to remove their hats as a sign of respect. Women, conversely, had to show submission to the divine order on the Lord's Day.

The meeting house was full, and members tried to squeeze into the boxes that were clearly occupied. They started to stand on either side of those who were seated, with hopes for a short sermon. Brown was known for his straightforward sermons, which were always shorter and more inspirational than those of the previous pastor.

The Reverend appeared on the pulpit, and Hannah took a deep breath. Her pastor, and friend, was dressed in his traditional black wool Geneva gown. Around his neck, resting on his shoulders were the fallen bands; two stark white linen rectangle strips, that represented the two tablets of law given to Moses. Hannah knew it to be a special day because he had chosen to wear the Periwig; the powdered wig was a symbol for a gentleman, one who was educated at Harvard. He was carrying his Bible and placed it on the lectern and raised both his arms.

"Shall we pray?" He asked his congregation.

Everyone stood, bowed their heads, and listened intently to the opening prayer. A reserved amen followed. Everyone remained standing, picked up their Psalm booklet, and opened it. The first Psalm was always the same; they sang *a cappella*, as musical instruments were not allowed during the meeting. Piety and prudence were the easiest ways to show devotion.

With the Psalm finished, he motioned for them to sit. He picked up his Bible and began to speak of faith, inner peace, and transformation. His sermon was directed to everyone, but Hannah knew that it was inspired by their conversations; she would always be grateful for his counsel.

When he finished, it was time for another song. The congregation stood and began another Psalm. Hannah sang the words, though she was outside her body looking down; it was a sobering thought to see her family and strangers coming out to celebrate with her.

She reflected on how long it had taken for her to be delivered to this place. Sixty-seven years after she had been baptized, it seemed that her father had the foresight to do that. The original sin loomed over all newborn babies in the colony, and Hannah wondered if Elizabeth's twins found salvation. It was her desire to be reacquainted one day with Elizabeth and her babies.

The Psalm was over, and everyone sat quietly. Hannah, deep in thought, remained standing; she had not noticed that the others had sat down. She felt a tug on her mantle and quickly sat; she could not afford any embarrassment that morning. She could not tell if anyone noticed but sensed people were looking at her. Carefully, she bent her head to peer in the direction of Thomas; he was looking directly at her. His smile was there; she sensed it and felt a level of comfort.

Reverend Brown opened his Bible and took out a folded piece of paper that Hannah knew was her words that he helped write. He spoke directly, his voice carrying the weight of the church and the thoughts of its newest member.

"Goodwife Duston is here this Sabbath morning to receive salvation from the church and enlightenment for our God," he told his brethren. "Let us welcome her; these are her words."

Brown stood tall and looked at Hannah. He assured her with his eyes that she did not need to be nervous. He would be her guide; it was time to begin.

"I desire to be thankful that I was born in a land of light. I have had a great deal of affliction, and I hope that it has begun to work for my good," he paused to draw a deep breath.

"I have been at a loss as to whether I should come to the table of the Lord. I have come to the resolution that I will no longer hold back. I desire the prayers of the church for me," Brown finished and folded the paper.

He did not speak of her history, the raid, the captivity, or the violence that she harbored in her heart. It was a confession shaped in careful language that her reliance on grace alone would give her the salvation she sought.

The meetinghouse was deafeningly quiet, not a sound from the attendees; it was truly a moment of reflection for everyone. The Reverend once again challenged them to an introspection of their own feelings. They all knew Hannah's story either through first-hand accounts or from idle gossip; it was time to put it all behind them for her sake and the sake of the community. There was no show of emotion; the applause that she had received in the streets was now only the sound of silence, which would be her approval.

Everyone stood and began another song; this Psalm was sung with lighter and more enlightened voices. Hannah felt a relief filled with joy and jubilation, something she thought she would never feel again.

The church deacons ritually placed the communion table in front of the pastor, along with the pewter cups filled with wine and bread on trays. The serving of communion was the next order of business; it was the Puritan view of a community meal. The Deacons went to their seats in their boxes. They were all regarded as guests at the Lord's table. They would start at the front with the men, followed by the women.

Hannah was happy that she was not singled out or made a fuss over. Her wait was over. After decades of self-doubt, she was finally counted among the faithful; her confession of faith had been received by her family, known to her neighbors, and now by God.

The deacons stood in front of her, one offering a bit of bread and the other a taste of wine. She paused for a moment and reflected on how she felt. Using both hands, she openly accepted the offering, sealing the covenant that she just confessed to.

She was now accepted, one soul at a time.

"God's holy providence, hath manifested itself in preserving us, and in disappointing the plots of our enemies and giving us peace in our borders."

John Winthrop
Journal Entry
Governor
Massachusetts Bat Colony

The conflicts between the English and the French were sustained for many years, one conflict followed another. With the alliance of the native Indians siding with the French, the reign of terror on the frontier was always a threating element to life.

From King Philip's War, King Williams, and the conclusion of Queen Anne's War in 1713 with the signing of the Treaty of Utrecht, the long-running frontier wars were finally over. France ceded most of their claimed territory to Great Britain. It is estimated that 10% of the population of New England met its demise during these conflicts.

Hannah Duston survived her husband by twelve years, living to a respectable age of 79. Thomas passed in 1724, at 72. She spent the last years of her life in silent meditation living with her son Johnatan, in Haverhill. Her exact date and burial location has always been a question for historians and folklore enthusiasts.

Her legacy was all but forgotten for nearly 200 years, when, in 1874 a figure in her likeness was erected on, Sugar Ball Island. The very first statue in the Americas of a woman, which quietly stands amongst the tall trees at the confluence of the Contoocook River and the Merrimac River. The Hannah Duston Memorial State Historic Park, is in Boscawen, New Hampshire and continues to instill controversy with visitors.

Acknowledgments

Hannah Duston and her story has been a tale of heroism, and self-preservation. It is what New Hampshire's legends are made of. Her survival has been both celebrated and vilified.

There have been many written and verbal accounts of her actions over the past 300 years. In her lifetime her notoriety was glorified by gossip and the writings of such learned men like the Reverend Cotton Mather. He wrote several accounts, starting with *Humiliations Follow'd with Deliverances*, in 1697.

Her actions have been revisited by Nathaniel Hawthorne in 1836 in his account entitled *A Mother's Revenge*, published in a Boston periodical, The American Magazine. Henry David Thoreau took his prose to tell her plight, using the Merrimack River and its landscape to enhance his words.

Generations later, her story continued to pique the interest of local writers, each telling a version of her story that they had interpreted. *Hannah Duston's Sister*, by Sybil Smith is a fictional account that gives yet another assessment of Hannah.

Richard W. Pyne wrote *The Trail of Hannah Duston*, blending fact and fantasy, creating a narrative of historical possibilities. Jay Atkinson's, award-winning book, *Massacre on the Merrimack*, held true to her story, letting the reader draw their own conclusions or judgments.

Each of these works provided a tremendous source of inspiration for recreating this period of time in my mind and on the page. I would like to give thanks for the support of Sonny, and the brilliance of Arna, and lastly to Patrick—for all the reasons he knows so well.

A Novel by Dave O. Dodge

In 1961, Betty and Barney Hill were returning to their home in Portsmouth NH. They experienced an unexplained and unimaginable event in the heart of the White Mountain National Forest, one that would change their lives forever.

The night sky was clear, the stars were brilliant and the moon rose across the horizon. Barney drove, and Betty watched the night sky and as if it was her private celestial light show. Shortly after 10 pm, Betty spotted an object in the sky and it appeared to follow them through the mountain passes. What happened next would haunt them for years.

The incident would go on to be called the "Hill Abduction," and would be chronicled in numerous official government reports. After years of secrecy and months of forensic hypnosis; their story was leaked and published in a prominent Boston newspaper. The Hill's lives were then capitulated into the limelight.

Betty: A Life Interrupted, is a biographical novel retelling the story of her life. She was a well-respected social worker, a devoted church member, an advocate of human rights, and a devoted wife to her husband. Her story begins on the night that was interrupted causing her trajectory of her life to take another course, one she had no idea of its destination.

The Seasons of Grace

The Unauthorized Back Story of
PEYTON PLACE
Dave O. Dodge

"I'm trapped," she screamed silently. No one in the room hearing her inner pleas. "I'm trapped in a cage of poverty and mediocrity and if I don't get out, I will die." Only the sound of her typewriter could be heard that night echoing throughout the shack she called home.

Grace Metalious wrote the stories that no one dared to write before that time. A midcentury tale of small-town life in New England to the hustle and bustle of New York City to the unforgiving film studios of Hollywood, her story unfolds. Her infamous first novel *Peyton Place* catapulted her from obscurity to the top of the literary world in the 1950's.

This is a case of where art imitates life and so does this biographical novel of the young author's life. *The Seasons of Grace* is a fictional account, sometimes dark, sometimes shocking, but always authentic.